return / renew by

KT-375-727

"There's plenty of Kadrey's trademark . . . , g . . . refer-
ences, and the only complaint . . . is that . . . this trip to Iphigene
didn't last longer."

—*RT Book Reviews*

"Kadrey again has painted a world that draws you in with its mysterious, yet frightening, beauty. . . . The imagery is just phenomenal."

—*Crimespree Magazine*

"An intelligent stand-alone tale of quiet horror that should appeal
to Kadrey's many fans, as well as to lovers of more subtle shivers."

—*Library Journal*

Praise for Richard Kadrey

"Witty, gritty, over-the-top mayhem to care. If you mixed Jim
Butcher with Christopher Moore, forced a kicking and screaming
Warren Ellis in after them, and shook well, you'd get . . . well, I'd
be careful opening the mixer. But the result wouldn't be too far
away from this."

—*Daytona Beach News*

"Kadrey's prose is raw and gutter-tough, Raymond Chandler meets
Lux Interior at the Whisky a Go Go at the end of days."

—*Austin Chronicle*

"Kadrey knows how to spin a story, his prose is crisp and effortless,
and the entertainment value is high."

—**Charles de Lint,** *Fantasy & Science Fiction*

"Don't compare Kadrey's prose with Stephenie Meyer's, or even Joss
Whedon's *Buffy the Vampire Slayer.* Those works are mere fluffy
soap operas next to Kadrey's writing. Richard Kadrey's imagination
is gritty, sleazy, and macabre."

—*Seattle Post-Intelligencer*

E ITEMS

Also by Richard Kadrey

Dead Set

RICHARD KADREY

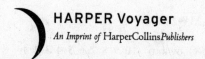

HARPER Voyager
An Imprint of HarperCollinsPublishers

This is a work of fiction. Names, characters, places, and incidents are products of the author's imagination or are used fictitiously and are not to be construed as real. Any resemblance to actual events, locales, organizations, or persons, living or dead, is entirely coincidental.

Harper Voyager and design is a trademark of HCP LLC.

DEAD SET. Copyright © 2013 by Richard Kadrey. All rights reserved. Printed in the United States of America. No part of this book may be used or reproduced in any manner whatsoever without written permission except in the case of brief quotations embodied in critical articles and reviews. For information address HarperCollins Publishers, 195 Broadway, New York, NY 10007.

HarperCollins books may be purchased for educational, business, or sales promotional use. For information please e-mail the Special Markets Department at SPsales@harpercollins.com.

A hardcover edition of this book was published in 2013 by Harper Voyager, an imprint of HarperCollins Publishers.

FIRST HARPER VOYAGER PAPERBACK EDITION PUBLISHED 2014.

Designed by Shannon Plunkett

Library of Congress Cataloging-in-Publication Data has been applied for.

ISBN 978-0-06-233928-7

14 15 16 17 18   OV/RRD   10 9 8 7 6 5 4 3 2 1

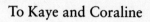

To Kaye and Coraline

Acknowledgments

Thanks to my agent, Ginger Clark, and my editor, Diana Gill. Thanks also to Pamela Spengler-Jaffee, Shawn Nicholls, Kelly O'Connor, Caroline Perny, and the rest of the team at HarperVoyager.

Thanks to Kami Garcia for good advice and Elsa Hermens for useful thoughts. Thanks to The Parlour Trick for the sound track to Iphigene. As always, thanks to Nicola for everything else.

Dead Set

Ône

For three straight nights Zoe dreamed about the black dog. It followed her through the empty streets of a strange city, trailing after her but never getting quite close enough to be threatening. It just watched. The funny thing was that these dreams weren't like regular ones. She was almost never alone when she dreamed, because Valentine was always there. But there was something different about the black dog dreams, something that made her not want to talk about them. Zoe had plenty of secrets in the real world, but she'd never kept one in her dreams before. It was depressing because it meant that, in the end, she wasn't safe anywhere.

The elevator wasn't working again. Zoe sighed and started the long walk up four floors. The stairway smelled of mildew and other people's cooking. When she made it to the top, a little out of breath, she fumbled in her pockets for the keys and let herself into the new apartment. It was her least favorite moment of the day.

Zoe didn't hate the new apartment. It just made her miserable. There were scrapes on the walls and floors from the previous tenant's furniture. A splotchy, stained rug in the hall and black mold around the bathroom window. Her room was smaller than the one she'd had back at the old house. Her old window had faced a green backyard with almond trees and low hills. The window in her new room faced the back of a run-down hardware store.

"It's not forever, dear," Zoe's mother reminded her. "Six months. A year at the most. Until we get the insurance straightened out."

Zoe nodded, not looking at her. Six months, she thought. Wasn't it a year already? No. Half that. Only a few weeks for the world to collapse and leave them stranded in the middle of nowhere. So, another hundred and eighty days to go. Or double that. How much more lost can we get?

She piled a couple of pillows on the bed, which was squeezed into the corner of the room. From her overnight bag she removed a stuffed Badtz-Maru and leaned him against the pillows. The worn doll had been a gift from her father on her tenth birthday. Six years later, it still had an honored spot at the head of her bed. For a long minute Zoe pretended that she didn't know her mother was standing in the doorway trying to think of something to say.

It was another one of those days. All afternoon she'd felt angry or sad or both at once and guilty for feeling any of it. She shouldn't be so attached to the old house, her school, and her friends. She should be bigger than that and hated that she wasn't.

"We'll get past this," said her mother.

Knowing she shouldn't even ask, Zoe said, "Can I use the phone?"

"Zoe . . ."

"I won't call anyone. I just want to check my e-mail."

Her mother looked at the floor.

"It's the end of the month. I'm already over our data limit and the few talk minutes left I need to keep for finding work. Can't you use a computer at the library?"

"What library? There aren't any around here. I checked," Zoe said. It was a lie. She hadn't checked because she didn't want to know. Before they'd even moved to the city, she'd taken BART to the library at the San Francisco Civic Center a few times, but gave up going a month earlier. A homeless guy followed her to a reading table, where he thumbed through a newspaper. It wasn't a big deal. A smelly guy always followed her when she went in. It wasn't until the man's breathing changed and she realized he was masturbating under the table that she left and never went back. She suspected any library in their run-down neighborhood, the Tenderloin, would be like that, or maybe worse. Throw in a few crackheads with the homeless.

"What about school? Don't they have one you can use?"

Zoe shook her head.

"The server's dead and the school doesn't have the money to get it fixed."

Zoe's mother leaned against the doorframe, her arms crossed in front of her.

Please don't ask about the other phone, Zoe thought. It was too humiliating to admit that the cheap prepaid phone her mother had given her had been stolen from her bag on the bus. Zoe had almost taken one from a RadioShack on Market Street. The phones were right by the door. She could grab one and run. But she didn't have the guts.

"I'm sorry. Next week. I promise," said her mother.

"It's okay," Zoe said. She smiled and the effort made her stomach knot. "It's no big deal."

"Sorry," said her mother softly.

"I know."

Zoe started folding clothes she'd piled on the end of the bed. A couple of minutes later she heard her mother unpacking things in the kitchen.

She sat on the edge of her bed, wanting to cry but not letting herself. The tears she held back weren't about sadness. She'd been through that already in the days leading up to her father's funeral six months ago. The tears that threatened to come now were made up of anger and fear and something else. Something deeper and darker and more forever feeling, but Zoe couldn't find a name for it. All she knew was that not talking made not crying easier and not crying was all that held the world together. That was enough for now.

She snapped the rubber band around her wrist, the one they'd given her at the hospital. She breathed deeply in and out. The relaxation exercise was one of the few useful things that the doctors had given her for the times when it all got to be too much and she thought, even for a second, about hurting herself.

In the morning, on her way to school, Zoe stopped to adjust one of the straps on the backpack where she carried her books. At the end of the block sat a dog, looking in her direction. It was dark enough she couldn't see its eyes. Zoe walked the last few blocks to school and at each corner looked back. The dog was always there, a half block behind. As she neared the school, it trotted in her direction. She crossed the street, and as she climbed the stairs outside school she turned. The dog sat quietly at the corner. Anyone watching, she thought, would think the dog was hers, waiting patiently to walk her home. Zoe went inside, and when she looked back through a window the dog was gone.

The new school was no better than the apartment. Zoe had just started the second quarter of her junior year at her old school when she'd been told to report to the principal's office and her mother took her home. And that was that. No more school until last week.

On her first day at the new school Zoe learned its real name: Show World High, the other students called it, for the strip club a few blocks away on O'Farrell Street. The place didn't look much like a school or a club, she thought. More like a supervillain bunker, without the death rays or computers. *An abandoned supervillain bunker,* all bare concrete, wire over the windows, and heavy front doors like someplace they used to store nukes.

In the lunchroom the student tribes were as plentiful and, thank God or Iggy Pop or whoever, as obvious as the ones at her old school. The jocks, the skate rats, the computer geeks, the Goths, and the stoners in their baggy Kurt Cobain thrift-store rags all had pretty rigid dress codes, so they were easy to spot. The computer geeks sat together at one table. Like the stoners, they mostly kept to themselves, so she didn't have to worry about one of them actually trying to talk to her.

Then there were the generally smart kids who got good grades without trying too hard and were still able to have fun, hang out, and just goof off. Zoe knew if she put her mind to it, she could fit in with them, but she couldn't work up the interest or energy, the necessary level of up-tempo bullshit it would take to break the ice with new people. She thought of Julie and Laura, the real friends she'd left behind at her old school in Danville. They'd probably texted her on her now-dead phone, and when she didn't answer they'd e-mailed her. Did they think she'd forgotten about them already? Found new friends and invented a shiny new personality for herself? Two more things to worry about. Maybe two more things lost.

None of her new teachers at Show World High were particularly bad, but they seemed either tense, exhausted, or flat-out bored. Zoe sat in her English, history, and geometry classes, and after each one couldn't remember a word anyone had said.

Then there was Mr. Danvers. He taught biology. The moment she walked into his classroom, the dull fog she'd drifted into since she'd started at Show World lifted. Mr. Danvers's classroom had enormous posters displaying the anatomy of humans, horses, and cats. Some were antiques that he found at flea markets and estate sales. Behind him were floor-to-ceiling shelves crowded with animal skulls, fossils, piles of bones, owl pellets, and jars of animal teeth.

While people were still getting to their seats, Mr. Danvers looked up from his papers and asked, as if the question was off the top of his head, "How tall was the tallest human being on record? And don't say Goliath because we don't really know how tall he was and, anyway, it was two thousand years and everyone else could have been Munchkins back then."

The talking in the room faded. Zoe found an empty desk near the back.

"No one? For your information," said Mr. Danvers, "the tallest human on record was Robert Wadlow from Alton, Illinois. He was born in 1918, and when he died, he was just under nine feet tall." Mr. Danvers climbed on top of the long black lab table and strode across it to the nearest wall. "That would put him about here," he said, leveling his hand with a mark a foot below the ceiling. "To give you an idea how big he was, the tallest player in the NBA right now is only seven foot seven," said Mr. Danvers, pointing to a lower mark, "making him almost a foot and a half shorter than Wadlow." Mr. Danvers stepped from the lab table onto his chair and back to the floor. He reached below the table, grasped an enormous pumpkin, and put it on top. "This pumpkin is just about the size of Mr. Wadlow's head. Imagine how big his skull was and how much it weighed. What it must have felt like carrying the thing around all day."

There was impressed murmuring in the room, a few giggles. Zoe sat forward in her chair, staring at the pumpkin. It was kind of cool having a mad scientist for a teacher.

Crossing his arms, Danvers leaned on the pumpkin. "Any of you jocks envy Mr. Wadlow? Don't. Humans aren't supposed to be nine feet tall. The weight of Wadlow's own body nearly crippled him. He had acromegaly, a hormone condition where his body produced too much growth hormone. André the Giant, the wrestler, also had acromegaly. He died in his forties. Mr. Wadlow died at twenty-two."

Another burst of murmurs.

"Like all humans, Wadlow was a mammal. In terms of humans he was huge. In terms of mammals he was a speck. The biggest mammal in the world is the blue whale. Ever seen an elephant? Imagine twenty-five elephants all strung out in a conga line. That's a blue whale." He pointed to the back of the room. For a moment Zoe's stomach tightened as she thought he was going to call on her. But he turned back to the class and said, "A blue whale wouldn't even fit in this room. And this enormous animal, maybe the largest animal that ever lived, eats one of the smallest: plankton. Microscopic shrimp. That has to mean something, but I don't know what. Maybe just some cosmic irony. And I'm not talking about Intelligent Design. The first person to say 'Intelligent Design' has to wear the Charles Darwin beard I keep in my desk for the rest of the year."

Zoe smiled. It felt a little funny, like exercising muscles she hadn't used in a while, but it felt good.

Later at the apartment, she tried hooking up the TV to the cable and was delighted to discover that it hadn't been turned off. She watched a documentary about how ancient Egyptians made mummies, taking out all the organs, finishing with the brain, and wrapping the hollowed-out body in layers of beeswax and linen. Zoe's mother got home after dark, wearing high heels, her good cream-colored job-interview suit, and carrying a big bucket of KFC under her arm.

"Hey, you got the TV working," she said.

"Yep."

"You know how I used to think this was my lucky suit?"

"You never told me that," said Zoe.

"Really? I didn't?" her mother asked. "Anyway, the luck in this thing has officially flown south for the winter." She dropped down onto the sofa and kicked off her high heels, groaning as each shoe slid off. "Whoever invented these things should be burned at the stake."

"You don't have to wear them."

Her mother sighed.

"Yeah, I do, darling. It's like part of the uniform when you're a woman looking for a job," she said. "Sometimes, out in the world . . . being exactly what people want and expect . . . well, maybe it isn't a good thing but it's a smart thing."

"But not today?"

"No, not today." Zoe's mother rested her head on the back of the couch and draped her arm across her face to cut out the light. After a moment she sat up and asked, "How's it going at the new school? Have you made any friends yet?"

"Sure," Zoe said. She knew the question was coming and had an answer ready. She'd even made up a friend in case her mother wanted details. A girl from the drama club who had a big part in the school's annual musical. She knew her mother would like her to know someone into music.

"Good. I'm glad you're not alone all the time."

Zoe nodded. "Classes are pretty easy compared to Danville. A lot of the teachers look like they're on Valium. Except for one. He's okay."

Her mother rubbed her feet through her stockings. "What's so special about him?"

"He teaches biology and has this pretty cool collection of animal bones and body parts," said Zoe. "He showed us the skeleton of a bat the size of your thumb."

Zoe's mother gave her a tired smile. "Nice. He sounds like Matt Everson. Did you ever meet him? He was a friend of your father's back in the old, olden days."

Whenever she said the "old, olden days," Zoe knew her mother meant back when she and Zoe's father had lived in an old warehouse populated by artists in the industrial part of San Francisco. Back then, Zoe's mother had been a graphic designer, designing album covers for little punk record labels. Her father had been road manager for a couple of bands and played around with computers in his spare time. Later, he wrote software all the time and started making money, but Zoe had been an infant and didn't remember when they moved from the leaking warehouse to the house in Danville with the backyard full of almond trees. Sometimes she wished they had stayed in the warehouse. It would have been so great growing up around paintings and sculptures, the plasma cutters, and the welding equipment the artists used. Maybe things would have turned out differently. Maybe Dad wouldn't be dead.

She heard her mother sigh. She'd picked up the mail Zoe had piled on the coffee table. Her mother was staring at a fat official-looking envelope. "Shit. More insurance papers."

"I still don't understand what the problem is. Do they think Dad's alive and hiding in the basement or something?" asked Zoe.

"I don't know," said Zoe's mother wearily. "It's some goddamn thing. A piece of paper that should have been filed with some department and wasn't. Or it was and got lost. Suddenly, to these people, your father never existed." She opened the envelope and looked at the papers. Very quietly she repeated, "Like he was never even here . . ."

Zoe turned up the TV. She couldn't stand hearing her mother talk like that. It hurt seeing her so lost and hurt. Zoe knew she should tell her mother she loved her but she couldn't do it because she didn't really feel it. Where that feeling, and a lot of others, should be was a deep dark void. Instead of talking and maybe saying the wrong thing and making things worse, she watched people on the TV screen praying to old, animal-headed Egyptian gods.

"I swear I'm not a stupid woman, but these insurance people speak Martian or something." Her mother shook her head and put the papers back in the envelope. "That's why we have a lawyer now, so he can speak Martian to the insurance company's Martians."

"Just make him make them believe that Dad was real."

"I know. That's the idea."

"I hate them," said Zoe.

"So do I. Are you hungry?"

Zoe nodded.

"Why don't you grab us some plates."

They watched TV while they ate the now-lukewarm chicken. A chubby English archaeologist explained how in the Egyptian underworld the dead were judged by Thoth, who weighed their souls against a feather. If the soul weighed less than the feather, it went on to the Western Lands, sort of like the Egyptians' heaven, he explained. "But if the soul weighed more than the feather," he said, "a crocodile-headed beast devoured it and the soul would vanish from the universe forever."

When they finished eating, Zoe took the leftovers and dishes into the little kitchen. Back in the living room she found her mother asleep on the couch. Zoe turned off the TV and went quietly to her room, closed the door, and undressed for bed.

Feeling so rotten all the time was exhausting, she thought. For a while after her father died the doctors gave her sleeping pills because she couldn't close her eyes for days at a time. Now, except on those nights when the black dogs came, sleeping and dreaming were her favorite things in the world.

Zoe stood in the almond grove behind the old house, though this one wasn't exactly like the real grove. It was better. The hills in the distance knifed high enough into the sky that they were topped by snow. Zoe's house wasn't there. None of the houses in the development were. In her dreams, the grove stood in the middle of a great green plain that stretched from horizon to horizon. The sky was the color of twilight and dotted with pale blue, trembling stars. Zoe always liked this time and this place because, although the light was fading, she could see everything, even in the darkest places.

Valentine, her dream brother, was waiting for her in the tree fort, throwing unshelled almonds down at her. Valentine had dark eyes and black, unruly hair that he was always pushing out of his eyes, just like her father used to do. Valentine wore the same dirty white T-shirt, ripped jeans, and sneakers he'd had on every night since she could remember.

She laughed and picked up the nuts as they landed at her feet, throwing them back at Valentine with one hand and shielding her face with her other. They ran around the treetops, through the wooden maze of planks and ropes, trapdoors, and stairs that made up their ever-growing fort, whooping and throwing almonds at each other. She felt lighter, almost like a kid, when she was with Valentine. She hadn't always felt that way. Things changed after her father died. Dreams became the only place where she could blow off steam and feel free and happy.

When Zoe made it to the roof of the fort, Valentine was standing by the wooden railing, looking at the distant mountains.

"Something is walking through the snow," he said, pointing. The mountains were hazy through a halo of fog. Zoe looked hard and thought she could see a tiny dot moving across one of the snowy peaks, leaving a trail of even, microscopic footprints.

"What is it, do you think?" she asked.

Valentine shook his head. "An animal, maybe. Maybe a person," he said quietly.

"Could it be Dad?" Zoe asked.

"Why would it be him?"

"I don't know. Maybe he's there looking out for us."

Valentine turned to her.

"Do you really feel like anyone is looking out for you?"

"Just you."

He squatted down to pick up some dried leaves that he methodically held up and dropped over the side of the railing, one by one. "On the other hand, it would be nice if whoever's walking on our mountain is someone we knew."

"Assuming it's a someone."

"Yeah."

Zoe had known Valentine for as long as she could remember. He'd always been a part of her dreams, but she'd stopped talking about him years before when she saw the looks she got from other children and their parents, and she realized that not everyone had a dream brother. She'd asked him once why she was the only person she knew who had a dream brother like him. Valentine had become very quiet and climbed high into the tree, too high for Zoe to reach, and he wouldn't come down or talk for the rest of the night.

"Maybe it's Mom up there," said Zoe. "Spying on us." She turned her back on the mountains and sat down, resting her back on the railing. She leaned back and looked up at the stars, willing herself to fall up into them. It didn't work.

"Are you and Mom still not speaking?"

"We're speaking," said Zoe. "Just not about anything."

"Just take-out chicken," Valentine said. He dropped a leaf onto Zoe's head. She batted it away.

"That's about as deep as it gets with us right now." Zoe turned around and let her legs dangle over the edge of the fort. The air felt good. "I feel so stupid. I'm lonely, but I don't want to see anyone or talk to anyone."

"What about your friends back at the old house?"

She got up, ignoring the question, and looked back

up at the mountain. Zoe tried to find the dot moving through the snow but the fog had moved in and she couldn't see a thing. "Sometimes I wish I could see you when I'm not asleep," she said. "You're the only one I can talk to."

Valentine knelt down beside her. He looked around conspiratorially, and then lifted up his T-shirt. He was skinny, and his ribs stuck out under his ghost-white skin. Valentine put his hand over his heart and slid his fingers into his chest. When he pulled his hand out, he was holding a small tin compass. It looked like the kind of piece of junk you'd get in a box of kids' cereal. Valentine put the compass in her hand.

"When you're awake and you need me, you can look at that," he said. "We can't talk but you'll always know where I am because the blue half of the hand will always point to me."

Zoe shook the compass, half expecting it to break, and walked around the tree fort. Just as Valentine said, the blue hand always pointed to him.

Zoe went back and hugged her dream brother. "Thank you," she said. Valentine hugged her back.

Later, they picked green, unripe almonds from the tree and threw them, in the special way that Valentine had taught her, straight into the sky. The almonds flew up and out of sight, every now and then hitting a star and sending it spinning.

When that got boring, Valentine turned to Zoe. "Why

do we always stay up here?" he asked. "Why don't we ever climb down?"

"It's dangerous out there in the world," said Zoe. "There are things down there."

They looked over the edge of the fort. Below them something large and scaly, like one of the animal-headed gods she'd seen on TV, swam silently through the green grass as if it were water.

Two

"In the wild, the differences between scavengers and predators are simple," said Mr. Danvers in class the next day. "A predator, say a wolf or a shark, will generally catch and kill its prey. What does that leave for the scavengers?"

A girl with short blue hair and black, kohled eyes said, "They find stuff to eat. Animals and things that are already dead."

"Exactly," said Mr. Danvers, reaching for something on his bone shelf. He pulled down a jar the size of a two-liter soda bottle and turned back to the class.

"They'll steal stuff, too," said Zoe. It was the first time she'd spoken up in any of her classes. She liked that Mr. Danvers didn't make you raise your hand if you knew the answer. "On this show I saw they said some predators, lions sometimes, would rather steal food from another animal than go and find it on their own."

Mr. Danvers smiled at Zoe. "Good addition, uh . . ."

"Zoe," she said.

"Good work, Zoe. Yes, stealing food might be rude, but it's a lot more energy-efficient than hunting for it yourself." Mr. Danvers unscrewed the jar and poured a pile of yellow-white animal teeth onto his lab table. "Everyone gather around up here. We're going to see what predators and scavengers use to catch and eat their lunch."

After class Zoe went to her locker and exchanged her books for a brown-bag lunch of leftover fried chicken. The blue-haired girl came over. "Cool shirt," she said. "Very retro."

Zoe had to look down at her shirt to understand what the girl was talking about. "Oh, I guess so," she said. The shirt was black and much too big for her. She'd cut off the sleeves and collar. There was a large blue circle on the front and the words THE GERMS: GERMICIDE.

"I grew up with it, so I never thought of it as retro. It was my dad's," Zoe said. "He knew all these guys, back in the day."

The blue-haired girl bugged her eyes in mock, sitcom shock. "Your dad hung with Darby Crash?"

Zoe nodded, nervous about the sudden and intense attention.

"Does he still do cool stuff like that?"

Zoe shook her head. "No. He's . . . he died."

"Oh," said the blue-haired girl. She took a step back. "I'm sorry. I'm pushy and I talk too much."

Zoe shrugged. "No. It's okay."

"I'm Absynthe," said the blue-haired girl. She leaned in conspiratorially. "Really Courtney. My mom says it's for Courtney Love but I think it sounds like I should be on TV with a monkey sidekick. All my friends call me Absynthe. With a *Y*."

"Hi. Absynthe with a *Y*. I'm Zoe."

"I was headed down to the cafeteria of doom to meet some friends. You want to eat with us?"

Zoe hesitated. Sitting with people meant she'd have to talk, and talking was still a black and frightening thing. Plus, she'd found a shady spot under an emergency staircase where she could eat her lunch alone. Still, being around people all day and never saying a word to anyone was getting old.

"Okay," she said. "Sure."

They walked to the lunchroom and Absynthe led Zoe to a table where three other girls were sitting. "This is Jessie, Molly, and Rexx," said Absynthe. "Everyone, this is Zoe. Her dad toured with the Germs." Absynthe said the names fast enough that Zoe wasn't sure she could put the right names with the right faces.

"He didn't really tour with them," said Zoe, sitting down. "He used to work in clubs and knew a lot of the bands."

"That's still pretty fucking hot," said a tall blond girl in a fifties gas-station shirt with rolled sleeves. The name over her breast pocket read STEVE, but Zoe was pretty sure she was Jessie.

"Was your dad in a band? Would I have heard of him?" asked a girl in a shiny black PVC top. Rexx, thought Zoe. The girl slurred her words and giggled enough that Zoe knew she was high.

Zoe shook her head. "No, he didn't play. Mostly he road-managed," she said, then quickly added, "But he knew everyone. You can see his picture in a bunch of books and on even some live records around the L.A. punk scene."

A short-haired, tough-looking girl in a black tank top and jean jacket said, "Your old man still into music? My band has a demo tape." Molly, thought Zoe.

"No," Zoe said. "He doesn't do music stuff anymore."

Out of the corner of her eye Zoe saw Absynthe trying to signal the other girls. When Molly started to ask about Zoe's father again, Absynthe shook her head so the girl would drop the subject. Molly looked away. Zoe opened her lunch bag and closed it. Looking at the cold friend chicken, she suddenly wasn't hungry.

"To the Germs and the other golden oldies," said Rexx.

Golden oldies? thought Zoe. Then she remembered that not everyone grew up listening to twenty-plus-year-old punk bands. To these girls the Germs and X were as old as Chuck Berry and the Beatles.

"And your dad," added Absynthe.

Rexx pulled a silver flask from her purse and poured vodka into the other girls' Cokes. Not high. Drunk, Zoe thought. When Rexx saw that Zoe didn't have anything to pour the vodka into, she looked baffled for a moment and then clumsily shoved the flask at her. "It's okay. Take a shot under the table."

Vodka splashed from the flask onto Zoe's shirt and into her eyes, burning enough to make her eyes water.

"Shit!" she yelled, jumping to her feet. The bag of chicken fell on the floor. She left it there.

"You okay?" asked Absynthe.

"I'm sorry," said Rexx, laughing so hard that she had to lean on Molly. She slurred, "Oh, man, I'm really sorry."

"Yeah," said Zoe. "I've got to wash this out of my eyes."

She walked quickly out of the lunchroom, went to a bathroom, and rubbed water into her eyes until the stinging stopped. When she stopped, her eyes were bloodshot and looked like she'd been crying. Instead of going back to the lunchroom, Zoe headed for the nearest exit and pushed her way outside. She went down the stone steps and kept going.

That's what you get for talking to people, she thought.

Her right eye hurt all the way home and her clothes were wet and carried the antiseptic reek of vodka. Zoe rinsed her face and the T-shirt in the bathroom sink. She was glad her mother wasn't home so she didn't have to explain why she stank of booze. She squeezed out the shirt in the sink and decided to hang it outside so that maybe the smell would evaporate. There was a fire escape outside her window, so she climbed out and up to the roof. A rusty pole that had once held part of a clothesline was a good enough place as any to leave the shirt. When she was done, she went back downstairs, wiping her wet hands on her jeans.

As she went, she remembered the last time she'd seen her father wearing the shirt. It was the day after his very last birthday party. He and Zoe's mother had bought a new cabinet to store their huge collection of old vinyl records. Zoe was helping her father sort the collection, first by genre, then alphabetically. They concentrated and didn't talk much, but it was a sweet and comfortable silence that said neither of them had to chatter just to fill the air with words. Still, Zoe couldn't help herself when she thought of exactly the right question to spring on her father.

"Riddle me this, how many members did Black Flag have over the years?"

Her father looked up and set down a beat-up copy of *Plastic Letters* by Blondie.

"Uh, eighteen or so. Around that," he said.

"Here's the real question: who had more members, Black Flag or King Crimson?"

Her father leaned back, looked at the ceiling as if thinking, then back at her.

"I don't know prog rock that well. Since when did you listen to the stuff?"

"I don't. I just wanted a question that would stump you."

"What's the answer?"

"Excluding session players, King Crimson had twenty-five actual members, so they win."

"You're quite the little music geek these days."

"Gee, I wonder where I get it from?"

Her father smiled at her.

They sorted records for a few more minutes. Zoe set aside a copy of *Double Nickels on the Dime* to listen to later. She said, "I know you were in bands back when dinosaurs still walked the earth—"

"What a lovely way to put it."

"You know, you never told me why you quit."

Her father put a stack of Martin Denny records to the side and paused for a second to scratch his ear. "I quit because I sucked," he said. "Okay, I didn't actually suck, but I was mediocre. One afternoon I was at the band's rehearsal space in this old warehouse off Mission Street and I could hear another bass player practicing in the next room. I never saw who it was, but he or she was a monster. Really beautiful sound. Loud, aggressive, but smart, too, you know? I knew I'd never be able to do that, even if I practiced all day for ten years. I was mediocre and that's all I'd ever be and I didn't want to spend the rest of my life being second rate."

"That must have been hard."

"It wasn't fun. On the other hand, if I had been good I'd have been on the road all the time living out of a van and I'd never see you or your mom."

"So, lucky us you sucked."

"Lucky us," her father said. He stopped for a minute to stare at a worn copy of *Fun House* by Iggy and the Stooges. "Okay, here's a philosophical question for you, is Sonic Youth punk?"

Without hesitation Zoe said, "Hell yes. Yeah, they played noisy avant-garde and stuff, but they did it punk, so yeah. They're in the club."

Her father smiled without looking at her. "You only say that because you want to be Kim Gordon when you grow up."

"Or a cowboy. I haven't ruled that out yet."

"I'm not sure your mom would let you keep a horse in the backyard."

"I won't tell if you won't."

"It's our secret," said her father.

Zoe sat on the sofa, alone in the apartment. Do I go back to school or hide here and watch TV all day? she thought. Neither. Both options were too depressing to seriously consider. She put on a ripped Clash T-shirt that she'd bought at a garage sale for fifty cents and went out.

Zoe walked along Ellis Street in the opposite direction of the school, turned north after a few blocks, and kept walking, heading nowhere at all, just killing time. She walked with her hands in her pockets and her head down, not even looking where she was going, only glancing up at streets corners so cars creeping through the red lights wouldn't mow her down.

She'd been walking for about half an hour and guessed she was somewhere along the edge of North Beach. Up ahead was an old shop with rusting metal grates over nearly black front windows. A hand-painted sign on the side of the shop said AMMUT RECORDS. RARE, USED & LOST."

Zoe went to the windows and peered in. The glass was so dark and dirty she wasn't sure if the place was open or had been abandoned years ago. But there was a dingy little sign in the front door that said COME IN. Zoe pushed and the door opened smoothly, without even a squeak.

Inside, the shop was cool and the air was pleasant, not musty like she'd been expecting. There weren't any lights on, so the place was lit by the little sun that streamed in through the dirty windows. But it was enough. Torn and dusty posters for bands that were old before Zoe was born were thumbtacked to the walls. There were rows and rows of bins, all full of battered vinyl LPs. Zoe had always found something mysterious about the old records stacked in her parents' closet. It made no sense to her that dragging a needle across a flat black piece of plastic could make all the music they'd grown up with and loved.

When she was six, someone had explained to her that the grooves on the LPs were really little hills and valleys and that the needles made music from bouncing through them. One day when she learned that her fingerprints were little hills and valleys, she got a sewing needle and dragged it across her fingers. All it did was draw blood. Lesson learned. People weren't records. Records were.

"Hello," came a deep voice. Zoe looked around and saw someone standing behind a counter near the door. The man was tall and completely bald. His skin was very pale. His forehead was high and smooth because it looked like he didn't have any eyebrows. It made him look a little like E.T., Zoe thought.

"Can I help you, young lady?" the man said.

"Are you Am . . . ?"

The man smiled. "It's a tricky name to say right," he said, and came around from behind the counter. "Just call me Emmett. All my friends do." He extended his hand and Zoe shook it.

She couldn't begin to guess his age. When Emmett turned his head one way, the shadows on his face made him look eighty. When he turned another way, he looked twenty. But she was sure that he couldn't be that young. His skin was strange. Smooth and stretched a little too tight, like Laura's aunt's face. She got Botox injections all the time and Laura said that she'd had about fifty face-lifts. Emmett didn't seem like the face-lift type, but who knew?

"What lovely eyes you have," he said. "Like a cat's."

"My mom used to say that all the time," said Zoe.

"Your mother is a smart woman."

Zoe nodded, not because she agreed but because she didn't want to talk about it with some guy she just met.

"Is there something I can help you find? We don't get many customers your age."

"I was just going by," said Zoe. "I don't want to buy anything."

Emmett waved a hand to the records. "That's all right," he said. "Look around. Maybe you'll find something for next time."

Zoe walked to the closest bin. It was so stuffed with ragged old records that they barely budged when she tried to flip through them. A plastic hand-lettered divider read TRAD JAZZ.

"Do you have any punk?" Zoe asked.

"We don't carry new releases, you know. No *Green Day* kind of stuff," said Emmett.

"I like the old bands," said Zoe.

"Good girl," said Emmett. He pointed. "Over against that wall."

Zoe went to where he indicated and found the "Punk" divider. The bin wasn't as crowded as the jazz section but it was just as beaten up. The first record was *Frankenchrist* by the Dead Kennedys, a San Francisco band her parents had played a lot when she was in elementary school. There were other records she recognized from the old house, now boxed up and put in storage like baby clothes and furniture no one liked in the first place. Toward the back of the section, Zoe found a single by the Cramps that looked familiar. She looked at the back and saw her mother's name at the bottom. She'd designed the cover.

Zoe put the record back and wandered through the rest of the store, running her hands along the smooth wooden bins and across the tops of the disintegrating cardboard LP covers.

"Why is it so dark in here?" she asked.

From behind the register Emmett looked up from a book. "It hurts my eyes," he said. "I can see fine like this. If you can't, I can turn some light on."

"No. That's okay," she said. Emmett went back to whatever he'd been reading.

At the back of the store was a beaded curtain and printed across it was a burning heart encircled by thorns. Zoe could see more record bins beyond the curtain. She looked around, and when she didn't see an "Employees Only" sign she pushed her way through.

The back room was different from the rest of the shop. It was brighter, but in a soft and diffuse way, like sun through water, though Zoe didn't see any lights on the walls or ceiling. The room had a thick smell, like burning pine. She followed the scent and found an incense burner in one corner. It was a chipped ceramic volcano.

Dark lumps, like brown sugar, burned at the bottom and smoke curled out the volcano's cone at the top.

Zoe circled the record bin. There weren't any plastic dividers saying what kind of records these were. She picked up a couple of LPs at random. They didn't have regular covers with a picture and the name of the band. Instead, they were wrapped in coarse brown paper printed with strange symbols that reminded her of the Egyptian hieroglyphics she'd seen in the mummy program. Some records only had a few symbols, while others were almost covered with them. Zoe slipped one of the records from its case to check the label, careful to touch only the edges of the disc the way her father had taught her. The record didn't have a label. It was the strangest record Zoe had ever seen.

The disc wasn't black, but milky white and translucent, shot through with a spidery red-and-blue web work that looked like veins and arteries. At the center of the LP, pierced by the round spindle hole, as if wounded, was a heart. In the strange underwater light of the back room, Zoe could swear the heart was beating.

"I had a feeling those cat eyes of yours would lead you back here," said Emmett. He was standing by the beaded curtain. Zoe hadn't heard him come in and the beads were silent and still, like he'd come through without moving them.

"Most people walk right by this room. They can't see

it or they don't want to and they stroll by as if it wasn't even here," he said, opening his hands. "But here it is."

Zoe held up the strange LP. "What kind of record is this?" she asked. "There's nothing written on it."

"Actually, there's quite a lot of information on the cover, but you have to know how to read it." Emmett gently took the record out of Zoe's hands. The heart seemed to beat faster when he touched it and he slipped it back into its case.

"These symbols, they tell names, places, incidents. The shape and texture of an individual's life on earth," Emmett said. "To answer your real question, these aren't records of music. Each of these records is a life. Not the recording of a life, but a life itself."

"I don't understand," said Zoe.

"I suppose it is a little hard to understand at first," Emmett said. "These are the lives of people who've passed on. They're what you might call souls. Or ghosts, but solid, not the wandering kind." He leaned on the bins and looked down at Zoe. "When some spirits depart this world they leave nothing behind. Like a baby coming out of its mother's womb, the transition is simple and complete and nothing more is necessary. Some spirits, though, get stuck. They get lost. Some don't even know that they're dead. And some of those spirits end up here." Emmett nodded toward the records.

"How?"

Emmett shrugged. "They just do. Like you."

"I don't know if I believe that."

"I wouldn't expect you to. You're a material girl living in a material world. See, I know some new music," he said proudly.

Zoe didn't want to be rude and tell him that the Madonna song was a standard on oldies stations.

"How can I show you what I'm talking about?" Emmett muttered. He clapped his hands together. "Would you like to see another life? Something old. Something from another time, so you can really feel the difference."

"It sounds like a virtual reality ride I went on once at a museum. All it did was make me dizzy," she said.

"I tell you what, try this and then you tell me if it's virtual reality."

Zoe thought about it for a moment. She'd already ditched school and lost a shirt. Maybe she could salvage something from this lousy day.

"Okay," she said.

Emmett looked through the bins and selected an LP with a complex collection of symbols on the front—fish, birds, plants, and jagged lines that might have meant water. He went to the incense burner and opened a large box standing next to it. Zoe followed and stood behind him, peeking over his shoulder. Inside the box was a strange machine about the size of an orange crate. Brass fittings gleamed in the diffuse light. Under a rubbery turntable there were delicate gears, lenses, and faceted jewels like insect eyes. Zoe thought it looked like a Halloween spook-house version of the record player her parents had in their bedroom back at the old house. Emmett set the LP gently on the machine and positioned six silver legs on different parts of the disc. Each of the legs had a barbed needle at the end. They made Zoe think of giant spiders.

"This is an Animagraph," said Emmett. "There are very few left in the world and fewer people who know how to use one. It's how we can see, touch, and experience the life of these lost souls." When he was finished setting up the Animagraph, he held up an elaborate set of headphones for Zoe.

She hesitated for a moment, then took the phones and slipped them over her head. They didn't seem to fit right. There were extra wires and straps.

"Allow me," said Emmett, sliding the phones off her. He put them back on her the other way around, with the part that looked like it should go over Zoe's head covering her eyes. The ear parts fit snugly, but then Zoe felt Emmett pulling more straps across her face. They went across her nose and mouth and wrapped around her throat. What the hell? she thought. She started to say something but the strap across her mouth kept her from opening her jaw. She pulled at the strap around her throat just as she heard a familiar scratching: the sound of a needle sliding into a record groove.

And she was standing on a green lawn behind an enormous white house. There was a badminton net a little off to her left, which was funny because until that minute she'd never seen the game, yet now she knew exactly how to play it. There were people around her, all dressed in strange old clothes, like photos she remembered of Steampunk cosplay. The older men wore dark suits while some of the younger ones had on jaunty striped jackets and flat straw hats that she remembered were called "boaters." The women, including Zoe herself, wore long, wide skirts that smelled faintly of some flowery perfume and starch. There was a tart taste in Zoe's mouth. Lemonade. She looked down at her hands. She had on white gloves and her hands were too large. An adult woman's hands. Then Zoe saw her belly. It was enormous. A man she knew to be her husband came over and laid his hand on her stomach. He smiled down lovingly at her.

"Are you comfortable, dear?"

"Yes," she felt herself say.

Squirm. There was something inside her. She was pregnant.

Zoe heard a soft scratch. A second later she was back in the record shop with Emmett unstrapping the headphones. At first she couldn't speak. She touched her stomach, relieved by its smooth flatness.

"You just experienced a few moments in the life of Caroline Lee Somerville from Manassas, Virginia. You were there right at the end of her life in 1904," said Emmett. "She died giving birth to that baby you felt."

"Holy shit," whispered Zoe. "That was so cool."

Emmett beamed. "I'm glad you enjoyed it." He set down the headphones and returned the record to its slip-case.

Zoe could still feel the life moving inside her. She could see her husband and the mansion. She knew every room inside.

As Emmett returned the LP to the bins Zoe asked, "Can I try that again?"

"I was going to suggest that very thing," said Emmett. He stepped over to another bin and picked up a record. "Would you like to see your father's life?"

Zoe went cold inside. She wasn't sure she'd heard him right, but she knew she had. There was a strange feeling in her stomach. Not fear exactly, more a feeling of being empty and queasy at the same time, like she might be sick.

"Your father is right here, with us," said Emmett, weighing the record in his hands. "And I can let you see him. But, of course, this is a place of business and I'm a businessman."

Zoe knew what he meant.

"How much do you want?" she whispered.

Emmett shook his head. "Money? I don't want your money," he said. He glanced at his watch. "It's almost closing time. You should be getting home."

"How much?" Zoe asked, quietly and insistently. If Emmett was telling the truth and she could see her father, she'd find some way to pay whatever he asked. And she knew he knew it.

Emmett set down the LP and led Zoe to the front of the store. "I don't want much at all, really," he said. He opened the door and gently pushed Zoe through. "Come back tomorrow at the same time and bring me a lock of your hair. Then I'll let you see your father." He locked the door and turned around the little sign in the window from COME IN to CLOSED.

That night, when Zoe got to the tree fort, Valentine was on the roof looking at the mountains through a telescope. The telescope looked old, patched together with duct tape, rusting rivets, and lumpy, ragged welds. Zoe had never seen it before and wondered where it had come from, but there were other, more important things on her mind.

Without waiting for Valentine to turn around, she said, "I met a man who can let me see Dad." He kept scanning the mountain. "He says Dad is a lost soul."

"There's definitely someone on our mountain," Valentine said. "But I can't get a good look through all this fog." The mist was heavier than Zoe remembered. It shrouded the mountain, roiling and swirling from the summit to the ground. It had even begun to send out white, ghostly fingers onto the green grass plain.

"Did you hear what I said?" Zoe asked. "I'm going back tomorrow to see him."

Valentine took the telescope from his eye and looked

at her. "How do you know you can trust this guy?"

"I guess I don't." Zoe shrugged. "But it's not like he copped a feel or asked for money, and he could have. I have to go back and see if he was telling the truth."

"If he didn't ask you for money, what did he ask for?"

"Nothing," Zoe lied, though she wasn't entirely sure why. She didn't want to have to explain about the lock of hair. She knew it was a little weird, but she couldn't take the chance on being talked out of going back to the store.

Valentine turned back to the telescope. "Mother is worried about you."

"You think so?"

He nodded, inching out the lens to change the telescope's focus. "She's afraid you're going to hurt yourself again."

Zoe tugged down her sleeves and snapped the rubber band, suddenly self-conscious. "You know I don't do that anymore."

"But you have razors hidden in your room." Valentine closed the old telescope and turned to her. "You took Father's shaving kit when you and Mother were packing up the old house."

"I'm not going to use them, I swear." Zoe sat, arms around herself, her knees drawn up to her chest. Valentine limped over and sat down next to her.

"Throw them away. Please."

"I can't," she said. "I need them. I'm not going to use them, but it helps to know they're there."

Valentine turned over his skinny, dirt-grimed arms, holding them up so Zoe could see. "When you hurt yourself you hurt me, too," he said. Seeing the long overlapping scars that extended from her dream brother's wrists almost to his elbows took Zoe's breath away.

"Why didn't you tell me?" she asked.

"Because you needed to stop for you, not for me. And you did and that makes me happy," said Valentine. "But I'm asking you, for my sake this time, not to start again."

She nodded, her arms and legs still tucked against her. Wrapped tight like a little ball of pain, Zoe leaned against Valentine. "I won't. I promise," she said. "I'll throw the others away."

"Thanks."

"But not Dad's razor. It was his and I'm keeping it."

"Okay," said Valentine. He didn't sound happy about it but he didn't argue with her.

"I'm going back to the store tomorrow. Maybe I'll get to see Dad."

Valentine opened the telescope and handed it to Zoe. "I'm going to keep watching the mountain."

He sounded more serious than Zoe had ever heard him sound before.

Three

Later, Zoe had another dream.

She was lost in a strange city and rain was coming down in blinding sheets, coming down so hard it was as if she'd been swallowed by an invisible monster. Through the beast's clear hide she caught distorted glimpses of buildings and streets, but she couldn't tell where she was. People rushed past her, bundled against the cold and the storm. She had a feeling that it had been raining for a long time. Maybe forever. The crowd swept her up and carried her along.

"Hello?" she said. "Can someone help me? I don't know where I am."

People kept moving, faster and faster until they were sprinting around her. Hands shoved her out of way. Shoulders bumped into her, almost knocking her down.

No one spoke or looked at her. Everyone just kept moving in a kind of desperate rush.

"Dad!" Zoe yelled. "Dad! Are you here?"

A noise came from behind. Deep and menacing. She didn't just hear it. She felt the growl in the pit of her stomach. It was the dogs. That's why everyone was running. There was a pack of the black beasts behind them. A faint shadow in the shape of a woman with something like a crown on her head had them on a leash. Then she released them.

The mob rounded a corner onto a long street unmarked except for a bus stop. The dogs were close on their heels. There was nowhere else to run. But running was becoming impossible. Zoe felt pavement turning soft under her feet. It rolled and squirmed like cement-colored taffy until deep cracks formed. The fissures split, pulling back like lips to reveal rows of gigantic, needle-sharp teeth. The great mouth moved down the street and, one by one, swallowed everyone in the crowd ahead of her. Each person disappeared without a sound. Zoe turned around hoping to find somewhere else to run. The dog pack waited at the end of the block for anyone foolish enough to try to double back.

Zoe broke from the group and started across the street. The mouth swam toward her, gaping wide, showing its black gullet. As she ran, she heard her mother calling, but when she tried to answer she slipped and the needle teeth rose like a wave from the pavement and swallowed her.

"Zoe!" yelled her mother, shaking her. She came awake with a start, her mother standing over her. "Your alarm's been going off for fifteen minutes. You'll be late for school."

Zoe blinked, her eyes crusty from deep sleep. She rubbed her face, trying to force the image of the pavement's teeth from her brain. Her mother balanced on one leg in her doorway, pulling on her high heels.

"I might to be late tonight," she said. "I have a couple of interviews, then I'm meeting with the lawyers. There's a frozen pizza in the fridge if you get hungry."

" 'Kay," said Zoe sleepily.

"You all right?"

Zoe nodded. "Yeah. Just weird dreams."

"I'm sorry I'm gone so much right now," said her mother. "It'll be better soon."

"It's okay," Zoe said. "I understand." Soon. Like everything else.

She smiled, knowing it would reassure her mother just enough to leave her alone.

"Wish me luck. I have an interview with the art director of a cool new tech and art magazine."

"That sounds great. Good luck," called Zoe as her mother blew her a kiss and disappeared. A moment later she heard the front door close. She waited for a moment longer, listening. When she was sure she was alone, Zoe got her hairbrush from the dresser. As she pulled hair from between the teeth she wondered what Emmett wanted with it. But how could she—or anyone—know what someone would be like if all they did was stack souls in boxes and hook themselves up to a machine so they could live other people's lives? It's like something an alien would do, thought Zoe. Maybe that's how the Martians are going to invade the earth. Through record stores no one ever goes into.

School was a kind of fever dream. Emmett had told her to come back at the same time, which meant she had to go to all of her morning classes and stay for lunch. If someone was trying to invent a new kind of torture, she thought, this was it.

Zoe didn't hear a word anyone, teacher or student, said that day, including Mr. Danvers. All that existed in the world was the record store and getting to it at the right time. It felt like she was in a kind of excited trance, trying to will the hands on the classroom clocks to move faster.

While she was putting her book in her locker after Mr. Danvers's class, she saw Absynthe.

"How are you?" Absynthe asked.

"Okay."

"You took off kind of fast yesterday. I was a little worried."

Zoe shook her head. "I was just surprised. It's all good."

Absynthe leaned against the lockers. "If it's any consolation, one of the teachers smelled the vodka—hell, it stank up the whole lunchroom—and Rexx got suspended."

"Damn. I was a little pissed, but I didn't want that." Zoe frowned.

"It's for the best," said Absynthe. "Her parents just split up and she's been tweaking hard about it. She's lucky that she got snagged at school and didn't pull a James Dean in her mom's Honda."

Great. Someone else creeping up on death. Was everyone dying these days?

"I'm sorry. I didn't know."

"Shit happens," said Absynthe. He shrugged. "They're making her go see a counselor and join a teenybopper AA group."

"I hope she's okay."

"She's a good girl. She'll be fine." Absynthe smiled at Zoe. "So, you brave enough to try lunch with us remaining dissolutes?"

"I can't," Zoe said, wishing she'd prepared a good lie in advance. "I'm only here for half the day."

Absynthe gave her a nod of deep understanding. "Lucky girl. You legit leaving or ditching?"

Zoe put the last of her books away and closed her locker. "Ditching, I guess."

"Where to?"

Zoe thought about it for a minute before answering. She still didn't know Absynthe very well. How much could she tell her?

"It's probably not a big deal," she said finally. "Really, it might all just be a waste of time." She immediately regretted saying it. For the first time since leaving the record shop, Zoe wondered if what she'd experienced might have been some kind of sick trick Emmett liked to play on girls and that he'd just laugh at her when she showed up, bag of hair in hand.

"Sounds like a guy," Absynthe said knowingly. "Most guys are a major waste of time. But they smell nice, so what are you going to do?" She started walking back toward the lunchroom, giving Zoe a little wave. "Let me know if you get lucky."

"I will," said Zoe, heading the other way, toward the exit.

On the walk to the record shop, Zoe had a couple of moments of panic. Yesterday she hadn't paid much attention to the route and she'd been so out of it on the walk home that she hadn't memorized the way. As she walked she nervously gnawed the inside of her check until she bit so hard it started to bleed. She cursed and spit blood in the street.

She wished she could talk to Julie and Laura. Julie always seemed so grounded and Laura was flat out the smartest person she knew. Zoe suddenly felt very alone and off balance without them, without anyone to talk to but Valentine. And Valentine just lived in her dreams. According to the doctor her mother sent her to, Valentine was her imaginary friend, a result of an acute emotional crisis. When Zoe told the doctor that she'd known Valentine all her life, since long before her father died, he'd talked about invented memories and how Zoe must have been suppressing abandonment issues since childhood. She decided the doctor was an idiot and she'd stopped listening to him. But now she wondered if he might not have been at least a little right.

If Valentine isn't real, then I'm just talking to myself and there's no one anywhere, she thought. And that's exactly how it feels sometimes, like I'm alone and trying to make friends with the echoes of my own voice. The full weight of that possibility, that Valentine might be nothing but her own bad wiring, made her feel worse. More alone than ever and possibly crazy. Zoe pushed the thought out of her head and looked around for something familiar.

And saw, with a shock, that she was standing at the front door of Ammut Records. She still couldn't remember the route she'd walked to get there. Maybe I'm not supposed to? she wondered. Maybe not knowing is the way. It didn't make much sense but it's what got her here and back home again.

Zoe reached for the door and stopped. She felt in her

pocket and found the compass Valentine had given her. Or had she had it all along and convinced herself that he'd given it to her? The compass pointed due west. Zoe shut her eyes and closed her hand around the toy.

I don't know if you're real or just me talking to me. Either way, wish me luck because I really need it right now.

She opened her eyes and entered the store.

Just like yesterday, it was cool and pleasant inside. The pine smell of burning incense hung thick in the air.

"Right on time," came Emmett's low voice.

She looked around, and through the dimness she saw him standing back by the beaded curtain.

"Did you bring me what I wanted?" he asked. In the strange light she couldn't see him step forward, just his shadow.

Zoe reached into her pocket and pulled out the plastic bag that contained strands of her hair. He accepted the bag, held it up to the light, and weighed it in his hand like they were doing a drug deal.

"Good girl," he said. "But next time when you bring me something, please bring it in a paper bag or wrap it in a tissue. Plastic is so"—he paused for a moment as if groping for a word—"unnatural."

"Okay," said Zoe, thinking, Next time? Right now I'm not a hundred percent sure I want a *this* time.

"Well," said Emmett conspiratorially, "I suppose you'd like to see dear old dad?"

"Yes," she said, and followed him through the curtain

into the back room, feeling a dizzy mix of excitement and fear.

Emmett already had her father's record out. It was leaning against the wall near the incense burner. While he put it on the Animagraph and adjusted the legs, Zoe looked at the bins. There must be hundreds of lives in there, she thought. It's like a cemetery for ghosts.

"Ready?" asked Emmett. He stood beside the Animagraph, holding up the elaborate headphones.

"Why did my dad end up here?" Zoe asked.

"His spirit got lost on its way to somewhere else."

Zoe ran her fingers over the coarse paper cover of one of the special records, tracing the outline of the symbols. "Then why isn't he a ghost like in the movies? How did he end up here like this?" she asked, spreading her fingers across the record cover.

Emmett did an exaggerated shrug. "God? Gods? The universe? I don't know who makes decisions like that," he said. "I'm just a small businessman."

"Yesterday you didn't ask my name or anything about me, but you knew who I was. You knew that my dad was here. How?"

"You found the back room. That meant there was something for you back here," Emmett said.

"How did my dad get lost? Did he do something wrong?" Zoe nervously chewed the inside of her cheek again. It hurt and the broken skin felt gross, so she stopped.

"Some spirits are too weak to go. Some can't let go of their previous lives." Emmett held up the headphones again. "Maybe you can ask him when you see him."

"I don't understand any of this," said Zoe. "And I don't believe in magic."

"And yet, here you are."

Here I am, she thought. She looked over at the bins. She couldn't stand the idea of her father lying there, forgotten and dusty, slotted between other lost souls. She went to Emmett and stood in front of him. "I'm ready," she said.

He slid the elaborate headphones over her head. As he wrapped the last cord around her neck, she felt a little jolt of claustrophobic fear again. She slipped a hand into her pocket and felt around for Valentine's compass. She closed her hand tight around it.

A moment later, Emmett patted her shoulder. Zoe readied herself, not sure what she was expecting or even hoping for. She knew in the still, small center of herself that didn't always hurt, that wasn't always on the verge of tears, that her father couldn't possibly be here, couldn't be anyplace where she could actually talk to him. But the rest of her wanted anything that would, for even a moment, bring back some sense of him from his shattering absence.

Zoe heard the scratch of a needle dropping into a record groove.

And she was in a club, sweating, pumping her legs to

the thrashing beat of a band. They were playing impossibly fast and at an impossible volume. The sound was like being punched in the chest.

The club was crowded, the air thick with the familiar smell of cigarette smoke and sweating bodies jammed together in too small a space. People kept bumping into her, but instead of knocking her back, the way crowds always did at shows, they just sort of bounced off her and kept moving. She was much taller and heavier than she was used to being. She could see over people's heads all the way to the stage, where Black Flag was raging through "Rise Above." She moved her arms and they felt huge. It took a few minutes but then Zoe understood that she was inside her father's life, looking out through his eyes, feeling his excitement and a sense of such utter well-being that she knew he had to be drunk or high, maybe both. And she was caught up in that, too, a part of him, smiling through the chemical euphoria that had buoyed him through some random night when he was just a few years older than she was now.

Through the noise and smoke her gaze—*his gaze*—fell on a girl. She was almost as tall as he was, with a dark Mohawk, lurid purple eye shadow, and a sleeveless denim jacket with FUCK YOU VERY MUCH stenciled across the back. The girl was idly, but methodically, peeling the label off a bottle of Bud with her thumbnail. When she noticed Zoe's father checking her out, she smiled and stood her ground. It was the smile of someone who knew exactly how hot she was and was utterly at ease with being stared at. It took a few seconds to sink in before she recognized the girl as her mother. The girl who would become her mother in a few years. She felt her father's heart beat faster at the sight of her. She—he—took a step toward her.

Then Zoe was somewhere else, tumbling through a cascading slipstream of memories, experiences, and sensory details, all colliding and piling up on top of each other. She was adrift, moving from her father's childhood to random moments of his life and back and forth across time. She called out to her father from inside him. It was like she was caught in a storm of sights and sounds, smells and textures, all hitting her at once. All the sensations and snapshots of his life. It was too strange even to be scared.

She was her father later that night kissing her mother (talk about weird) as a bouncer tried to steer them outside after the show. She was her father in a hospital sitting by his own mother's bedside waiting for her to die. He wanted to reach out and tell her that she'd been a lousy mother, that he'd been a rotten son, and how he loved her anyway. But he'd bottled up everything for so long that he couldn't get at the words. So he just sat beside her bed, waiting.

She was her father sitting at his desk in a software company wondering what he'd done with his life. How did I get here? Is this it? I hack code and drive home for dinner until I die? he, *she,* wondered. She was her father looking at her as a baby crawling to him across the dirty warehouse floor. When he picked her up and held her infant self in his arms, she felt his deep mix of love and fear, the pure animal devotion he felt for his daughter and the stark fear that was a mantra running through his head. *What do I know about anything? How can I take care of her? Can't I just run away and pretend it never happened?* Zoe didn't feel hurt by the thought or his fear because she felt it all coming from the deep, desperate love he felt for her and her mother.

She was her father in the parking lot, at the end of another twelve-hour day spent punching code, trying to get the new release out the door, knowing that the company's next round of financing depended on it. She felt a pain start in his chest, like a hand reaching through his skin and bones, squeezing his heart until the whole world collapsed into a crushing knot of agony that cut off his air and pushed away every thought or sensation but the pain. Zoe had never felt anything like it, and just when she thought the pain had gone as far as it could go, a new wave hit. She felt him fall, felt the sun-scorched asphalt dig into his knees and sear his face where he, she, lay.

Zoe felt her father dying. And in the small, fragile space she held around herself that separated herself from him, she screamed.

She was still screaming when Emmett pulled the headphones off. For a moment the shock and the strange light combined to make him look weirdly out of focus, like a ghost of himself. It was over in an instant, though, and he was just Emmett again. Zoe sagged to the floor, and at last, barely breathing in the adrenaline rush that had left her cold and shaking, her head still spinning with the shock and fear of feeling her father die, she put her head down and began to cry.

She didn't let the tears go on too long. Emmett brought her toilet paper from the restroom so she could wipe off the makeup that had run down her face. Zoe's hands still shook when she said, "I was him. I was inside him but I couldn't talk to him."

Emmett nodded. "Yes. But I didn't cheat you. I said I could let you see your father, and that's what you did."

"I saw him die."

He nodded matter-of-factly. "It was an important moment for him. I'm not surprised you ended up there."

Zoe sat on the floor, drew up her legs, and rubbed the place on her chest where she felt her father's heart stop.

"It wasn't what I was expecting at all."

"Most people, even the ones we hold dear, are seldom what we think."

"I didn't want to just see him. I wanted to talk to him."

"Ah," Emmett said. "Seeing is easy. Talking, that's a harder job." He took the record from the Animagraph and slid it back into its cover. There was a symbol that looked like a bird in one corner, a snake biting its own tail in another, and then a line of Xs made of bones. "But it can be done."

"It can?" asked Zoe, feeling her despair lift a little.

"Almost anything can be done. If the customer can pay the price."

"What do you want?"

"Don't you mean how much?"

"You didn't want money before, why would you want it now?"

"You learn fast," Emmett said. He winked at her and closed the Animagraph.

"So, what do you want for me to talk to my dad?"

"Hardly anything at all."

"Tell me."

"A tooth," he said.

"A what?"

"A tooth. A baby tooth will do, or a recent one. It doesn't matter really."

"Why would you want my tooth?" asked Zoe. Leaning against the wall, she pushed herself to her feet.

Emmett walked to the counter in the front of the store and she trailed after him. The regular, normal LPs in their labeled bins looked strange and crude, like props in a movie. On the counter lay old 45s with torn covers stained by coffee and cigarette butts. Zoe picked one up. The cover was a picture of a costumed man in brilliant red ostrich feathers and a headdress that looked like something from an old western. The man didn't look like an Indian, she thought. More like a voodoo witch doctor. The 45 was called "I Walk on Gilded Splinters" by Dr. John. She didn't think he looked much like a doctor either.

"Why would you want my tooth?" Zoe asked again.

"Curiosity killed the cat. Don't you know that?" asked Emmett, a gentle chiding in his voice, but he smiled as he said it. He opened the cash register, took a cigarette and a white plastic disposable lighter from one of the wooden cubbyholes. "It's an unusual business, you know, minding the dead, running the Animagraph. It shouldn't be a shock that the payment for those services would also be unusual."

"I guess," Zoe said. *This thing, whatever it is, is getting stranger by the minute. But I can't stop now.*

Emmett lit up an unfiltered Camel, inhaled deeply, and blew a smoke ring at the ceiling. "It's your choice, of course," he said. "You've seen your father, with those pretty cat eyes. What you have to ask yourself is 'How much do I really want to talk to him?'"

Zoe didn't say anything. Emmett put the cigarette in the corner of his mouth and busied himself stacking the 45s and clearing clutter off the counter. She wondered where the records and papers could have come from. There hadn't been anyone but Emmett in the shop either time she'd found it. As she looked around it didn't look like anyone else had ever come inside.

"How do you even know I have a tooth?" she asked.

Emmett cocked his head to the side. "I get a lot of different kinds of people in my shop. I watch them. Watch them move and think and make the million small decisions that will lead them to the back room or out the door. You get to know people that way, the way I know you. You have toys. You have clothes. You have books. All sorts of childhood trinkets from a time when you were happy. You keep these things close to you. Some people call these objects 'souvenirs.' Others call them 'talismans.'"

"Is that why you want my tooth? It's a talisman?"

"Who knows?" Emmett said. "However, it is the price."

Zoe sighed. What choice did she have?

"I'll take it," she said.

Emmett smiled, showing his big white teeth. "I'll have everything ready for you tomorrow. Your father will be so happy to see you."

Zoe walked home the same way she'd arrived at the store: by vague wandering and eventual luck. It seemed insane to her that she could navigate that way, but she was getting used to it.

It was dark and the streets seemed unusually quiet, the lights unnaturally bright. Like the last time, instead of feeling nervous wandering in a city she barely knew and couldn't really navigate, she felt a thrilling rush of energy. *If this is what seeing Dad again will be like, it's worth it, whatever crazy things Emmett might want. Be-sides, what's he going to do with a tooth?*

She let herself into the apartment as quietly as she could. To her relief, her mother was asleep on the couch with the TV on, her shoes off, her jacket and purse in a pile on the one chair in the room. Zoe went straight to her room and closed the door without making a sound.

Already the trip inside her father's life had begun to recede in her consciousness until it was like the memory of a dream. She wasn't sure if this was an effect of what-ever magic powered the Animagraph—and *magic* was the only word she could think of for it—or the shock of feeling her father die. What she was certain of was that she had accepted a whole new idea into her life, just as she had begun to accept that she could never remember the exact route to Emmett's store.

Magic, she thought. Why not?

She could hear the word now without judgment or irony. It was becoming just one more fact in the innu-merable facts that she learned every day at home and at school. Algebra. The name of the largest mammal. The number of days in a row you can eat fried chicken with-out barfing. Ways to communicate with the dead.

She went to her closet and pushed the clothes on hangers out of the way. On the floor was a box. She picked it up and tore off the sealing tape. Inside were her baby shoes, snapshots of her parents back at the ware-house, small stuffed animals, and a small pink plastic bottle with a white kitten on the top. My talismans, she thought. Zoe shook the bottle. Something rattled inside. Popping the top, she poured out the contents. Her last two baby teeth, the ones that had come out together, rested in the palm of her hand.

She held the teeth up and looked at them, amazed that she'd ever been small enough for the tiny things. Then she put them back in the bottle, sealed it, and set it on top of her dresser.

She took the compass from her pocket. "Tomorrow," she said, holding it tight. "I'll talk to him tomorrow."

Four

Zoe awoke early the next morning before the alarm went off. While in the bathroom for her morning pee, she realized that she was starving. She hadn't eaten lunch or had any dinner after coming home last night. Even bone-dry KFC leftovers seemed appetizing at that moment. She went into the kitchen to forage for breakfast and found her mother sitting at the table, red-eyed and smoking. When her mother had quit smoking a couple of years earlier, she had threatened to strangle Zoe if she ever started, so Zoe made sure her mother never knew. There was an upturned peanut-butter-jar lid on the table, overflowing with burned-out Marlboro Lights.

Official-looking papers were scattered on the table. Zoe had seen enough of them by now to know that they were legal documents. She tried to read them upside down, but the kitchen lights were off. All she could make out were a few words at the top of one page, words printed larger and darker than the rest: DENIAL OF CLAIM.

"Your father doesn't exist," said Zoe's mother. "Didn't exist."

"Don't say that. *Dad existed*."

"Not according to these assholes," said her mother. Her voice was raspy from the smoke. There were dark rings under her red eyes. She looked like she'd been up all night.

"Just please don't say that about Dad."

"I know, baby. I know," said her mother with a kind of exhausted resignation. "I just don't know what we're going to do. We can't live like this forever." When her father's software company had gone bankrupt, it took their savings with it. After that, the little money they had in a family trust disappeared frighteningly fast. Zoe's mother kicked an empty moving box lying on the floor near the table.

The way the flat morning light came in through the grimy little kitchen window, if she tilted her head just right, Zoe could almost see her mother as the girl in purple eye shadow. Beautiful. Happy. Confident. If she tilted her head back and looked at her straight on, it was her mother, raw-nerved and bone-weary.

The girl in the purple eye shadow is dead. As dead as Dad.

Zoe remembered her father watching his own mother die, how he'd been made mute by despair and hopelessness. How he'd carried the guilty memory of it his whole life.

"It'll be okay," said Zoe, feeling like a liar as she spoke. She looked down at her feet, willing them to move. She took a couple of tentative steps. "It'll be okay." One more step and she was standing by her mother. She was afraid to look at her, but gently laid a hand on her shoulder. She felt her mother's hand close over hers.

Zoe's mother put her arms around her and pulled her close, crying like Zoe had never seen her cry before. There was a flutter in Zoe's stomach, a heat that rose to her cheeks. Part of her wanted to cry, too. But she'd already lost control in Emmett's record store and the tears had stung, like her body was trying to force broken glass out through her eyes. Now she held the tears back, telling herself that she would never lose control again. Zoe rubbed her mother's back as she cried.

"It'll be okay," she repeated. It didn't matter if she herself didn't believe it.

She saw her father by his dying mother's bed.

I just have to say it.

School felt entirely new and strange. Not impersonal and oppressive, the way it had when she'd first arrived, just . . . strange, but not in a bad way.

As she stood at her locker, the distance Zoe had felt toward the other students had changed. All the kids, the different tribes . . . they all looked different. A little less odd and a little more something else. What? Forgivable, maybe. Seeing through her father's eyes, feeling his life pass through her, had changed something in her, but the sensation was even stronger here than it had been the night before.

Zoe looked around the crowded hallway. The girls were all beautiful, all variations of the youthful version of her mother from the club. The cheerleaders, all smiles, texting each other madly, were more graceful than her mother. A cluster of girls in Dr. Who T-shirts and super-hero and science-fiction backpacks seemed kinder, and some of them seemed more shy. Some of the girls were prettier, but not many. And none of them, not one, possessed the confidence her mother had had, that magic rock-star arrogance. The kind that didn't push you away, but drew you to her.

And then there were the boys. Zoe couldn't remember the last time boys had registered on her radar. Since the funeral, boys had all blurred together into a kind of vague cloud of maleness that was easier to ignore than individual boys. Now she was looking at them again and remembering their mystery and allure. Boys' walks fascinated her, so full of their random and unfocused animal energy. Zim, the boy she'd hung out with at her old school, had shared her first kiss with, had mutually copped first feels with . . . he had a great walk. Too bad he turned out to be such a jerk, Zoe thought, remembering him drunkenly hitting on Julie at a party.

Until now, Zoe had stayed mad at Zim, but even he seemed forgivable now—as young, stupid, lost, and over-whelmed by the world as Zoe herself. And there was his great hip-swinging walk. She remembered that he had always been much more handsome walking away than standing still.

Around her twelfth birthday, when she'd first become vaguely interested in the mystery of boys, Valentine starting give her advice, especially on which ones to talk to and which to avoid. His general rule was to look out for the ones having too good a time. Happy was all right, but too happy was a big biohazard warning. These were the boys who were usually the kings of their cliques— jock heroes, drama-club darlings, and the rest. Valentine said that they were the ones who listened and believed it when some idiot teacher on a nostalgia high would tell their class, "These are the best years of your life." Knowing all that as she did, though, didn't always help when the less discriminating part of her brain kept her gaze locked on the boys' gliding arms, their strong legs and hips.

One of the shy girls, in glasses and a Wolverine T-shirt, dropped a book and a handsome boy in a basketball team jacket didn't see. He started to trip. A little switch went off in Zoe's brain and she saw her father falling down next to his car in a parking lot. The handsome boy caught himself, shot Wolverine girl a dirty look, and continued down the hall. Zoe felt a tightness in her chest, but it was over in a second. She turned back to her locker, closed it, and hurried away.

"To continue our discussion from yesterday," said Mr. Danvers, "who can remind us of the definition of a predator?"

Zoe was doodling on a piece of paper in her notebook. She couldn't concentrate on much of anything, even a topic as cool as predators. She distractedly drew long, ragged sets of triangles. Gradually they linked up into long rows.

Teeth. There were dozens of sets of teeth leering up at her. She'd covered that whole page with them.

"Care to join us, Zoe?"

She looked up, suddenly embarrassed. The whole class was looking at her.

"Yes? Sorry."

Mr. Danvers gave her a quick, reassuring smile. "Holly was kind enough to remind us of the definition of a predator. I wonder if you remember the name of the act predators carry out?"

Zoe glanced down again at the jagged teeth and shook her head. She was letting her mind drift off to the dark place again. Like before, when she wouldn't talk for days at a time and her mother would be crying while on the phone to the doctors. It was stupid. She was happy now. There was no reason to let the darkness swallow her. *I'm going to see Dad*. I'm happy, Zoe told herself. I'm happy.

"Predation," she said.

"Excellent," Mr. Danvers said. "And what do most predators eat?"

"Other animals."

"Making them?"

"Carnivores."

"Give that girl a cigar," said Mr. Danvers. A few kids in the class laughed. He turned and wrote CARNIVORE on the blackboard, then added a few more notes underneath.

Absynthe caught her eye and gave her a little wave. Zoe waved back. "How's the boy?" mouthed Absynthe. Zoe glanced up at the board to make sure Mr. Danvers was still writing, then she mouthed to Absynthe, "I'll tell you later." Absynthe nodded and turned back to the front of the room.

"All predators have special skills and adaptations that help them hunt and catch their prey," Mr. Danvers told the class. "Great white sharks are a good example. In their snout, they have an organ called the ampullae of Lorenzini." He paused to write this on the board. Zoe copied the words, though she had a feeling that by tomorrow she'd have forgotten what they meant.

"This organ," Mr. Danvers continued, "can detect the tiny electrical currents generated by all living things. Sharks also have an incredible sense of smell. Great whites can detect a drop of blood in the water from five kilometers away. Anyone know how many miles that is?"

A shaggy, blond boy in a plaid shirt a couple of sizes too big for him thrust up his hand, then blurted out, "Three point one one miles."

Mr. Danvers nodded. "Thank you, Alex. I'd have settled for three, but you get extra brownie points for knowing about the point one one."

Zoe tried to write down everything that Mr. Danvers said, trying to stay focused so she wouldn't start drawing teeth again.

"Snakes are another advanced predatory species. They use highly developed organs in their tongue and mouth to literally taste the air. And they do it very accurately," said Mr. Danvers. "Most snakes have lousy eyesight, but a lot of snakes, pit vipers, for instance, make up for this by seeing their prey another way. They have infrared—heat—sensors in pits on their face, between their nostrils and their eyes. They use these sensors to hunt prey at night."

In Zoe's mind's eye a picture formed of Emmett in his dark store, lurking there all day, and maybe all night, happily dusting the record bins in total darkness. At first it was funny but then the image of him moving around the store in the dark, just another shadow, nothing more than a trick of the light, made her uneasy.

It's just your mind playing tricks on you, she told herself. Trying to drag you back to the dark place. Emmett was odd, maybe even a full-on fruit bat, but he'd never done anything creepy or hurt her. In fact, he'd shown her a whole new world. Emmett was giving her back her father. How could that be a bad thing?

Mr. Danvers went to the shelves and took down the big jar of animal teeth. "Everyone come on up. I'm going to show you the kind of specialized teeth predators have." He dumped the jar on the tabletop.

As Zoe followed the rest of the class to the front of the room, she heard a girl say, "Ew! Are those people's?"

Mr. Danvers held up a couple of yellowed, flat-topped teeth. "They look like it, don't they?" he asked. "They're chimp molars. Very similar to ours."

Zoe squeezed in and looked at the teeth Mr. Danvers was holding. They did look very human, if a little bit big. I really don't want to lose my last baby teeth, she thought. And how would Emmett know the difference in that dark store? An idea formed in her mind while Mr. Danvers went on about sharks biting through steel cables and how some snake teeth were like needles and perfect for injecting poison, but she wasn't listening anymore.

As class ended, Zoe busied herself at her desk, shuffling papers and stacking and restacking her books, waiting for the other students to file out of the room. Mr. Danvers sat at the lab table writing in a black spiral-bound notebook. Zoe walked to where he sat, rehearsing the question in her mind, trying to sound relaxed and spontaneous.

"Mr. Danvers?"

He looked up, a little surprised. "Yes, Zoe. What can I help you with?"

Zoe set her books down on the lab table. Animal teeth were still strewn across its surface. Some had been moved into little piles during class. Canine. Feline. Bear. Snake. Shark. Zoe picked up a shark tooth the size of a shot glass. It was heavy and she remembered that it had belonged to a kind of prehistoric shark the size of a school bus.

"We talked about all these killers and carnivores, but they all seem the same to me, you know?" she asked. "I mean, lions and tigers and bears are all killers, but you haven't said which one is the best predator."

"Ah," Mr. Danvers said, raising his eyebrows in mock surprise. "I thought the answer to that was obvious. It's us. Humans have hunted and killed every species of animal on the planet, many to extinction. No other predator can claim that." Then he added, "None that we know of."

"What do you mean?"

Mr. Danvers set down his pen and laced the fingers of his hands together. "Back in the early eighties, a hand-ful of important biologists thought that we could pretty much close the book on mammal species, that we'd found every single kind of mammal on the planet. Then, in Madagascar, people started discovering new species of lemurs, a kind of primitive primate. Suddenly there were a lot more mammals around than a lot of smart people had ever thought possible." He paused for a moment and opened his hands. "Who knows what else is out there, hiding in the deep rain forests, on mountains, or in underground burrows? The dinosaurs ruled the world for more than a hundred million years before we came along. Maybe there's something out there that will knock us humans off our perch as king of the food chain."

Zoe set down the shark tooth and picked up one Mr. Danvers had said was from a lion. It was bigger than her thumb and curved like a dagger. "I don't like the sound of that," she said.

"Don't worry," said Mr. Danvers. "We've got another million years or so before we have to worry about poodles and tabbies taking over."

Zoe smiled. "Want to help me put these away?" Mr. Danvers asked, reaching for the jar he kept the teeth in. He put the empty jar in the middle of the table and began dropping handfuls of teeth inside.

Suddenly the plan Zoe had been thinking about evaporated. She didn't want to steal from him after all. "Shouldn't we be separating these by species or something?" she asked.

Mr. Danvers shrugged. "I like a little chaos. When things get all mixed together, sometimes you see things you would never have seen otherwise."

Zoe nodded, wondering how she could ever have thought about ripping off someone as genuinely okay as Mr. Danvers. She dropped handfuls of animal teeth into the jar, mentally kissing her baby teeth good-bye.

A teacher Zoe didn't recognize, an older woman wearing lipstick just a little too bright for her prim dress, came into the room. "Mr. Danvers," she said. "The vice principal would like to see you."

"Thank you, Ms. Messina," he said. The woman nodded, giving Zoe a quick, inquiring glance before she left.

Mr. Danvers got up and took a sport coat that Zoe had never once seen him wear off a peg on the far side of the shelves. "Would you mind putting away the teeth for me? Just set the jar back on the shelf."

"Sure," said Zoe.

"Thanks," said Mr. Danvers, and he left, giving her a quick smile before closing the door behind him. Zoe continued dropping teeth into the jar, but her mind was racing.

This is a sign, she thought. The universe wants me to take it.

Still, she dropped teeth into the jar. If she hadn't already decided to be a good girl, to not steal and just give Emmett her own damned teeth like she'd promised, this wouldn't be a problem.

What the hell does he want my tooth for, anyway? she wondered. The idea was bothering her more and more.

Zoe dropped the last of the teeth into the jar, hesitated, and then screwed the lid shut. Another second of hesitation, then she took the jar and set it on the shelf with Mr. Danvers's other science specimens.

As she picked up her books, Zoe was again hit by the image of Emmett sitting quietly in his dark shop all night, waiting for her to bring him her tooth. She set down her books and took the jar from the shelf, going down on her knees behind the lab table. She twisted the lid, but it wouldn't move.

She heard the door open. A voice filled the room. "Jim?" It was an adult. Another teacher's voice. Whoever it was took a couple of more steps into the room. "Jim?" There was a pause. Zoe didn't move. She held her breath, and from her crouched position, it felt like her heart was going to beat right out of her chest. A moment later, though, she heard an annoyed exhalation of breath and the teacher leave the room, closing the door behind.

Zoe let out her breath and sucked in air. Her hands were shaking. She tried the lid again, but it still wouldn't move. She tapped the top of the jar on the floor a couple of times and tried again. This time the lid twisted off easily. She dumped the teeth on the floor and sifted through them quickly. In the jumbled mess she couldn't find the one she wanted. Then she wondered how long she'd been looking and when Mr. Danvers would get back. Panicked, she started scooping teeth back into the jar. When she picked up the last handful, there it was: one perfect human-looking chimp tooth. She pocketed it, screwed the lid back on the jar, and left the room as quickly and quietly as she could.

Absynthe was coming down the hallway, hiding an unlit cigarette cupped in her hand. She looked surprised, then put her hand over her mouth, her eyes widening in amusement. "Outside," she said. Caught off guard by the order, Zoe followed her.

Absynthe led Zoe around a corner of the school and into a cul-de-sac under a set of rusted, cobweb-covered emergency stairs that looked like they couldn't support even one of the skinny fashionista girls, much less a bunch of panicked students.

Absynthe held out the pack and offered Zoe a cigarette. Zoe shook her head. "No thanks. I quit," she said. She had to cut herself off. She almost said, *I quit when I was in the hospital.* She wasn't ready to talk about any of that yet.

Absynthe put her hand on Zoe's shoulder. "Please tell me the guy you're sneaking off to see isn't Mr. Danvers."

Zoe stared at her for a second. "What? No!"

Absynthe gave her an appraising look. "So, what were you doing in there? Checking your grades?"

"Yeah."

"Liar," Absynthe said, more amused than accusing.

Zoe leaned back against the wall. "The guy I'm going to see. It isn't what you think. It's more complicated. I don't know exactly how to explain it."

Absynthe lit the cigarette and nodded. "I get it. An older guy, right? Yeah, I've been there. Watch your back. Those college boys can turn weird on you."

Zoe almost laughed. An older guy. You're right about that, she thought. But if you only knew the rest.

"I'm a little mixed up about some of what's going on right now," she said. "When I work this out, maybe I'll tell you all about it. Okay?" She looked up at Absynthe and the girl's face was more serious than Zoe had expected. "I'm going to have to tell someone and my mom is totally out of the question."

Absynthe nodded. "Moms are like that. First they kill you with kindness, and then they ground your ass." She nodded to the nearby exit. "Run off to your secret rendezvous that's not what I think. But remember that when you're done you owe me a story."

"Deal," said Zoe.

Absynthe gave Zoe the appraising look again. "You know," she said, "you're cuter than I think you want to be. I was considering luring you out here and kissing you, but it seems like maybe you have enough going on right now."

Zoe blinked at the girl a couple of times. "Oh. Yeah. I think I do."

Absynthe smiled. "Don't worry. You're safe. For now."

"Uh. Okay," Zoe said, trying not to look as surprised and confused as she felt.

"Go see your sugar daddy," said Absynthe, waving her hand toward the street.

Zoe started back along the cul-de-sac. Halfway down

she spun on her heels. Absynthe was puffing away on her cigarette and looking at her. "Wait a minute," Zoe said. "Older guys turn weird? And now you want to kiss me? I think you owe me a story, too."

Absynthe laughed. "Deal."

Five

The day was hot and bright. Zoe walked to Emmett's on autopilot, not paying attention to where she was going, knowing her feet would find the way. Her mouth was dry and her pulse pounded in her temples.

Then, as always—as if the store found her instead of her finding the store—she was there. She pushed her way inside, welcoming the sensation of being swallowed by the cool darkness.

When her eyes adjusted to the light, she spotted Emmett near the back of the store. He had piles of LPs stacked on top of the record bins and was sorting them into their proper slots.

"You came back," he said conversationally, not looking up from his work.

"Sure. Why wouldn't I?"

Emmett pulled one of the white record dividers

toward him, then hefted a pile of battered old Johnny Cash albums into the empty space behind it in the bin. "You'd be surprised at how many people, once they've had a taste of a loved one's real, undiluted life, never set foot in here again."

"Not me," said Zoe, shaking her head. "I want to see my dad."

"Did you bring what I asked for?"

Zoe reached into her pocket, removed the chimp tooth, and held it out. She seemed to finally have caught the man's full attention because he put down the records and came to her. Zoe made sure to stand in the darkest part of the store. She didn't want Emmett to get too good a look at the tooth until she was already under the Animagraph's spell. She didn't have any real idea about how the machine worked, but she was fairly certain that it wasn't something you could just turn off with the flick of a switch, even if you realized that you'd been slipped a counterfeit molar.

Emmett plucked the tooth from Zoe's open palm. He held it up before his eyes, like a jeweler appraising a diamond. "Ohhh. A grown-up one," he said. "How lovely. Thank you, Zoe."

She nodded, her throat tight, her heart hammering, waiting for him to figure out her trick. But he didn't. Emmett beamed at her like her parents would do when she'd brought home straight A's.

"Can we do it now?" Zoe asked.

"Of course." Emmett led the way to the back of the store and held the beaded curtain open for Zoe like a doorman. He seemed much happier than usual. Like the tooth had made him feel a little giddy, Zoe thought.

Then his face turned serious and Zoe's heart sank. But relief rushed over her when he began to speak.

"I need to get formal for a minute and tell you that you can change your mind and leave now," said Emmett. "What if what you see is more than you can bear? You're going to the land of the dead. It's not an easy journey."

Zoe shook her head. "I don't care."

"This is your last chance," said Emmett. "What if you get stuck? What if you're so overcome with grief and longing that you can't let your father's spirit go? What if the Animagraph breaks down? It's an ancient machine. Things can go wrong. You'll be stuck with your body in the world of the living, while the thinking, feeling part of you will be lost in a world of ghosts."

Zoe clenched her jaw. Emmett's infuriating, exasperating questions had knocked her off balance and were bringing back some of the darkness and doubt.

"I don't fucking care."

"Okeydoke," said Emmett lightly. He tossed the tooth in the air once, caught it, and dropped it into the breast pocket of his work shirt. "I have to ask. Make sure you're going of your own free will. Standard disclaimer stuff."

"Please, just hook me up."

"At your service, ma'am."

He put his hands on Zoe's shoulders, steered her to the Animagraph, and began fastening the claustrophobic crisscross of straps and buckles around her head. Before he pulled the blinders over her eyes, he said, "Hold out your hand." Zoe obliged and he dropped three objects into her palm. All were white. Two were circular and one was shaped like a little plastic tube.

"What are these?"

Emmett went back to the straps. "The two round ones are aspirins. The plastic tube is a kind of herbal smelling salts. Believe me, you're going to need them all when you get back." He stopped talking while he tightened a couple of extra-small buckles. "When you return, just swallow the aspirin and break the tube under your nose. Or, if you prefer, I could do it for you."

"That's okay," said Zoe. She didn't like the idea of someone else doing something that sounded so strange and oddly intimate, much less him. She wished he'd shut up about sending her away and just do it.

"I'm ready," she said.

Emmett pulled the last few straps into place. "Blast off in three. Two. One."

Zoe heard the familiar sound of a needle hitting a record groove. Then the ground opened up and she began to fall.

Soon the feeling of falling became a feeling of rushing, as if she were being swept down a river in powerful rapids. Only there was no water and no sound, just the ceaseless push and pull of her body as she tumbled through the dark. The air smelled wet and rank and she might have brushed against stone a few times. Zoe felt as if she could let herself be swept along forever. There was something comforting about the idea of just letting go.

She was sitting in the window seat of a crowded bus. Next to her was an old woman in a yellow floral house-coat and an elaborate hat covered with fake flowers. Like a crazy Easter bonnet, she thought. Other passengers filled the aisle, holding on to overhead straps. There were old men and women, their faces liver-spotted and lined with age. There were people her parents' age and some hers. There were even some children packed together in the back.

This wasn't like a normal San Francisco city bus. It looked very old. The interior angles were rounded and there were small patches on the ceiling where the paint had peeled off. The seat sagged and the fabric had been repaired with thick, coarse thread. The big diesel engine under her feet groaned and strained at every turn.

Long shadows lay along the road but the bright lights inside the bus made it impossible to see much outside. Zoe cupped her hands around her eyes and stared out the window. Specks of rain jeweled the glass, and when she looked down, she could just make out the road sliding by.

No one on the bus spoke. No one looked around.

So, these are souls, thought Zoe. Are they new souls or old? She wondered if there was some way to tell. She leaned to the old woman next to her and whispered, "Do you know where this bus goes?"

The old woman looked at Zoe and smiled kindly. "There's only one route, dear. The buses go to and from and back again."

"But where do they go to and from?"

She patted Zoe's arm. "It'll be all right dear. You'll see." A moment later, the bus slowed and pulled to the curb. The doors hissed opened and the passengers started filing off.

When the old lady stood, Zoe followed her off the bus. They were parked near the corner of a very ordinary-looking street.

"Ma'am, I'm looking for my father," Zoe said.

The old woman nodded. Off the bus, she seemed more animated, more like a real old lady and not a dreaming ghost. The other passengers were also more relaxed, moving and talking to each other, like regular people.

The old woman sighed. "How lovely." She popped open her purse, pulled out something yellow, and put it in Zoe's hand. A piece of butterscotch candy. She gave Zoe a small wave and walked around the corner with some of the other passengers.

Zoe walked to the corner, too, as the other passengers wandered off in all directions. Everyone was moving, talking, excited. Zoe tried to get the attention of one or two of them, but they all seemed in a rush to go somewhere. Soon the street was empty. She stood under a streetlamp on the corner and watched the bus pull away.

The rain along the road hadn't made it to town. It felt like late afternoon. A fat orange sun hung midway down the sky. She was standing on a long, wide street across from a boardwalk that ran along a beach. Beyond the boardwalk, Zoe could see an old-fashioned Ferris wheel, carousel, and a wooden roller coaster that reminded her of Coney Island. The sound of tinny carousel music made her feel a little better.

She crossed the street and stood on the boardwalk, leaning on the rusting metal fence and staring out at a calm black sea, wondering what to do next. She could see people down on the beach, moving among the amusement-park rides. It was so beautiful in the late-afternoon light. It nearly made her cry. She suddenly felt very alone and lost.

Something moved in the corner of her eye. She turned around and saw a man in a dark gray overcoat. Like her, he was staring out to sea.

"Dad?" said Zoe.

The man looked up. He stared at her for a second.

"Zoe?"

She ran to him and almost jumped into his arms. They held on to each other for a long time, neither of them speaking, just holding each other. A moment earlier she'd been lost in a strange city, and now she left like her heart could burst from joy.

Finally, her father stepped back a little and looked at her. "What are you doing here?" He froze, the color draining from his face. "You're not . . . ?"

Zoe shook her head. "No. I'm not dead. I just needed to see you."

Her father pulled her to him again. "It's wonderful to see you, but you shouldn't be here."

Zoe pushed him away, but held on to his sleeve. "Dad! Don't say that! Don't say you don't want to see me?"

He put his hand on her cheek. "It's wonderful to see you. But you still shouldn't have come here."

Zoe pushed her father harder this time and stepped back. "Why do you keep saying that?" she yelled, not caring if anyone heard her. Tears welled up in her eyes. "What did I do wrong? Why did you have to go? Do you blame me and Mom?"

Her father took a step toward her, but Zoe took another step back. He stayed where he was and said, "Baby, I would never leave you and your mother if I could help it. But I died, and the dead can't live in your world."

Zoe nodded, hugging her arms across her chest. "One minute you were there and then you were just gone."

"I miss you both. And I'm mad, too, you know. I was taken away from the only people I ever really loved."

"I used this weird machine. I saw your life from inside

your head," she said. "You were so unhappy working all the time. It felt like you wanted to go."

"Not for a second," said her father. He put his hands on Zoe's shoulders. "Yeah, I was unhappy with the way things were, but that was about bad choices. Work and money and things. It was never about you or your mom. Your mom and I were already talking about me working less and her working more, trying to find a little more balance for all of us."

"Really? You swear?"

"I'd never lie to you." Zoe's father put his arms around her and she let him. Zoe cried against his chest and this time the tears didn't feel like they were being torn out of her.

After a few minutes, her father asked, "What do you think of my new home?"

Zoe looked around. "What is this place? Heaven?"

Her father laughed. "That's everyone's first question."

"It's not hell, is it?"

"That's everyone's second question," he said. "We're in a place called Iphigene. It's a kind of way station. A place where you spend time before moving on."

"How long do you have to stay here?"

He shrugged. "I don't know. I think it varies. A lot of things are like that here. You kind of feel your way along. Not much is written down," he said. He grew quieter, more thoughtful. "I think you have to figure out the rules for yourself. Iphigene is kind like a video game, you know? What do you need right now, the golden key or the flaming sword? When you figure that out, you get on a bus and move on to the next level."

"Iphigene," said Zoe. "It reminds me of Coney Island. Kind of old and messed up, but in a cool way. Can we look around?"

Her father nodded. "Let me give you the tour." As they crossed the street, he took her hand. Zoe smiled, feeling about six again.

They walked back to the corner where the bus had dropped her off. There was an open-air newsstand with a dark green awning. They sold magazines and newspapers in what looked like a hundred languages. A clothing store, with mannequins modeling different coats, stood next to it. Farther along was a movie theater with an old marquee where the name of the movie was announced with removable plastic letters: JEAN COCTEAU'S ORPHÉE. At the end of the block was a bar with a big picture window looking out over the ocean and a crescent moon on the door, where people talked and laughed in the semidark.

"Look at all the restaurants," she said as they crossed to the next block. "Do you eat here?"

"Some do," said her father. "I think it's another choice. I haven't eaten a bite and I've never been hungry. Some souls never leave the restaurants. They just eat and eat. I guess it's comforting. Some don't seem to know they're dead. Hell, I wasn't sure at first. But you learn."

Zoe stopped walking and hugged him. "I hate that you're dead," she said. "Everything's wrong. Nothing works. My life sucks."

"I'm so sorry. I wish I was with you. But your mother will take care of you. She's strong."

Zoe let out a harsh laugh. "She can't do anything. We lost the house. We live in a shitty little apartment. I don't have any friends. Mom just cries all the time."

They sat down on a bench and looked out at the calm, black sea. "Your mother is the strongest person I know. She might be upset now, but if you can help her, you'll both get through this okay."

"But everything is such shit."

"And everything is going to be shit for a while," he said. "That's what happens when you lose someone you love. Then, one day, weeks or months from now, things aren't quite so shitty. Then, little by little, they start to get better. Eventually, you'll get back to who you really are, and what your life is supposed to be." He sighed. "But for a while, things are just going to be rotten and it helps to have someone to help you through it. You and your mother can do that for each other."

Zoe nodded. She sat back and laid her head on her father's shoulder. He said, "When you two aren't fighting, what's your mom doing with herself?"

"She's trying to find a job, but it's been so long. It's really hard for her."

He shook his head. "So many stupid choices," he said.

"That's another lousy part about being dead. You can see your whole life laid out in front of you. Every stupid, mean, and pointless thing you ever did. Me working all the time and your mother not working was a terrible idea."

"Mom did all this art before."

"She stopped a little while before you were born so she could be a stay-at-home mom," he said. "We wanted you to have a kind of home neither of us had." He fell silent for a minute. Zoe sat up and looked at him. He was frowning. Deep lines creased his forehead, and crow's-feet at the corners of his eyes darkened his expression.

"You know, it could have been me who stayed home," he said. "I wouldn't have minded being a house husband. But I'd played with computers and was good at it, so when a friend started his own company, a job just landed in my lap. And your mom ended up being the one who stayed home."

"That's funny. I thought what you did, working all the time, was the sacrifice."

He laughed at that. "Did you see any of the album covers your mom designed? She had a really savage talent," he said. Zoe could hear the pride in his voice. "She'd stroll into the offices of these little labels and all the tough-guy wannabe artists would try to intimidate her. She'd just stare 'em down."

"I remember," Zoe said. "Some of those old covers were really good."

"If I'd worked less I could have spent more time with you, and let your mom do more of her own art." He shrugged. "But I didn't. That's one of my biggest regrets."

The sun was getting lower, burning a deeper, redder shade of orange as it slid toward the horizon. Below them on the beach, the amusement park was lit up like a birthday cake.

"Let's go on the carousel," her father said. He took her hand and they ran across the street, down a wooden staircase, and across the light, clean sand to the park.

There weren't many people on the rides, and no ticket sellers. No one was in charge to tell them to stay behind the yellow line or to wait until the ride stopped, so they both leaped onto the carousel while it was still turning. Zoe chose a white stallion, trimmed in gold and crimson. Her father chose a snarling sea serpent, painted in lurid pinks and purples. After the carousel, they rode the spinning teacups and then the Ferris wheel. At the top of the wheel, Zoe could see Iphigene laid out below her. Behind the long street that ran along the ocean, row upon row of giant apartment buildings stretched into the distance as far as she could see. At the far end of the long street, off to her left, was a huge white marble building. It looked like a strange combination of a fairy-tale castle and a cathedral.

"What's that?" she asked, pointing to the building.

"That's City Hall."

"Dead people have a city hall?"

"We prefer the term *postlife*."

It was the kind of dumb joke he used to make back home, and hearing him say something so ridiculous felt really good.

Next, they went on the roller coaster. It was enormous, bigger than any coaster Zoe had ever seen in the living world. She was a little nervous getting into the front car, but her father was so happy and confident that she went anyway. The coaster was like the one at Coney Island, old and made of wood. It clacked and creaked the whole time their little car crept to the crest of the first drop. Near the top, Zoe looked down and the city was nothing but a bright toy at the bottom of the Grand Canyon. She closed her eyes and grabbed on to her father's sleeve. He put his big hand over hers and they stayed like that the rest of the way up.

Then the clicking stopped, and they began to fall. Zoe's stomach rose up into her throat. Then she heard something new. It was her father screaming at the top of his lungs, the big, insane whoop that people always made on roller-coaster drops. She felt her father's arms go up into the air as the whoop went on and on. Zoe opened her eyes a crack at the bottom, just as the roller coaster whipped them around the first corner. She let go of her father's sleeve and tried to whoop, too. He took her hand and held it up with his, and they whooped together, screaming like idiots, with pure joy as the sun came down slowly over the sea.

Something unclenched inside Zoe, almost without her being aware of it until the feeling had begun to pass. For the first time in what seemed like a million years, she felt all right. She might even have called the feeling happy. She smiled and it wasn't the rueful half smiles of her recent life, but a real one. She and her father were together, side by side, and she felt whole and healed in a way that all the words and doctors and pills in the world couldn't have fixed. And she saw that he was happy, too, just to be with her. And that was enough.

Later, as they strolled along the boardwalk, Zoe asked, "Where do you live?"

He nodded toward the apartment buildings. "Back there a few blocks."

"How many people are there here?"

"I don't know. The buses bring new people all the time."

They stopped and leaned on the rusty metal fence separating the boardwalk from the beach. The sun was just falling below the horizon, and night was spreading like a dark tide across the sky. A few yellow stars flickered faintly high above.

"I hate to say it, but it's time for you to go," her father said.

"Can't I stay a little longer?"

"When I came down to the beach tonight, it was because a little voice whispered in my ear that I should go to the bus stop at the boardwalk. Now that voice is telling me that I have to take you back."

"You can get on the bus, too. Come back with me."

"I can't leave here yet. It's not my time."

"I don't want to go."

"You have to go. I want you to go," he said. "This is a place for the dead, not a living girl. No matter how beautiful she is, or how wonderful it is to see her."

Zoe looked down at her feet. "Walk me back?"

"Try to stop me."

Zoe looped her arm in her father's and held on to him tight all the way to the bus stop. Lights had come on in the restaurant and the bar. The movie-theater marquee was lit up. The street looked like something from a pleasant dream of the perfect small town.

A bus was already waiting when they reached the end of the boardwalk. Zoe's father pulled her close and kissed the top of her head.

"Go and live your life," he said. "Be happy. Be crazy. And always remember that I love you."

"I love you, too, Dad."

At the bus's entrance, her father said, "Your mother doesn't know about any of this, does she?"

Zoe shook her head. Her father nodded and smiled. "It'll be our secret," he said. "But when you get home, promise to kiss her for me."

"I will."

He held her hand as she got on the bus. Zoe found a window seat and pressed her palms against the glass, as if she could reach through it and touch her dad's arm one more time. The bus engine rumbled to life. Her father blew her a kiss as the bus pulled away. Zoe closed her eyes. She thought she was going to cry, but she felt the ground open up and the powerful sense of falling. Then the surging tides that had carried her to her father and Iphigene swept her away.

Zoe gasped when she came down, back into her body. But she was happy. Excited even. A few small tears lingered on her cheeks. She took a long, deep breath and wiped them away.

"So, was it what you wanted?" asked Emmett.

"Oh, man. It was a million times better than I hoped for. I feel like I'm flying."

"Good. Not everyone is so chipper when they come back. I'm glad you are."

Zoe felt Emmett bustling around her, loosening the straps, unhooking wires. Suddenly the blinders came off her eyes and she could see again. The old store looked wonderful. Even Emmett looked wonderful. Everything was perfect. She didn't even need the aspirin Emmett had given her.

"I want to take him home with me," said Zoe.

"You want your father's disc?"

"Yes. I know it'll cost me something, so just tell me the price and I'll pay it."

He tugged at the last few Animagraph straps. "Look how eager you are," he said. "You must have had a wonderful time."

Zoe recognized his tone as the beginning of a negotiation. "I did. Thanks for helping me get there. What do you want for the disc?"

"You don't even have an Animagraph. What will you do with him?"

"I don't want to play the disc," Zoe said. "I just don't like the idea of my father's soul stuffed in some dusty bin like old socks."

"Of course," replied Emmett, nodding and scratching his chin like he was thinking. "The price is this: your blood. Not much. Just a few drops of blood on a tissue or cloth. Give me that and you can take dear old dad home with you."

Zoe looked at Emmett and didn't hesitate. "I'll bring it tomorrow."

"I can help you do it now. I'm sure I have a straight pin or box cutter behind the counter somewhere."

Zoe looked at Emmett's rumpled clothes and dirty fingernails. The dust on the record bins. "No thanks. I can do it."

"I was just kidding," said Emmett with good humor. "This will be a snap for you. You're a strong girl."

"Keep my dad's disc handy," she said. "I'll be back at the same time tomorrow."

"We'll be waiting with bows on." Zoe left the shop

while Emmett was still putting away the Animagraph, too filled with restless energy to stand still.

Outside, the San Francisco night air was crisp and perfect. The fog was rolling in from the ocean. Emmett's quirks couldn't touch her buoyant mood. Besides, she'd finally figured him out. He was like those Japanese businessmen she'd read about. The ones who pay all that money for schoolgirls' panties. *Fine, let him have his creepy collections. What he wants is easy. It's nothing. One last time with the razor and then never again. I'll do it after dinner.*

The night remained perfect, beautiful, a frozen moment of goodness, but she had to admit she was getting chilly in nothing but her jeans and an old Circle Jerks T-shirt. She stuffed her hands deep into her pockets to warm them up. Something crinkled against her fingers. She pulled it out. It was the butterscotch candy the old woman in Iphigene had given her. Zoe unwrapped it and popped it into her mouth. It didn't taste like much of anything at all, but that was all right. She sucked on it all the way home, wondering where she should keep her father's disc. Maybe on her dresser, so she could see it when she got up. Maybe on the wall near where she'd tacked up that old single her mother had designed for the Cramps. There were lots of possibilities.

Six

The elevator was out again when Zoe got home. She stumbled up the stairs as exhaustion numbed her arms and legs. The trip to Iphigene and back had taken more out of her than she'd realized. According to the clock in the liquor store window down the block, it was almost eight. She'd been gone for hours. Still, nothing could break her buoyant mood and the new optimism bubbling inside her. Today she'd seen her father and tomorrow she'd bring him home. What could be better than that?

"Zoe?" Her mother was sitting on the living room sofa. The room smelled of cigarettes and blue-gray smoke curled from the fresh butt in a saucer on the floor. Her mother looked as tired as she felt, Zoe thought.

"Hi. Sorry I'm home so late." She leaned against the

wall on the other side of the room, trying to look relaxed, like nothing had been going on.

"Where have you been?"

"Nowhere. Out walking around."

"Don't lie to me. Where have you been?"

Zoe stood up straight as a familiar old tension filled the room.

"At a record store," she said.

"Till eight at night? What record store?"

"This used place in North Beach. They have a lot of old punk vinyl. I even saw a couple of covers you did." She should have seen this coming. The buzzkill and her mother's seemingly magical ability to start in on her just when she was feeling good. Zoe stared down at her shoes.

"Don't change the subject," barked her mother. "Your school called me today. You've been cutting classes."

Zoe closed her eyes and tried not to groan. The scene they were starting was way too familiar.

"Just a couple," she said.

"More than that, according to your school."

"Well, they're wrong," Zoe shouted. "No one knows me here. They wouldn't know if I was there or not."

"So, you don't answer when they take roll?"

"Not always," said Zoe, hating how stupid she sounded telling such a feeble lie.

"I don't believe you."

Even though she knew she had no right to be angry, Zoe couldn't help herself. Why did this have to happen now, just when things were getting better? "Believe what you want. Nothing I say matters around here, anyway."

"What does that mean?" her mother asked, her voice getting low, her tone wary.

"You brought us here. This apartment. The new school. This whole stupid life we're living was your idea."

"It's starting again, isn't it? The lies. The disappearing." Her mother reached for the cigarettes, caught herself, and dropped them to the floor.

"Nothing is starting again," mumbled Zoe. She pressed the palms of her hands to her forehead, trying to force down the headache that was building behind her eyes. "Why are you acting like this?"

Zoe's mother stood and tried to grab her. "Let me see your arms."

Zoe crossed them tightly over her chest. "No!"

"What are you hiding?" Her mother grabbed again, caught Zoe's sleeve, and pulled. Zoe twisted away, got loose, and backed into the hall.

"I'm not hiding anything," Zoe said. "But I don't want to be examined when you say it like that."

Her mother came closer, red-faced and furious. "How the hell am I supposed to say it, Zoe? 'Please, dear, if you don't mind, let me see if you've decided to start mutilating yourself again.' How's that?"

"I don't do that stuff anymore, I swear," Zoe said, her voice small and childlike, a tone she hated.

"Then show me."

"Not when you're like this!" she yelled.

"I want to believe you," said her mother, turning away. She walked back into the living room and stood with her back to Zoe. She seemed to be thinking. "What about all the classes you've been missing?" she asked.

Zoe sighed. "The school sucks. My teachers are jerks. The only decent one I have is Mr. Danvers. Sometimes I cut after his class."

"That's all?"

"Well, the other day this stupid bitch snuck some vodka into the lunchroom and spilled it all over me."

"You were drinking at school?"

"No!" shouted Zoe. "Will you listen to me?" Exhaustion and the pointlessness of an argument she knew she couldn't win left her with the overwhelming desire just to give up and lie down on the floor. Let her mother yell until her voice was gone. Maybe, if she stayed on the floor long enough, she'd turn to stone like one of Mr. Danvers's fossils.

"I didn't even know this girl," Zoe said. "She pulled out this vodka and spilled it all over. I was angry and I smelled like a wino, so I came home. What was I supposed to do? They don't know me there. Should I go to class smelling like booze and get expelled? If you don't believe me, the shirt is still on the roof. I wanted to see if I could get the smell out."

"Which shirt was it?"

"The Germs."

"Damn. I always liked that shirt."

"Me, too."

Her mother dropped down onto the sofa and picked up the cigarettes. This time she lit one. When she spoke, her voice was quiet and calm. "I know our situation right now is hard, but I can't get us through it alone. I need some help."

"I know," said Zoe. She went to where her mother sat and pulled up her sleeves, showing her unmarked skin. "It's Dad who's gone. I'm here and I'm not going anywhere."

Her mother closed her eyes for a minute. When she opened them again, they were red and wet. "Thank you," she said. She puffed at the cigarette. "I thought you were hurting yourself again."

"I'm not. I'm okay," said Zoe, trying to sound reassuring. She showed her mother the rubber band and snapped it.

"Okay. But listen, you can't keep ditching classes. The school said you can make up the classes you missed, but you'll have to do a lot of extra work. Maybe stay late some evenings and weekends. Understand?"

Zoe nodded. "Yeah, I understand."

"Okay." Her mother leaned back, rubbing her eyes with one hand and holding the cigarette with the other. Her hair was a mess. Between that, her red eyes, and the lines the harsh living room light etched into her forehead, she looked a hundred years old. Nothing at all like the girl with the purple eye shadow.

"Mom?"

"Yes?"

Zoe slipped past her and sat on the sofa. "When I was born, did you quit working so you could stay at home and take care of me?"

Her mother pushed some stray hairs off her forehead. "Your dad and I thought it would be good if you had someone around."

"I understand that part. But why didn't you keep designing? Do freelance work, like when I was at school and stuff?"

Her mother frowned, not the furious kind Zoe had grown used to but something more introspective. She leaned back into the sofa cushions. "I used to be really good, you know? Then I stopped when you were little. When I thought about going back to work, it felt like everything had passed me by. There was all this new software I didn't know and there were these kids who were so damned good at it. I didn't know how to get back in the game." She puffed the cigarette, made a face, and crushed it with the others in the saucer. She shook her head. "That's a lie. I choked. Simple as that. Once I stopped, I was too scared to fight my way back in."

"But you wanted to?"

"Hell, yeah," she said. "It's funny, you asking about this. Before he died, your dad and I were talking about it. He could get me discounts on some digital graphics classes through his company. What made you ask about this now?"

"No reason. I just wondered," Zoe said. She took a long breath and let it out. "I'm going to my room now, okay?" Her mother nodded.

Zoe got up and started for her bedroom. Halfway there, she turned around and came back. From the chair, her mother looked up at her. When Zoe leaned down, her mother looked unsure and flinched a little. Zoe kissed her on the cheek.

"I promised someone I'd do that."

"Who?"

"I promised I wouldn't tell."

"Set your alarm a little early," said her mother. "I rented a car. I'm driving you to school in the morning and picking you up after school until you're caught up on your work."

Damn. "Yeah, okay. 'Night."

"'Night."

Zoe was still shaky, but she was also exhausted. She felt like a deflated balloon, limp and shapeless. She tried to push the fight with her mother out of her head, and she lay down without taking her clothes off. It's just for a minute, she told herself. Just until I catch my breath. She snapped the rubber band twice.

A couple of minutes later, she was fast asleep.

In her dream she was near the tree that held the fort, but this was one of those rare nights where she didn't materialize in the fort itself. Looking out across the field, she knew why this time was different. The normally empty field tonight was full of carnival rides. Zoe instantly recognized the carousel and Ferris wheel that she and her father had ridden in Iphigene. She called up to Valentine to come down and go on the rides with her. She started toward the spinning carousel, then stopped. A black dog sat on the edge of the platform. A woman-shaped shadow, darker this time, rode one of the carousel horses, a fierce black war-horse in shining armor. Zoe took a step back and her foot came down on something soft. It hissed. A snake.

The field was covered in a black, writhing river of glistening fangs and dead green eyes. Zoe froze, one hand on the ladder that led up to the fort and the other up defensively by her throat. Her mouth remained closed, but somewhere in the back of her brain she was screaming. She knew that all she had to do was step up onto the ladder and climb the few feet and she'd be out of danger, but she couldn't move. Her eternal, primal fear of snakes paralyzed her, froze her in place. The snakes seethed around her feet, their bodies sighing through the short grass until it sounded to her like a crack in the earth letting out the world's last wheezing breath before it died.

Something fastened around Zoe's wrist. She started to scream, but her throat closed up and she couldn't make a sound. She felt herself being pulled upward. Zoe looked up to see Valentine reaching down from the top of the ladder, trying to haul her up. Seeing him above her snapped her out of her frozen fear and she began to climb. When she got to the top, Valentine pulled her up the last few feet into the fort. She fell back against the railing, out of breath. Valentine was panting, too.

"Thanks," she wheezed, then coughed drily.

"Breathe," said Valentine between his own deep breaths. "In through your nose and out through your mouth."

Zoe nodded, following his instructions. She already felt calmer, and in a couple of minutes the breathing slowed her heartbeat and she was no longer gulping air. When she could talk again, she said, "Where did they all come from?"

Valentine shrugged. "From the mountains, I think. Did you bring the carnival?"

Zoe looked over her shoulder at the bright inviting lights on the rides. "I guess so," she said. "I was just at a park like that. I must have dreamed the rides here."

"You went to an amusement park?"

Zoe nodded. "Yeah. Dad was there."

Valentine looked at her for a moment, like he was carefully considering his words. It wasn't the reaction Zoe had been expecting. "You saw Father? Where?"

"This crazy town called Iphigene. That's what I wanted to tell you tonight, but the snakes spooked me."

"Don't worry about them. They're scary, but not poisonous."

"That doesn't help much," said Zoe, embarrassed at how small her voice sounded.

Valentine pulled her to her feet, grabbed a handful of almonds that had fallen from the tree, and dropped them over the sides. The snakes ignored them. He leaned over the railing, hawked up something in his throat, and spit over the edge. There was no reaction from below. The snakes were too busy striking at swarms of fireflies that swirled out of the nearby grove.

"See?" Valentine said. "They're not too bright."

Zoe remained unconvinced, but nodded at Valentine.

"Tell me about Iphigene," he said. He tried to make the request sound spontaneous, but Zoe could hear tension in his voice. "How do you even know about the place?"

"I told you. I was there. It's where the dead go and wait before they go on to wherever."

"How did you get there?"

"By bus!" Zoe said, laughing, happy to reveal the craziest part of her trip. But Valentine didn't smile back. He looked concerned.

"Emmett sent me," Zoe said. "With this old machine. An Animagraph."

Valentine kicked a few more almonds down onto the snakes. "Did Emmett ask you for anything?"

She didn't say anything. She didn't want to be yelled

at twice in one night, and she especially didn't want to be yelled at by Valentine. Why couldn't someone just be happy for her?

"You said before that he didn't ask for anything, but I don't know if you were telling me the truth. People like Emmett, they always ask for something."

"How do you know?"

"I see a lot up here." Valentine nodded to the telescope propped against the tree.

Zoe looked out at the spinning carousel. "I gave him a tooth."

Valentine whirled around. "You gave him one of your teeth?" Valentine said, fear or anger edging into his voice.

"No!" said Zoe. "I gave him a tooth. Not my tooth." It felt like everyone was after her tonight.

Very quietly, Valentine said, "What do you think he wanted with one of your teeth?"

"I don't know. He's a lonely old weirdo who bribes girls for souvenirs. He probably beats off to them when he goes home."

"I wouldn't be so worried if that's all it was."

"What do you mean?"

"I mean there's only one reason someone like Emmett would want a tooth from someone like you. That's to gain power over you."

"What kind of power?"

"I don't know exactly," said Valentine. He crossed his arms and frowned. "The point is that anyone who asks you for something like that isn't your friend. Emmett is dangerous and he wants a lot more from you than a tooth."

"But he sent me to see Dad. He's going to let me take Dad's spirit home tomorrow."

"And what does he want for that?"

Zoe bit the inside of her cheek. It hurt immediately, so she stopped. She wanted to yell at Valentine the same way she'd yelled at her mother. She'd come here to share something wonderful with him and he was spoiling it by being more scared of a silly old creep than she was of snakes. And snakes were real and could really hurt you. Zoe wasn't scared of Emmett. She'd handled jocks trying to cop feels in the hallways at school and her friends' stepfathers when they got too touchy-feely. Zoe knew she could take care of herself, but knew Valentine wouldn't believe her. It was still Valentine, though, and she didn't want to lie to him again.

"Some of my blood," she said.

"Blood," said Valentine flatly. He shook his head. "You can't see him again. No matter what he promised you."

"Look, if he's as bad as you say, then I can't leave Dad with him."

"Father can take care of himself. He wouldn't want you putting yourself in danger."

"I don't believe this," said Zoe. All the frustration

and anger she'd felt earlier with her mother was coming back. "What do you mean control me? For what? You think he wants to rape me or something?"

"Maybe," said Valentine evenly. "But there are some things even worse."

"Like what?"

Valentine shook his head and walked to the far end of the platform.

"I'm only going back one more time," said Zoe. "Then I'm never going to see him again."

"You're in danger already."

"You know what? I don't care," Zoe shouted. "I've seen a lot of stuff in the last few days and I'm willing to sacrifice a little of my safety for Dad because I know he'd do it for me."

Valentine picked up the telescope and walked around to the far side of the tree without saying a word. When Zoe came around the tree, he was holding the telescope up and was looking at the mountain.

"Want to hear something funny?" Zoe asked.

"Always."

"A girl told me she wanted to kiss me."

Valentine slid the telescope sections in and out, focusing it. "I can see that."

"What do you mean?"

"Well, you're pretty. Why wouldn't she want to kiss you?"

Zoe looked away, embarrassed by the compliment.

"Is she cute?" Valentine asked.

"Yeah. You'd like her."

"You'll have to introduce me sometime."

Zoe grinned and leaned back against the tree. "Anyway, I just wanted to tell someone."

Valentine came over and hugged her. "Thanks," he said. Zoe nodded. She reached up, grabbed a low branch, and lifted up her feet. She hung there until her arms got tired and she had to put her feet down again.

"Come here," Valentine said from over by the railing. He pulled a book of matches from his back pocket. As Zoe came up next to him, he struck a match and let it drop. The match became a microscopic meteor streaking to the ground. But before it could hit, a half-dozen snakes struck at it. He lit another match and dropped it. The snakes struck at that one, too. He handed the matches to Zoe and let her toss a few. Each time she tossed a burning match toward them, the snakes attacked. She remembered Mr. Danvers saying that snakes had lousy eyes, but could sense the heat their prey gave off.

"See? They're easy to fool," said Valentine.

When Zoe got bored teasing the snakes, she gave the matches back to Valentine and looked over the field to the rides. "It's too bad we can't go over there."

"That's okay," Valentine said. He was back looking through the telescope. "It'd be kind of weird with whatever's on the mountain." He handed the telescope to Zoe and pointed to the mountain, at a spot near the peak. Zoe put her eye to the lens and peered through.

The mountain was still swallowed by mist. It raged in brutal gusts, forming a slow whirlwind like a procession of angry ghosts. Through the mist, Zoe could just make out a shape that looked like a man hunkered down in the snow. There was a glint of something shiny nearby. The mist cleared for a second and Zoe got a better look at him. The man's face was covered, but she saw that he, too, had a telescope. And he was looking right at her and Valentine. She remembered something Emmett said: "I watch people." But she knew it couldn't be him in her dream, so she pushed the thought out of her head.

"I don't want you to go see that Emmett guy again," Valentine said. "But I know you will, so you need to be careful."

Zoe looked at him. "I still have Dad's razor."

"Keep it with you for a while. Don't let it out of your sight."

Zoe got up early and went straight to her closet. At the bottom of the box where she'd retrieved her baby teeth, she found her father's shaving kit. She'd found it in the trash when they were packing up the old house, which had really pissed her off. Her mother had been on a rampage to get rid of sharp objects, and maybe there was good reason for her attitude at the time. Zoe had been a little crazy during the weeks between the funeral and the sale of the house. But so was her mother, she thought, which maybe explains why she thought it was a good idea to throw away the whole kit. Good thing that Zoe had made a point of sifting through the trash cans during the night, looking for lost treasures.

She took the straight razor from the shaving kit and went to hide it under the T-shirts in her dresser. When she opened the drawer she could tell that the T-shirts had been moved. She always stacked the East Coast and West Coast punk bands in different piles. Now they were mixed together, which meant that her mother was looking for contraband in her room yesterday. Good, she thought. She's already checked the drawer, so it's the perfect place to hide something. When she'd slid the kit under the shirts, Zoe tucked the straight razor into her back pocket and put on one of her father's old Fear T-shirts, one that hung low and loose over her hips. She checked herself in the mirror and nodded, satisfied that the shirt covered the outline of the razor.

There was a soft knock at the door and her mother stuck her head in. "You ready to go?"

"Yep," Zoe said, grabbing her backpack from the floor. She tried to look cheerful on the way out but felt too weird, so she settled for trying to look relaxed.

The drive to school was mercifully short. The car wasn't even too embarrassing—a relatively new, red, four-door Honda Civic. Zoe found a song she liked on the radio, but when she turned it up, one of the speakers in the back crackled and died. She sighed and turned it off. They rode the rest of the way in silence.

She was hoping that her mother would drop her and speed away in the rented car. She had to suppress a groan when, after they stopped, her mother shifted the car into neutral.

"Thanks for the ride," Zoe said, and reached for the door handle. Her mother put a hand on her arm.

"I have to go see the lawyers today and then I have a second interview at a place I went last week," she said.

"That's great. Good luck," said Zoe.

"Thanks. Promise me you'll go to your classes and be good. I'll pick you up at four."

"I promise," she said, feeling funny and wondering how she could possibly keep the promise and still make it to Emmett's.

"I know there's something else going on that you're not telling me about," said her mother. "I won't push you on it. When you're ready, I want you to know that you can talk to me and tell me anything."

"I know. Thanks," Zoe said, feeling gratitude for her mother reaching out, but fear that the timing was all wrong. "See you later."

She got out of the car, feeling pure relief as her mother drove away.

It was like she had a fever all day. Zoe felt hot and her classes were all a complete blank. She'd sit through

English or history, and as she walked out the door realize that she hadn't heard a word or remembered a thing that anyone had said. Not even Mr. Danvers's class got through the fog that enveloped her brain. He was talking about reptiles again, but her mind kept leaping from one thought to the next, one problem to another.

How was she going to get to Emmett's and back without breaking her promise to her mother? Not that breaking promises or lying had stopped her from much of anything recently . . . And if she did ditch her afternoon classes, could she make it back to school before four?

And if she did make it to Emmett's, then what? She kept playing Valentine's warning over and over in her head. She wondered about the man on the mountain, looking at them through a telescope. Had it been Emmett? Why would it be him? She'd gone back to him day after day and given him what he wanted. Well, except for that last time, she thought. Still, he got a tooth, another creepy trophy for his collection. What more could he want from her? Then she shifted in her seat and felt the razor in her pocket, which brought back Valentine's warning.

Absynthe wasn't helping. Sitting a couple of rows ahead of Zoe, Absynthe could always find the perfect moment, when the other kids were distracted by one of Mr. Danvers's skulls or a drawing on the blackboard, to turn and shoot Zoe an inquiring look. She mouthed, "How did it go?"

Zoe just shrugged and mouthed, "Talk to you after class."

When the bell rang, Zoe lost Absynthe in the mad rush as people ran off to lunch or the bleachers for a beer or weed break. When she didn't see Absynthe by the lockers or in the hallway, she went outside and around the building to the staircase that Absynthe had led her to yesterday. Sure enough, Absynthe was there, leaning against the wall smoking a cigarette. Her hair looked very blue in the sunlight. She wore a black thrift-store little girl's party dress, trimmed in moth-eaten white lace, and green-and-black-striped tights tucked into the tops of shiny thick-soled boots covered in laces and buckles. They looked like something from a science-fiction movie. Zoe smiled to herself.

"What are you smiling at?" asked Absynthe.

"I like the Aeon Flux boots," she said.

Absynthe put her hands together with her index fingers steepled like a gun and made shooting noises with her mouth. Zoe grabbed her chest and fell against the wall like she'd been shot. When she was done dying, she leaned against the wall looking down the cul-de-sac at the other girl.

"Listen, I didn't mean to freak you out or anything yesterday," Absynthe said. "About the kiss thing."

"Don't worry about it," said Zoe. "It's fine."

"We still friends or whatever?" Absynthe asked. The

question surprised Zoe. It was funny thinking of Absynthe as uncertain about something.

"We're cool," Zoe said. "I'm much more tweaked about other things today."

"Then come over here and tell me about it." Absynthe sat on the steps in front of an old fire door and patted the space next to her. Zoe came over and sat down.

"So what's the big deal about today?"

Zoe sighed. "Aside from being grounded, I need to see someone and get back to school before my mother gets here later."

"Is this about your mystery man?"

"Which one?" said Zoe, and laughed ruefully.

"There's more than one? Damn, girl. Here I was thinking I was corrupting a little suburban girl and you've got a secret harem."

Zoe leaned back against the pockmarked surface of the fire door. "I wish it was that simple. There's one guy I'm worried about helping and another I just have to deal with to do it. And I want to finish this all up today so it's over with and I don't have to see him anymore."

"Then why don't you just go? Do the deed and get back before your mom's any the wiser?"

Zoe shrugged. "I wasn't before, but now I'm a little weirded out by the guy."

"Did he hurt you?" asked Absynthe. There was real concern in her voice.

"No. He never did anything but what I asked him.

But he's always been a little weird and yesterday someone warned me about him."

"Maybe you should take the advice and forget about this guy."

"That's the problem. I can't. He has something of mine, and I really need it. I don't know what I'll do if I didn't get it back."

Absynthe puffed the cigarette, dropped it on the ground, and stubbed it out. "Then do it fast and do it now. It's daytime and people aren't as crazy as they get after dark. Don't chitchat, just do what you have to do and get out." She leaned forward on her knees and clasped her hands together. "I can wait for you. If you like."

"Thanks a lot," said Zoe. "I'm probably blowing this way out of proportion. Like I said, he never did anything to me and he could have. I'm just being a big chicken."

" 'Hope is the thing with feathers,' " said Absynthe.

"What?"

"It's an Emily Dickinson poem about not being afraid, even in the middle of a shit storm."

"Wish I had feathers like that." Zoe hadn't pictured Absynthe as a big reader or someone into poetry at all. And if she did read poetry, not Emily Dickinson. Bukowski maybe. She set the thought aside as one more thing to ask her about when she had Dad and was free of Emmett. "It's been a weird few weeks, you know? Even weirder since we came here."

"Please." Absynthe let out a sarcastic laugh. "Don't go playing innocent with me. I know your dirty little secrets now."

"No, you really don't. But I might tell you. Tomorrow. When it's done."

"You sure you're going to be all right? Endings for stuff like this can get kind of messy."

"Don't worry. It's all settled except for this one thing."

Absynthe lit another cigarette. "Tell me what you want when you want. I'm all ears."

Zoe snapped the rubber band on her wrist.

"When it's over, I will."

Before she ditched school, Zoe went into one of the bathrooms, locked herself in a stall, and got out the straight razor. When she'd cut herself before, it had always been with skinny little double-edge blades she'd shoplifted from the mall. She'd never used anything like the straight razor, and the sight of it now—big in her hand, a tarnished metal blade with a bone grip—made it even more intimidating. It still carried a faint scent of her father's aftershave. She didn't want to do anything to spoil that, but she knew that this was the price she'd agreed to.

She tugged at the rubber band on her wrist, but she didn't snap it.

Zoe wondered if Absynthe ever cut herself, or let someone cut her. She knew kids who gave each other ritual scars, mostly because they were too young or too broke to afford professional tattoos or piercings. Absynthe, she thought, might have been fierce enough to play games like that. She might even have offered some of her own blood so that Zoe wouldn't have to cut herself. Why not let her, if she offered? Zoe had fooled Emmett once. She could do it again. But the bell had already rung and Absynthe was gone, back to class. No option there. No option but one.

Her arms were off-limits, she knew. Just the thought of it brought back bad, dark memories of the days before and the weeks after her father's funeral when she'd cut herself just to feel a different kind of pain for a while. In the stall, Zoe undid her pants and quickly, without giving herself time to think about it, made a shallow slash across the upper part of her left leg.

She took a few sheets of toilet paper and dabbed up the blood. It was only a surface cut, but Emmett said that all he wanted were a few drops, so she thought it should be enough. When the blood stopped flowing, she wrapped the red-blotched sheets in more toilet paper, pulled up her pants, and stuffed both the razor and the bloody paper in her pockets.

When she left school the hall clock said it was one-thirty. That meant she had to be back in no more than two hours. She walked quickly down the familiar, inexplicable path that always led her to Emmett's. Before, the walk had always seemed timeless and Emmett's shop had always magically appeared in front of her, right on cue. This time, however, the walk felt like it took forever. Zoe grasped at every vague landmark. A pink awning on a Laundromat. A shuttered bodega. When she saw a little church with Korean characters on the roof, she started running and kept running until she saw the shop.

She stopped for a second to catch her breath, then went and pushed on the front door. It was locked. The sign in the window said CLOSED. Zoe cupped her hands and peered through the glass. As always, it was cave dark inside, and she really couldn't see anything but the counter and the first few record bins by the door.

She banged on the glass with her knuckles. The door shook and rattled, warped and loose in its ancient wooden frame. After knocking for a minute or so, to her relief, Zoe saw Emmett coming from the back of the shop. He unlocked and opened the door, but only halfway.

"Yeah? What do you want?" Emmett asked.

"Hi. I'm here for my dad's record," said Zoe, still a little out of breath.

Emmett stared like he'd never seen her before. "What? Your father made a record? Was he in a band? What was it called?"

"No. My dad's record. The one where his soul lives."

"Hey," said Emmett, "I don't know what you're on, but I don't have time for this." He started to close the door, but Zoe caught the edge and pushed her way inside. The two of them stood across the empty space by the front counter, just looking at each other. Zoe was breathing hard and Emmett stared at her blankly.

"Look, kid, if you know the name of the record you want, maybe I can find it for you. But I can't stand here all day playing Name That Tune."

"Emmett, it's me," said Zoe. "Why are you acting like this?"

"I don't know what you're talking about."

"I found the back room with the soul records. You let me use the Animagraph."

"I don't know what the hell an 'Animagraph' is, and the soul records are against that wall under the Al Green poster."

"Not those soul records, the ones in the back room that people can't see." Zoe turned to the back of the shop, to the room where the Animagraph and the special records were stored. The entrance wasn't there. The dirty beaded curtain was gone. The wall was solid.

"What's going on?" she asked. "Did you change your mind about the price? Do you want something else? I brought what you asked for." She reached into her pocket and retrieved the bloody tissues. She held them out to him.

Emmett took a step back, his eyes widening. "What the hell are you doing, kid? Are you crazy?"

"Emmett, please. I just want to take my father home."

Emmett held up his hands, palms out, as if trying to hold Zoe off. "Listen, I don't know if this is the crank or the acid talking, but I just run a shop. I buy and sell old junk that no one wants."

"I know, and I want to buy something from you."

"With that? I don't think so."

"Then what do you want?"

"Nothing from you, with your bloody Kleenex. I sell real merchandise to people who can pay for real. If someone can't pay, I find someone else who can. And you, kid, can't pay."

"I don't understand what's happening here," said Zoe miserably.

"That part I believe. Now it's time for you to get out. I have a business to run."

"Please don't do this. I'll give you whatever you want," Zoe said. She pressed a hand to Emmett's chest. "I'll do whatever you want."

"You don't have anything I want," he said, and pushed her away.

Emmett grabbed her by the upper arm so hard it made Zoe gasp. He pulled her to the front door, opened it, and shoved her through. Zoe stood in the gray alcove between the bright street and the enveloping darkness of Emmett's shop. As he closed the door, she felt a tickle in her ear. It was as if some invisible presence were leaning over her to whisper a secret.

"I know you cheated me. That wasn't your tooth," said the phantom voice.

She turned, but Emmett was gone and the door was locked.

Zoe banged on the glass. She screamed and cursed at him. She kicked the door. There was no response, no help there. No way to fix things. There was nothing but ruins. Ruins that she'd made.

She started back to school, slowly and miserably. She wiped tears from her face and the snot from her nose with the underside of her sleeve, not caring how she looked or who saw her. Then she began to run. She ran by instinct, following the blind path away from Emmett's as she always did, but now full of fury and reckless anger. She ran against red lights. The sounds of squealing brakes and drivers' curses were a distant, meaningless noise in her ears. The world had collapsed into a narrow tunnel of pain and loss. All she could hear in her head was a single word pounding over and over again, *No, no, no, no, no . . .*

Zoe hadn't run from her father's funeral but now she wanted to run forever. To obliterate herself in motion. No past. No future. It was tempting. She could make it happen. All she had to do was cross against a red light and stop in the intersection. There wouldn't be any squealing brakes. There wouldn't be time. Just the thud of a car's bumper into her side and then nothing. Nothing forever. How beautiful that would be.

• • •

It was two-thirty when she got back to the school. She was sweating and shaking. Going back to class wasn't an option. She went around the building to Absynthe's secret corner, curled up against the fire door, and closed her eyes. She tried to sleep, hoping she could find Valentine. She took off her rubber band and threw it under some half-dead bushes with the beer cans and cigarette butts.

An hour later, Zoe was startled by the sound of the final bell. This was followed by the thunder of feet as the first kids hit the doors and made it outside like they were going to win a prize for their speed. These sounds from the normal world shook Zoe out of her trance and she went in through a side entrance, walking against the flow of bodies. Inside her locker she found an old T-shirt and wiped the last of the sweat from her face. Then she gathered her books together and went out through the front entrance to wait.

Her mother drove up a few minutes later, honking twice as she pulled to the curb. Zoe got into the car and smiled at her mother automatically, but without meeting her eyes.

"Hi," she said.

"Hi yourself," said her mother. "How was it being back in your classes?"

Zoe didn't answer for a minute. "Same as always," she said.

"Which means what?"

"The only teacher I have who isn't an idiot is Mr. Danvers."

"I don't remember. What does he teach?"

"Biology."

"What did he teach you today?"

Zoe had to think for a minute. What had Mr. Danvers talked about? She hadn't been listening, but his talks always got through, even on bad days.

"Teeth," she said finally. "For different species. Cow's teeth for chewing grass. Lion teeth for ripping flesh. Snake's teeth for injecting venom."

"Did he say anything about our teeth?"

"We're omnivores. We have a bunch of different teeth, but none of them are very good for fighting or killing." Then she added quietly, "Which isn't fair."

Her mother nodded. "I know what you mean. The insurance company and all these job interviews the last few weeks, I've wanted to bite a few people myself."

Zoe didn't say anything. She just stared out the side window, watching the streets roll by.

"Aren't you going to ask about my day?" Zoe's mother asked.

"I'm sorry. How was your day?"

"Well, Maggie at the law office finally got the insurance company to admit that losing your father's paperwork was their fault. That's the first piece of good news from them."

Zoe sighed. She imagined her father being packed away in a dusty box with other dusty boxes in Emmett's back room. "They finally believe Dad existed. Good for them."

"And there's something else," her mother went on. "I might have a job. It's not a dream job. It's just a junior designer position, but it's with a cool clothing-design company called Kitty with a Whip. Have you heard of them?"

"Yeah. Lots of kids at school wear their stuff."

"The owner is Raymond, this really sweet older guy who remembered some flyers I did for a gay club he used to work at about a million years ago. And there are a lot of great young designers. I could learn a lot working at a place like that."

Zoe couldn't remember the last time she'd heard her mother sound so excited. She wished she could feel happier for her.

"That sounds really great, Mom. I'm really happy for you."

Zoe's mother looked at her. "Are you all right? You mad at me for picking you up and making you study?"

"No. I just don't feel so good right now."

Her mother reached across the car and put a hand on Zoe's forehead. "You do feel a little warm."

"I'm fine," said Zoe, wanting her mother to lose control of the car and plow into a gas station or cross the center line and drive head-on into a bus.

"When we get home, you can study in bed," said her mother. "I'll bring you some lemon tea."

"Thanks," said Zoe, wanting to tell her mother everything, to confess it all and beg for her help, yet knowing she couldn't say a word.

The elevator wasn't working again, so they walked up the four flights to the apartment. Her mother took off her office shoes and went up in her stockings. Neither of them talked on the way. They were both out of breath when they reached the top. Zoe was sweating again and felt cold.

Her mother went straight to her bedroom to change and Zoe went to hers. She set her books at the end of the bed, took off her sneakers, and crawled under the cool covers. Her mother came in with a cup of microwaved tea a couple of minutes later. Zoe sipped it politely, but all she wanted to do was lie down and ease herself into the dark for a while.

"I'll come in and check on you later," said her mother.

"Okay. Thanks."

When her mother was gone, she pulled the covers up to her chin and closed her eyes. She wanted desperately to see Valentine. He was older, and although he didn't always understand exactly how her nondreamworld worked, he was smart and clever. He'd largely planned and built the tree fort on his own. He was always full of plans. He'd know what to do.

But sleep wouldn't come. She tried breathing exercises she'd learned at the hospital—counting backward from a hundred and relaxing all her muscles one at a time. Nothing worked. She got up and looked in her dresser for the Xanax she'd taken from her mother's purse months ago, but she couldn't find them. She lay back down, closed her eyes, and just let her mind drift.

Would it really be so terrible if I can't get Dad's record back? she wondered. She'd seen him and spent a wonderful afternoon with him. He was all right and Iphigene was kind of a cool-looking place.

But Emmett had figured out the tooth she'd given him wasn't hers. And someone was watching Zoe and Valentine from the mountain. Valentine didn't trust Emmett. And Emmett had gone out of his way to tell her that he sold things only to people who could pay.

Would Emmett do something with Dad's record? Something that could hurt him? There were so many LPs in that back room. Who were they for? Who would make them or buy them? Even Emmett didn't know, or that's what he claimed. Zoe's father said that some people got stuck in Iphigene forever. Had Zoe done something that would trap her father there forever?

Her stomach churned like she was going to throw up, so she went into the bathroom and opened the toilet lid. She sat down with her back against the bathtub and waited. But nothing happened. And then she remembered something.

Emmett didn't say anything about the record. It could still be in the shop somewhere. She had to know if it was there, and if it was, she had to get it, whatever it might cost.

Later, her mother came in and put a hand on Zoe's forehead. Zoe kept her eyes shut and her breathing shallow and regular, pretending to be asleep. After a couple of minutes, her mother left. Zoe heard her in the kitchen. Then she was in the bathroom, where Zoe heard running water and her mother brushing her teeth. Finally, her mother went to her bedroom and the apartment became quiet. Zoe looked at the alarm clock by her bed. It was just after eleven. Another hour, she thought. Just to make sure Mom is asleep.

When midnight finally came, she slipped out of bed, trying to keep her mattress springs from squeaking. Padding around her room in bare feet, she gathered up the things she'd need. She opened the window and set an old pair of surplus-store boots on the fire escape. Then she changed into the Runaways T-shirt Joan Jett had given her father back in the day. She pulled on her lucky black hoodie, the one with cat ears on the hood. She slipped out the window and closed it behind her thinking, I know this is crazy, but what else is there left to do?

She started up the fire escape when she realized she'd forgotten something. She opened the window just enough to squeeze through and grabbed her father's straight razor from where she'd kicked it under the bed to keep her mother from seeing it. She closed the window and ran up to the roof.

There, she sat on the gravel and pulled on her boots under the moon's wasted, colorless light. Something moved in her peripheral vision. Turning, she saw her vodka-soaked T-shirt hanging where she'd left it. She made a mental note to bring it down when she got back.

As Zoe climbed down the ladder she was hit with a sense of fear and sadness so deep that it made her stomach cramp. Doing what she was doing, going where she was going secretly in the middle of the night, it felt like she was crossing a border that she'd never be able to uncross and that she might not ever find her way home again.

She shook her head to clear it. At the bottom of the fire escape, she pushed the final collapsible section all the way down just like she'd seen in a hundred TV shows, climbed to the bottom, and jumped the last few feet. The night air was cool, and because it might disguise her, she pulled her hood up.

The walk to Emmett's was long and dreary. She wondered at herself now, at how she could have found previous walks to the shop so pleasant and magical. The path wound through grubby streets full of ugly people and buildings and stores that all looked like they were about to collapse.

A few men spoke to her as she walked. They stepped

out from the doorways and alleys of dim, unreal buildings. Some of the silhouettes grabbed their crotches and made kissing sounds as she went past.

A shadow man, tall and wide, stepped out from behind a tree just as Zoe was passing. One of his big hands gripped her shoulder, then slid down her shirt and over her breast. She didn't even think about it. The straight razor was out. Her arm moved and the blade sliced deeply into the shadow man's wrist.

He staggered back. "You bitch! You little bitch. I'll kill you," he yelled, but he stayed where he was. Zoe kept walking, trying to look brave. She kept the razor tucked in her hand for another block.

The light was still on in the record store. She ran across the street and hid in the shadows next to an old Dumpster. Did Emmett always work this late? *No wonder he likes to collect girls' things. If he spends all his time in that dreary store, he really doesn't have a life.*

Zoe trembled a little in the cool San Francisco dark. She looked down at her hands. She was still holding the razor, and it was open. There was a thin streak like India ink across the edge of the blade that she knew was the shadow man's blood. An old newspaper lay nearby. She took a couple of pages and wiped off the blade, refusing to think about how the blood had gotten on the razor. Still, it felt like one more step away from a safe life she'd never have again.

For a moment Zoe wondered if this might all be some awful fever dream. Maybe she was really at home in her bed in the old house. Her father and mother would have breakfast with her before she went to her old, familiar school, where she'd tell Julie and Laura about this crazy nightmare where she went to a carnival with her father's ghost, gave trinkets to an old pervert, and slashed a mugger like *Elektra: Assassin*. It was a comforting thought, but the night wind gusted through her, making her shiver, and she knew this was all real.

After she'd spent an hour standing in the cold, the lights went off in Emmett's shop. He came out the front door with a stack of records under one arm. Zoe squinted, but couldn't tell if they were regular records or the special ones.

Emmett walked to the corner and stood under the traffic light. It turned from red to green. The pedestrian sign said WALK, but Emmett didn't cross. He turned his head, looking up and down the street. Apparently satisfied that no one was around, he stepped off the curb. Instead of crossing the street, he crouched by the corner. Zoe crept forward and stood on her toes to see what he was doing. When Emmett stood up he was holding a sewer grate in one hand and the records in the other. To Zoe's amazement, he seemed to be shrinking. No. He was climbing into the sewer. A second later, she heard a dull clank as the metal grate dropped back into place.

Zoe ran from the shadows. At the corner there was no sign that the grate had been moved. She went to Emmett's shop and looked in through the dirty window. Do I break in? she wondered. What if there's an alarm? I should have brought a flashlight. How am I supposed to find Dad's record in the dark, if it's even in there? If Emmett took the record with him and I waste time inside, it won't matter. He'll be too far away for me to follow.

She wanted desperately to go into the shop. It was safe and dark and known. The idea of following Emmett into some unknown underground labyrinth terrified her. But there was this terrible feeling in the back of her mind, a feeling that told her that her father's disc wasn't in the shop. That out of spite or something worse Emmett had carried it underground, and that if she didn't go after him soon, her father would be lost forever. She would have failed him twice.

Zoe went to the corner and knelt down to get a good grip on the grate. She pulled, but it didn't budge. She knelt down and pulled again. Nothing. Zoe remembered Emmett's grip on her arm and the surprising strength with which he'd held her. She sat down in the street and braced her feet against the curb. She wasn't going to get this close to Emmett and her father and lose them both.

With both hands, she grabbed the far edge of the grate and pulled. The metal was wet and slimy, hard to hold on to. Finally, she felt the grate rise slowly away from the street. When it was a little more than halfway up, she let go and it fell backward toward her, leaving the sewer open.

She leaned her head into the opening. The smell reminded her of the time she and some friends had sneaked into the house where old Mrs. Asher had died and no one had found her for a week. Zoe pulled up the edge of her hoodie, covering her nose and mouth. Just inside the opening, she could see steel rungs, like a ladder, set into the concrete.

She turned herself quickly into position and lowered a foot into the opening. When one foot touched a rung, she stepped down and pulled her arms inside. Below street level, she was instantly swallowed by impenetrable darkness and a death-house reek of dead old women.

Zoe held her breath and started down.

Seven

At the bottom of the ladder the ground was a soft and yielding soup of slippery muck. It compressed beneath her, as if she were walking on damp leaves. No matter how hard Zoe tried, however, she couldn't pretend that what she was walking on was anything but the collective filth and waste of the city that loomed twenty feet over her head.

The damp soaked through her sneakers and socks, but she kept walking, breathing through her mouth, afraid she might throw up. She moved quietly, carefully, trying not to splash or make any noise. She kept a hand on the wall, feeling her way along as her eyes adjusted to the dark.

Even when she grew accustomed to the gloom, Zoe couldn't see much, just the vague outlines of the tunnel's edges where concrete sections were joined and metal service doors dripping with a colorless fungus that hung in ragged strands like Spanish moss.

Every now and then she'd pass under a manhole or a street grate and shafts of feeble light shone down to her. Then she would be submerged again in the dark, and each time it was like a black wave pulling her down to the bottom of the ocean.

She followed Emmett by listening for him. He was well ahead of her, and because he thought he was alone, he didn't make any effort to be quiet. He splashed casually through the black sewer muck, singing as he went. His voice echoed down the concrete tunnels, sounding to Zoe like a ghost choir. The tune sounded like something very old and from far away. She'd heard it in the shop, a song full of mystery, vengeance, and death: "Walk on Gilded Splinters."

Zoe focused her mind on the sound, on Emmett's song, and not on her surroundings. With each step the stronger part of her mind, the part that kept her panicky self in check, repeated, *I'm not afraid. Dad is waiting for me. Just keep walking. I'm not afraid.*

She lost track of the time. The dark never let up, nor did the stink of the place, but something changed ahead. There was faint yellow light around the next turn. She walked as fast as she could, careful not to splash. In a few minutes, Zoe reached one of the rusted iron service doors. It was half open, and when she listened, she could hear Emmett's song echoing from the passage beyond.

Lowering her head to get through the door, she took a tentative step inside the new passage. The light was brighter a few yards ahead. She stepped into the passage and stopped in surprise at what she saw. The air, the bare stone walls, the ancient rotting carpet that ran along the floor, a whole different world from the sewer tunnels. But it was more than the carpet and the light. The place gave off a static charge like it was alive and very old. Zoe started toward the light.

She could breathe through her nose here. The horrid stink of sewer didn't seem to extend beyond the metal hatch. The bare stone walls were smooth and covered in glyphs, like the ones on the special records in Emmett's shop. The marks covered the walls down the whole length of the corridor. Water. Snakes. The moon. Black dogs.

The light in the tunnel came from candles held in sconces all along the walls. Wax dripped down the wall like the liquid on stalactites and pooled on the floor. Rats ran ahead of Zoe, zigzagging across the carpet.

The passage ended at a stone staircase that descended at a steep angle to another tunnel below. The gray stone steps looked polished, worn smooth by centuries of use. But who used them? Zoe wondered.

Going down the steps, she wondered if she'd hurt herself without realizing it and thrown herself off balance. Each step she took was more uncomfortable than the last, and more than once she fell as she moved from one step to another. A few steps later, she realized that there was a simple explanation: the staircase was changing as she descended, with each step slightly higher than the one before. By the time she reached the bottom, she had to lower herself over the edge of each step and jump to the one below.

She was in a tunnel that was much larger than any of the others. Its vaulted ceiling towered over her head, lost in the moving shadows cast by the flickering candles set along the walls. Ahead of her was a set of enormous wooden doors, towering almost as high as the tunnel itself. An entrance for giants, she thought. The doors were ajar, so it was easy for her to slip between them. As she stepped through the doors she paused. Emmett's song was a distant echo ahead of her.

Beyond the doors were a series of dark stone chambers. Each of them was filled with lost trinkets and abandoned junk washed down from the city. Nearby was a pile of broken dolls as big as Zoe's house. Their tattered faces and glittering black eyes stared blankly at the ancient walls. Scattered throughout the chambers were mountains of rusting bicycles, water-swollen books and porn magazines, snowdrifts of wedding photos and hills of wallets, many open, creating shiny plastic islands of driver's licenses, credit cards, and school photos of smiling children, now lost and sodden underground.

There was a chamber filled with women's shoes and one with money—coins pushed to one side and bills to the other, a lost fortune. Enough to last her mother and her for the rest of their lives, Zoe thought, if she could figure out some way to bring it all home with her. Stacks of glittering gold coins lay at her feet and she was tempted to take some, but Emmett's song was growing fainter, so she moved on.

The next chamber brought her to an abrupt stop. It was divided into separate rooms, each almost as large and packed as the previous chambers. But instead of junk, these rooms held more personal items. In one room were bundles of hair, neatly tied with string and attached to a paper label holding a name and more of the symbols Zoe knew from Emmett's records. Next to that was a room full of small bottles, each of which contained a single tooth. The teeth, too, were labeled. In another room were stacks of marked vials that each held a drop of blood. In the final chamber were thousands of small, clear bottles. Each bottle was labeled with the word *Tears* and a name. Zoe stared at Emmett's awful collection, feeling cold inside. She wondered if Emmett had bothered to add her false tooth to that pile.

Shit. Emmett!

She could barely hear him now. Zoe turned and ran through the rest of the chambers, following the sound of Emmett's voice. There was little light past the chambers. She blundered in the dark, groping and stumbling along the walls until she came to an underground crossroads, tunnels leading in four directions. She couldn't hear anything. Emmett had stopped singing.

She didn't know what to do, which way to go. A wrong decision could waste enough time to let Emmett get away. But standing there forever would accomplish the same thing. Zoe closed her eyes. This wasn't the time to lose her shit, she thought. She'd come too far for that. She breathed and looked around for clues. As she stared at the ancient stones, the image of Mr. Danvers flickered into her mind. He'd know what to do. He was smart and would figure out some cool science trick to follow Emmett. But she didn't know enough science for anything that James Bond–like. Did she know anything at all, anything useful? No, she decided, but she had to make a decision, and knew she needed a push. She pulled out Valentine's compass and held it close to her eyes so she could see where the little pointer settled. It came to a rest pointing west, to her left. That was better than nothing. She started down the left tunnel.

At first she walked very quietly, even covering her mouth and nose in an effort to muffle the sound of her breathing. The tunnel dropped her back into darkness almost as deep as the sewers, but there were candles here and there that kept her from bumping into the walls. There was something else, too. A whisper, like a voice. And maybe a melody. It was Emmett, singing again. Zoe sprinted frantically toward the sound.

The tunnel took sudden sharp turns and there were two-foot blind drops where the candlelight didn't reach.

She fell. She slammed her shoulders into the walls. She twisted her ankle, but she kept running, and Emmett's singing grew louder with each step. She gulped air and her chest burned from breathing so hard. Her arms and head ached from tension, but she closed in on the sound. She could tell Emmett was just ahead as she rounded a final corner . . .

. . . And she found herself in a cul-de-sac of bare, rough limestone. A dead end. Emmett's voice still hung in the air, a dying echo, like the smell of a room that had once held flowers.

Zoe's legs shook, and it was hard to catch her breath. She touched her fingertips over the walls, feeling the cold, damp stone. There was nothing in the cul-de-sac, no sign that Emmett or anyone else had ever been there. She looked wildly around the floor for footprints, a dropped piece of paper, anything that might show her that she'd gone the right away. There were just murky puddles, stones, and trash-speckled silt in small dunes in the corners. Zoe fell back against the wall.

Lost, she thought. Everything lost. Emmett. Dad. She bit the inside of her cheek and tasted blood. She wasn't even sure if she could find her way back.

Zoe held up her hands. They were almost black, covered in filth and ragged cuts. Her sneakers and jeans were ripped in a dozen places. She felt empty, as if, in the last few hours, she'd used up everything she was.

I should have stayed in that room with the teeth and hair and tears. That's where I belong. That's all I am . . . Just pieces of a person.

Something snapped inside her, and without thinking, Zoe screamed and kicked the stone in front of her. It hurt, but she didn't care. She grabbed garbage from the floor and hurled it at the wall—cans, old magazines, a motorcycle chain, a beer bottle. The bottle shattered against rough rock, sending shards flying back at her. She covered her face, but felt blood running down her arms where pieces had cut her. The blood mixed with the black filth on her hands. The sight of it made her very tired. Tears ran down her face. She wiped them away and sagged against the wall.

From far below, something rumbled. Zoe stepped back and the noise stopped. She pressed her weight into the stones, but nothing happened. She touched the stones to see if she could feel any movement. The rumbling came again, faintly. A moment later, the wall started to open, but stopped when she pulled back her hands. Zoe looked down and understood. She wiped her hands over her face, smearing her tears onto them, then touched the wall again. When her wet fingers came in contact with the stone, the wall swung back like a door opening.

Another tunnel lay ahead, crowded with the skeletons of rusted-out old buses half buried in mud. There was a narrow pathway through the debris, and at the end of the path was an opening onto what looked like a street.

Slowly and carefully, Zoe made her way between the mounds of garbage, limping on her twisted ankle. Rats scrabbled along the tops of the buses, their small, sharp claws ticking on the metal. Zoe could see their glittering eyes and twitching, inquisitive noses as they followed her passage through their kingdom. There was nothing threatening about the rats. They were just curious and cautious, but she also got the idea that the rats were partly staring at her in wonder, as if they knew something she didn't.

A light rain was falling where the tunnel ended. A street spread out before her and a cloudy sky hung above. It was night and the rain was stinging cold, but to Zoe it felt like the most glorious shower in the world. She held out her hands and rubbed them together, washing off as much of the grime as she could. Then she looked up and let the rain rinse her face clean. There was a full moon, high in the cloudy sky over a calm, black sea. It was a beautiful sight. A sudden blast of wind came from the direction of the water, carrying an ocean chill. Zoe shivered in her wet clothes. By the far wall a heavy black overcoat hung off the end of a bedpost. She picked up and inspected it. The coat was relatively clean and no rats seemed to have claimed it for their own, so she put it on. The weight and warmth made her feel better instantly. But that good feeling only lasted for a moment. Above the bedpost where the coat had hung, a single word was carved into the high granite wall:

IPHIGENE

Eight

There must be some mistake. The garbage-strewn passage and this dreary, pitted road couldn't be part of the same town where she'd just spent a day with her father, could they? Maybe there was more than one Iphigene.

A horn blared at her from nearby. Two bright lights crossed over her. A screech echoed off the rocky cliff as tires tried to grip the wet road. Zoe lurched back and pressed herself against the hill. She'd wandered to the center of the road without even realizing it. A bus swerved around where she'd been a second earlier and continued on, disappearing around the curve. Everything was suddenly quiet, except for the rain, which was coming down harder than ever. Wind from the ocean threw itself against the hillside and the rain seemed suspended in the air, like shuddering Christmas lights. Iphigene, whatever version of Iphigene she'd stumbled into, lay just around the corner ahead. She'd come much too far to simply turn back without a look, so she started walking.

Her right leg hurt. She'd twisted her ankle coming down the giant stairs and now her whole leg throbbed. Her sneakers were soaked through, but she could live with that. It meant they couldn't get any wetter. She pulled the coat tighter around her, hoping it would warm her up. It helped a little, but not much. As she neared the town, the rain turned to a fine mist. Zoe heard the sound of the surf breaking quietly on the shore below the boardwalk. The fat, ice-white moon cast its reflection onto the dark water. For just a moment, no more than a heartbeat, the moon looked to Zoe like a giant eye watching everything and everyone in Iphigene, including her. Then the feeling was gone and it was just the moon again.

Ahead, the bus that had almost run her down sat idling by the curb. The front and rear doors were open and people were stepping down to the pavement. Many of the new arrivals stood on the corner, seemingly confused. They turned in slow circles like lost dogs trying to catch a scent that would lead them home. A few walked up the street, drawn by the sounds coming from the bars, while others crossed over to the boardwalk to stare at the ocean.

Zoe approached a plump man in a dark brown suit at least a size too small for him. The rain plastered his straw-colored hair across his forehead and his white shirt across the ample curve of his belly. He and a handful of others seemed unwilling to move far from the idling bus.

"This isn't right," murmured the fat man.

"Uh, excuse me," said Zoe.

He looked down at her. "It's all wrong," he said.

"I'm looking for someone."

The plump man turned in a slow circle, his arms held out in a gesture of confusion. "It's not supposed to be like this." He wrapped his thick hands around the bus-stop sign and shook it, as if to see if it was real. When the sign stayed firmly rooted to the street, he seemed to shrink a little. He shuffled away, around the corner, muttering to himself, "This isn't right."

Zoe put up the collar on her coat and held it closed with one hand. She went down the strangely-familiar-but-unfamiliar street, keeping her head down, trying to blend in with the new arrivals. At least then she'd have an excuse for checking the place out so much.

What had gone wrong with the city? Zoe wondered. She passed the newsstand with the green awning. The newspapers and magazines lay in bloated piles, water-logged and black with mildew. The clothing store where, she remembered, they sold coats like the one she now wore was empty. Broken mannequins lay among the sodden shadows, broken limbs scattered across the cracked linoleum floor.

On the next block, one of the big restaurants where, as her father had explained to her, nervous souls ate endless, pointless meals, was dark. The shattered front window had been carelessly repaired with cardboard and tape. Fireflies moved in sluggish lines inside the dirty glass. No, not fireflies, she thought as her eyes adjusted to the dark. People were moving around carrying miniature oil lamps made from ancient apothecary and liquor bottles. Zoe could make out a few faces inside the restaurant. They stared out at her with such hunger and dark resentment that it scared her. She turned away and crossed over to the boardwalk.

There were fewer people by the beach. An old man a few feet to her right was staring out at the moon, rubbing and flexing his arm as if it hurt. When he moved it, the arm squeaked. In the moonlight, Zoe saw that the man's arms were tarnished metal pipes, sort of like what they used in the bathrooms at school. The man's ragged coat was a patchwork of other coats, pieces of plastic, and what looked like vinyl from a car seat. All the pieces were stitched together crudely with string and wire. Zoe turned her head, looking down the length of the boulevard. A woman limped along on a carved leg from a piano bench. A young boy tossed a ball in the air and stabbed it in midair with a short knife that protruded from the end of his arm where his hand should be. Everyone on the street seemed to be held together with rags and junkyard plunder.

She looked back at the beach, but was startled by the old man, who had drawn closer to her. His pale face was so worn and heavily lined that "old" didn't begin to describe him. He looked "ancient," and Zoe flashed on things from Mr. Danvers's class. Carved scarabs in Egypt. Fossilized skulls from Kenya. Mammoths frozen in Siberian glaciers. The old man's face could have been as old as any of those things.

He smiled and put his metal hand on her arm. "You remind me of my daughter," he said in an airy, thin voice.

"Thank you," said Zoe, not knowing anything else to say.

The old man's face changed. He leaned close to Zoe's cheek and sniffed. "You smell like . . . I don't know." He seemed lost for a moment. Then his smile grew wide and wild. "The world! You smell like the world!" His hand closed tighter on her arm. "You're alive!" he whispered.

Zoe pushed the old man hard and backed away. But he came after her, dazed and excited. "You're alive!" he repeated over and over, getting louder each time he said it. People on the street stopped and stared. Zoe kept backing away, fear creeping up from her stomach. A couple of people broke away from the crowd that had gathered on the sidewalk and started toward her. Zoe bolted from the old man, back toward the bus stop. At least there were lights there.

But a curious crowd had gathered there, too. Zoe spun and started down a side street between the newsstand and the bar. Out of the corners of her eyes she caught glimpses of stripped cars tilting on flat tires and small fires in vacant lots where lost souls were huddled around jets of burning methane that leaked from the ground. The souls turned to look at her.

Zoe turned a corner and slipped on the wet pavement, going down hard on one knee, twisting her bad ankle. From both ends of the street, she could hear what sounded like all of Iphigene, wood and metal limbs clanking and scraping as the inhabitants of the city closed in on her.

She struggled to her feet and took off running, moving without direction or thought, propelled by her desperate need to stay ahead of the mob. When the street came to a sudden dead end, she darted down another alley and dashed by what looked like a row of derelict warehouses. Her breath caught in her throat. The throbbing in her leg was making her sick to her stomach. She couldn't run forever, she knew, but for now, she kept moving.

A hand closed on her arm and jerked her hard to the side. She tumbled down a short flight of stairs into a damp, dark basement. It only took her a moment to get back to her feet, but when she tried to scramble back up the steps, someone grabbed her from behind. A hand clamped over her mouth and a voice whispered, "Shhh. They're right behind you. Keep quiet."

A moment later, the mob came stumbling down the alley. Zoe froze on the stairs, hoping she was down low enough to be invisible to the street. Whoever was behind her pushed her head down so that she could only see the rough concrete steps on which she lay. Soon everything grew quiet. She could hear her own heart beating and the nervous breathing of whoever was holding her. A moment later, his hand moved away from her mouth, and she felt his weight lift from her body. Still on the steps, she turned and looked back into the basement.

"Thanks. I think," Zoe said.

She didn't see anyone at first. Then she heard someone move and could just make out a pair of feet in tattered sneakers illuminated by a slash of light near the far wall.

"You okay?" asked whoever was wearing the sneakers. A boy, definitely, she thought.

"I guess. Why are you all the way over there in the dark? Come out where I can see you."

"I'm cool over here right now," said the boy.

Zoe put her hand in her pocket and closed her fingers around the razor. "You can't keep me in here," she said firmly.

"You're not so smart, are you, if you can't tell the difference between a kidnapping and a rescue?"

"I'm feeling about as rescued as I need," she said, rising. The pain in her ankle made her wince. "Thanks. I'm heading out."

"Where?" the boy asked. "Do you know your way around Iphigene? Do you even know where you are?"

Zoe wanted to tell the voice to fuck off, but knew the boy had a point.

"How far are you going to get on that leg?" he asked.

"Okay," said Zoe. "But how am I supposed to trust you if you won't let me see you?"

The boy's feet shuffled on the dirt floor. Now it was his turn to be nervous, she saw.

"I'm not much to look at. Kind of ugly, in fact," the boy said. "I didn't want to scare you."

"Okay, but this voice-from-the-shadows thing is a little too Freddy Krueger. If you're trying to be my friend, come on out."

"I don't know."

"Hey, I've seen *The Evil Dead*. As long as you've got a head, I can deal."

Zoe watched the sneakers take half a step forward, revealing a length of filthy, torn jeans.

"I didn't want it to happen like this, you know," the boy said. "I had it all planned different. But then those assholes started chasing you."

"What did you have planned? Who the hell are you?" She was ready with the razor.

A pause. "I was hoping maybe you'd know. But why should you? The real thing isn't much like in dreams."

Zoe sat on the steps, her mind racing. There had been something familiar about the voice from the moment she'd heard it. It tickled something far in the back of her brain, like some deep memory or half-remembered dream. She let go of the razor and said, "Valentine?"

The boy took a step back, disappearing completely into the shadows. "This is dumb. I should go."

Zoe was up on her feet and crossed the room in a couple of painful steps. When she plunged her hands into the dark, all she felt was the rough stone of the basement wall. Off to her right, she could hear breathing, so she reached out in that direction. Her fingers brushed heavy cloth, and she closed her hand on the boy's arm. There was no flesh there. It was as hard and unyielding as steel. Zoe stepped back into the middle of the room.

"Come into the light, Valentine. Please."

The boy shuffled forward, his shoulders hunched, head down. Dark, unruly hair covered his face. Zoe reached out and touched his other arm. It felt as hard and artificial as the first one. She thought of the people she'd seen on the street, the ones with wood and metal limbs. She put her hand on Valentine's shoulder and felt something more familiar there, like skin and bone. The boy kept his head turned away from her and all she could really see of him was his heavy, patched greatcoat. It had a stiff collar so high that he could hide half his face behind it, but Valentine's familiar brown eyes glittered at her from behind the wall of the collar.

"It *is* you," she said, and for the first time outside of her dreams, Zoe put her arms around her brother.

Valentine's body was thin. He went rigid when she hugged him, and he didn't make any move to hug her back. When she tried to kiss his cheek, he pulled back suddenly, stepping into the dark again.

"Valentine, you don't have to be afraid of me."

"I'm not afraid."

"Then why are you hiding? What's wrong with you?"

A skeletal hand spotted with rust slid from the dark, pointing toward the stairs. "We shouldn't stay here. They'll be back."

"Did I do something to hurt you?" asked Zoe.

Valentine stepped past her, moving quickly to the stairs. "It's all right. We need to go."

Zoe followed him, limping on her injured ankle, which, after her fall into the basement, felt like there were pins sticking into the bone.

"You're hurt," Valentine said. Her took her hand and helped her to the stairs. "Sit."

Kneeling on the dirt floor, Valentine pulled a long, dirty white rag from the pocket of his greatcoat. He pulled off Zoe's sneaker and socks and carefully wrapped the rag around her ankle and foot, slipping her sneaker back on when he was done. As he worked, all Zoe could see of him was the top of his head and the occasional glint of light off his iron hands.

"Try that," Valentine said.

Zoe stood, slowly putting weight on her bad leg. It stung, but the pain didn't make her want to retch anymore.

"That's a lot better. Thanks."

Valentine nodded and started up the stairs. At the top he turned and said, "Keep your coat buttoned and your head down. Walk slow, like you've got nowhere to go and all eternity to get there."

"Do we have to go back out right now? I'm kind of freaked by this place."

" 'Course you are," said Valentine. "You're not supposed to be here. None of us are."

He stepped out first, then motioned for Zoe to follow him. They walked down the wet night street away from the direction in which Zoe had been running. The rain was misting down, making tiny diamonds on her overcoat as she and Valentine came to better-lit streets. Zoe looped one of her arms around one of Valentine's. She felt him stiffen for a moment, but he didn't pull away.

They crossed a broad street that she recognized. They were near the bar and boardwalk where the crowd had spotted her, she thought, a little afraid. But this time she wasn't alone. She looked at her sleeves, staring at the rain jewels there.

Heavily muscled, with bodies and huge heads that reminded her of the granite gargoyles on churches, enormous black dogs were eating something that lay in the gutter. The dogs from her dreams.

Zoe felt Valentine tug her arm. "Don't look," he said. "They're Queen Hecate's spies."

Zoe couldn't help glancing back. "What are they eating?" The dogs hungrily ripped into their food. "It almost looks like a body."

"I told you not to look."

• • •

Zoe closed her eyes for a few seconds and let Valentine lead her. All her life she'd wanted to live in her dreams with her brother and now her dreams had come true. But they weren't alone and it was both wonderful and horrible.

When they were well past the dogs, Zoe whispered, "Valentine, what happened to the city? I was just here a day ago and it was beautiful."

Valentine shook his head. "Nothing happened. The city's been like this for as long as anyone can remember. Father tricked you with pretty pictures and sweet lies. He showed you what you wanted to see so you'd get the hell out and never come back. Why *did* you come back?"

"I think I did something bad. I just wanted to see if he was all right."

"You think you're going to fix anything? Look at this place. Look at these people. Look at me." He lifted his head a little way out his high collar. She caught a glimpse of stitches in his face. Not the kind the doctor had given her after she'd fallen as a kid. These stitches were thick and crude, like wires in cheap leather. "Don't worry. Father hasn't been here long enough to look like me. But he's not exactly what you remember."

"What the fuck is this place? Are we in hell?"

"Yeah, but not the one you mean." They turned off the well-lit streets into a darker industrial area. Broken fences ringed fields full of strange and fearsome machines: cranes with what looked like claws, bulldozers with teeth. What lay ahead was even stranger.

Just a few blocks off the main road, the streets weren't straight anymore, and neither were the buildings. They twisted around, over and under each other, like weeds and vines in an abandoned garden. Some buildings stood straight up while others lay on their sides like snakes, wrapping around other twisted buildings, strangling the upright ones so they shrank to almost nothing at the middle but bulged at the tops and bottoms.

Valentine said, "The city used to be called Calumet. That means 'peace.' Now it's Iphigene. Only Queen Hecate knows what that means, and no one's asking her."

"That's the queen the dogs spy for?"

He nodded. "She rules Iphigene. We're her loyal subjects. She's been the queen here for over a thousand years. Maybe thousands. No one can say exactly."

In the distance, Zoe thought she could see a dark apartment building rise from the ground, windows and doors sliding into place as the place unfurled like a blooming flower.

"She doesn't sound like much of a queen."

"The city wasn't always like this. Before Hecate, we had day and night just like anywhere else. They say that when she crowned herself, the first thing she did was steal the sun out of the sky and hide it somewhere in her palace."

"Why?"

"She's the moon. The moon is Hecate." He looked up

at the bright white orb hanging over the sluggish ocean. "We can only love her and worship her under the moon. Anyway, that's what the old-timers told me."

The road took them under a kind of arch where two buildings had collided and grew upright against each other. Zoe could swear she heard a subtle crunch and creak as the buildings continued to move and grow above them.

"Old-timers. Old spirits, you mean? Old souls." Zoe was suddenly cold again. "It's all so real and solid here. It's weird to think that everyone here is dead. That you're all ghosts."

"But that's what we are."

"But I can see you and touch you."

"Spirits are real. And this is a place for spirits. You're the strange one around here."

She smiled a little at Valentine. "Thanks for letting me hold on to you. I know you don't like it, but I really need to right now."

"I'm just not used to it. It's kind of nice, in a weird way. No one's ever really, you know, touched me before."

Zoe tightened the arm she'd looped through his and pulled him a little closer. He didn't resist. "There's Dad. He's here now."

"So? I'm just some strange guy in your dreams, remember?"

"No, you're not. Otherwise you wouldn't be here. You wouldn't have . . . well, died."

"If you're going to get technical," he said. Valentine drew in a long breath and blew mist into the night air. "Anyway, I know Father, but he's doesn't know I'm around. That's how I like it, so don't go doing nothing dramatic."

"Are you mad at him?"

"Nope."

"You're hiding from him like you hid from me that time I upset you up in the tree fort."

"Maybe. Or maybe just because, okay? Stop asking so many damned questions," he snapped.

"Sorry." Two black dogs were fighting over a dead rat in the middle of a deserted intersection. They stopped and watched Zoe and Valentine intently as they passed, then they went back to their fight.

"I'm sorry," said Valentine. "I didn't mean it."

"It's okay. Can I ask you one more question?"

"Sure."

"You're here, but Mom and Dad never talked about you. You're not . . . Mom and Dad didn't . . ."

"Am I an abortion, you mean?"

Zoe looked down at her feet. "Yeah."

"A miscarriage. And that's your last question about that. You've got other stuff to worry about." On a street of derelict garages, Zoe followed Valentine up a fire escape two floors onto the tilted roof of one building. From three stories up, Iphigene was laid out at Zoe's feet.

Gazing out toward the beach, she thought that the city didn't look so bad. Kind of old and run-down, but not in a bad way. But the city was stranger when she looked inland. Nothing made sense. Streets bent and buckled and circled back on each other around buildings that lay like earthworms after a rain. It reminded Zoe of an M. C. Escher print Laura had of crazy stairs that ran into each other at impossible angles. Laura, Zoe thought. What would she think if she could see me now?

Valentine called her to the edge of the roof and pointed to a building at the far end of the boardwalk. "That used to be the city hall. Now it's Hecate's palace." It was an ornate, sprawling building of brilliant white marble. She remembered it from her first visit, but like the rest of Iphigene, the building was different now. There were long curved spikes running around the edge of the roof, like cobra fangs. Towers stood at each corner of the palace, topped with a carving that depicted different phases of the moon, from crescent to full.

"It's beautiful," Zoe said.

"Old bones," said Valentine. Zoe looked at him. "They say when you get close, the walls look like old bones."

"My friend Absynthe would love that."

"I remember her. Your Goth girlfriend."

"She's not my girlfriend," said Zoe, and she shoved him a little. Without hesitation, he shoved her back. She smiled and for a second everything was normal. She was in a familiar place, high in the air with Valentine teasing her about some silly thing or other. It's him, she thought. It really is Valentine.

"Listen. There's something I haven't told you. The real reason Father didn't want you here." Valentine's voice was low and slow, more serious than she'd ever heard him before.

"Queen Hecate is as crazy as the sea is black. She's been dead and crazy for so long, she doesn't even remember that she used to be alive. She can't leave Iphigene, or she won't. Maybe she forgot that this is just a way station and we're supposed to move on. But every day the buses leave empty." Valentine stared out at the palace. "She hates the living. That means she hates you. You need to be careful every moment you're here."

Zoe nodded, trying not to look scared. "What should I do? Is there somewhere I can hide until I can figure out what to do?"

"Of course." Valentine pointed to the next roof. "My house. It's right over there."

Valentine's house was a sprawling shack made of scavenged wood, sheet metal, parts of buses, and tar paper from nearby buildings. The inside was a forest of tools, old clothes, books, and old comics, all junk washed down from the city above. The place reminded Zoe of their tree fort, and she felt safe and at home. Valentine pointed to a relatively clean cot in the corner.

"It's not much, but I call it nothing," he said. For the first time he showed Zoe his face and smiled. He seemed more relaxed on his home turf. He took off his greatcoat and hung it on a meat hook by the door. Zoe finally got a look at his arms. They looked like lengths of rebar and pipe held together by wire and ragged welds. When he crossed the room, his legs moved strangely, swinging at odd angles under his loose jeans. She wondered if all his limbs were homemade, and had to remind herself not to stare.

"I have about a thousand more questions," she said.

"Everyone does when they first get here." He took a match and lit a small camp stove by a truck windshield that served as a window. "I'll answer what I can tomorrow. You must be tired now. Why don't you lie down while I make some tea."

"Do all ghosts drink tea?"

"Only the ones that know where to find it or steal it."

Zoe sat on the bed, not feeling at all tired, and watched Valentine move happily around his little home, getting cups and finding sugar. Seeing him made her happier than she'd felt in months. She lay down and looked out at the stars through the truck windshield. Then, without realizing it, she was asleep.

It was strange, waking up in the dark. It took Zoe a minute to remember where she was. The sight of the tools and old, broken toys hanging from the ceiling reminded her that she was in Valentine's rooftop home, but the memory didn't make the place any more real to her waking mind. It all felt too much like a dream. When she sat up and put her feet on the floor, however, the pain in her ankle told her that this was very real.

Valentine was over by the window. "Hey, you're awake. How are you feeling? I have some food, if you're hungry." He brought her a bundle wrapped in a white paper napkin. Zoe unfolded it and found a couple of slices of toast with strips of crisp bacon.

"Thanks," she said, and bit into a strip of bacon. It was like Styrofoam. When she sniffed it, the bacon didn't have any smell at all. She bit into the toast and found that it was the same, spongy and nearly tasteless.

"Something wrong?" asked Valentine.

"No, it's fine," said Zoe through a full mouth. She smiled and tried to look happy.

"Don't lie. You can barely choke it down." He picked up one of the bacon strips and sniffed. "Funny. It smells all right to me."

"An old woman ghost gave me a piece of candy that tasted like this. It's not really like food. More like the memory of it."

"I don't usually eat, myself. Never got the habit. And this is ghost food from one of the restaurants by the boardwalk. I guess I'm not surprised a live person can't taste it."

"It was nice of you to try. Thanks. So, if you live up here away from people and don't go to the restaurant or the bar, what do you do all day?" She thought about that for a second. "Night, I guess. You know what I mean."

"Yeah, I know. I scavenge. The streets. The canals. The beach. Wherever." He opened his hands to his packed-to-the-rafters room. "It keeps me sharp and awake, not in denial like the people in the restaurants stuffing their faces forever. Where do you think I got the things for our tree fort? Where do you think I got the telescope?"

Zoe smiled. Valentine almost looked happy talking about his stuff. Her smile faded when she thought about it and understood that this was all Valentine had. An endless night of picking through the world's castoffs. She tried not to show how sad that made her. "Where are we?" she asked.

Valentine nodded at the floor. "This building we're in is where people used to make and fix the buses that took people away. But we don't need them anymore. No one leaves, so all that's left are the ones that bring in new souls." He looked out one of the windows at the apartment buildings that crawled over the hills and disappeared into the far distance. "I don't know how big the city is. Big. Bigger than the living world, maybe. It grows and changes all the time, trying to squeeze in new souls. It's pretty modern up here, but over those hills, there are people that speak Latin, and others, I don't know what they speak, but they write with pictures. I'll look out for you, so you don't have to be afraid, but you can't let down your guard here. Not for a second."

"Well," said Zoe, having no idea how to respond.

"Sorry. I shouldn't have said all that at once."

"No, it's all right. I want to know the truth." She looked at the hills where Valentine had been staring a moment before. "If it wasn't so scary here, I'd like to see the people who write in hieroglyphics."

"We can't do that," Valentine said. "But I can give you what you came here for. I can take you to see Father. I know where he lives."

"I'd love that."

"How's your ankle?"

"Much better."

"Then let's go."

They crossed the roofs under the moon, back the way they'd come the previous night, and descended the fire escape to the street. Then they turned inland, headed toward the heaps of giant apartment buildings she'd seen from the roof. At the corner Valentine stopped her. He turned up the collar on her coat so that it covered more of her face. After studying her for a moment, he ran his hands down the sides of a telephone pole and wiped smeared dirt across Zoe's forehead and cheeks. He ended by popping a final dot of dirt on the end of her nose with his thumb. "Now you look more like one of us," he said.

She soon lost track of time as they walked. In the day that was exactly the same as the previous night, the idea of seconds, minutes, and hours became fantastical, like something from a fairy tale. She tried counting the streets, but they were so twisted around she had no idea where one stopped and another began. But they were definitely in an older part of the city. They crossed tall stone walkways lit by bent gaslights and descended long flights of cobblestone staircases to narrow catwalks just inches above murky canal water. Since she couldn't make out streets, Zoe tried remembering landmarks along the way. There was a half-burned billboard with the remains of a woman's smile beneath one of the stone walkways.

As they walked, Valentine dragged his boots through debris in the gutters and picked up anything he could find that was shiny, sometimes throwing it away and sometimes pocketing it. She understood now how his little house had become so crowded. His delight when he found something he liked was almost like that of a kid, Zoe thought. In fact, even though he was older, in some ways Valentine felt more like a little brother. She guessed it had something to do with his being dead so long. He never had the chance to go out into the world and grow up like Zoe and her friends did. He started collecting junk when he got to Iphigene and never stopped because there wasn't anyone to show him that there was anything else to do. He'd been cheated of so much. It didn't seem fair, but then what was fair in this strange place?

At the bottom of a staircase, in a circle of stones made where twisting buildings left an open patch of land, were the remains of what looked like a campsite. Ragged beds, tables, chairs, and lamps had been dragged outside.

"Why would people take their stuff outside where it rains?" asked Zoe.

Valentine didn't even turn his head.

"Not all the apartments are that nice. Some people prefer the street."

The camp was all just wreckage now. Splintered wood and gutted mattresses. The place hadn't been dismantled the way police would do it. It was torn to pieces, as if by angry animals.

Zoe's bad ankle hurt and Valentine had to help her limp over heaps of trash that filled some twisting streets by some of the old apartments. They were back on a street that looked more like a normal modern city. "Sorry about the trek," he said. "Truth is, you can take that big street over there most of the way back to the ocean." He pointed over his shoulder. "But I thought if Hecate's dogs had maybe heard about you, it would be good to go the long way round."

"It was a good idea," said Zoe, panting. She sat and retied the rag Valentine had put around her ankle. She still limped a little but she could walk just fine.

"Anyway, we're here." Valentine nodded to the nearest building. The address was 5,111,304 Ouroboros Street.

The apartment building across the street wrapped around the building, tightening it in the middle so it was shaped like an hourglass.

"This is where Dad lives?"

"Yep. Fifth floor, all the way in the back, on the right."

Zoe nodded, feeling both excited and nervous.

"Before you go in, there are a couple things you need to know. I'm not going in with you for the reasons I told you about last night."

"Just because," she said.

"Right. The second thing is that when we're out like this, if something happens and we get separated, you head straight back to my house. Got it?"

"I don't think I can find my way back the way we came."

"Then take the street that leads to the boardwalk and come back that way. And if you're ever alone, don't ever, no matter what happens, ever go down *any* unlit streets. Dim is okay, just not unlit. There are souls a lot worse off than me and you don't want to see the worst of 'em. The dying dead. More important, you don't want them to see you."

"Okay," she said. Zoe wanted to ask more about the dying dead but knew it wasn't the right time.

"I'm going to go wait over there." Valentine nodded toward an alcove at the side of a nearby apartment building. "Take as long as you need."

"Thanks." Zoe leaned forward and quickly pecked him on the cheek. He stiffened a little, but didn't pull away. She took that as a good sign, then hurried into the building.

There was an elevator in the lobby, but when she looked closer she saw it was just an open elevator shaft.

Someone had moved a bed and chair into the opening and it looked like they'd been living there. She found stairs around the corner and climbed to the fifth floor. At first, the building seemed utterly silent, but as she climbed, she began to hear small sounds of habitation. Footsteps. A drawer opening and closing. The tinkle of a glass on a table.

Zoe's heart raced as she stepped onto the fifth-floor landing. Her ankle hurt but she couldn't help herself, and ran all the way down the hall to her father's door. She knocked but didn't hear anything from inside. She knocked again. "Dad?" she whispered to the door. No response. She quietly turned the knob and the door opened.

The inside of her father's room was so spare it was almost empty. Like a prison cell, thought Zoe. While Valentine's place was stuffed to the rafters with goodies he'd plucked from the city's overflow, her father's room held a bed, a table, and a dresser with a vase of plastic roses on top. There was a discolored spot on one wall where a mirror or a picture might have once hung.

A straight-backed wooden chair had been dragged from the table and set before the room's one window. Every surface in the room seemed to be covered in dust, except for the windowsill in front of the chair. That area was clean. He leans on the sill right here, she thought. He sits here all day and night. This is his real life in Iphigene. Her breath caught in her throat and the stab of grief and loss made her fight back tears. Zoe reached for the rubber band on her wrist but it was gone.

She went back downstairs and found Valentine in the alcove. She told him what she'd found in the room. "He wasn't there," she finished.

"Don't worry," he said. "There's another place where he spends some of his nights. Maybe we'll find him there."

They took the shortcut to the beach. The route was much quicker, and Zoe could see the reflection of the moon in the sea after just a few minutes of walking.

"Remember, walk slow," Valentine warned her as they crossed the street to the boardwalk and climbed down to the beach.

The wet sand was heavy on Zoe's sneakers, but it sparkled like snow under the moon. They were headed for the old amusement park where she'd spent the happy afternoon with her father. Zoe knew that she was getting used to Iphigene because it wasn't at all surprising to her to see that the park was a wreck, a heap of collapsed timbers and rides that had slipped off their foundations and lay lopsided in the sand. She had to admit, however, that the place still held a kind of sad beauty, like a winter carnival frozen in a blizzard.

People were wandering down onto the beach behind them. Zoe turned in terror and was ready to run from the mob. But Valentine grabbed her shoulders and held her where she was, pointing to the street.

"Look," he said.

Several buses arrived simultaneously and what looked like a hundred people were suddenly milling around with the dazed look of all the new arrivals. Some people headed to the restaurant or the side streets, but more poured down onto the beach, as if being near the water would wake them from a bad dream. At first they walked. Then they ran, a solid wall of bodies. Zoe was knocked onto her knees and had to scramble to her feet to keep from getting trampled. The crowd carried her along with them, like a tidal wave of grasping hands and running feet. Finally, she worked her way to the side and shouldered her way free of the crowd. The rag around her ankle was loose. She fell and had to crawl onto the tilting turntable of the carousel.

Limping behind the carousel animals, she watched the last of the mob rush down to the sea. She couldn't see Valentine anywhere. The idea of going back into the crowd was too much. She decided to stay where she was until the beach cleared out. Then she'd sneak out and go back to Valentine's house.

Someone grunted nearby in the dark. Zoe whirled around and saw a man curled up asleep under the figure of a golden sea serpent. He had on the same shapeless overcoat that almost everyone seemed to wear in Iphigene, and his head was resting on a couple of the stuffed-animal toys that she'd seen scattered all around the abandoned rides. He grunted again and rolled over, facing her.

"Dad?" said Zoe, her voice hoarse from the sand she'd swallowed when she fell.

The sleeping man opened his eyes. They were blood-shot and wet. He was unshaven and his hair was wild, as if he hadn't brushed it in weeks. Slowly, drunkenly, the man pushed himself into a sitting position. He rubbed his eyes and ran his hands through his hair, pushing it out of his face.

"Dad?" said Zoe, though she was certain who he was this time.

The man turned and looked at her, his red eyes wide and full of fear. He tried to crawl away from her.

"No, no," he said. "I'm dreaming."

Zoe crawled after him and grabbed his leg. "Dad, it's me!" she yelled, and he froze on the spot. His shoulders sagged and he lay facedown where he was. For a moment neither of them moved, then her father sat up. When he looked at her this time, it wasn't fear she saw in his eyes: it was anger.

"What the hell are you doing here?" he yelled. "Didn't I tell you not to ever come back?"

Zoe crawled closer to him. "I had to. I did something bad back at home and I thought you needed help."

"There's nothing you can do back in the world that will hurt me here."

"But Emmett had these records and one of them had your soul or something on it . . ."

"Yeah, those." Her father drew up his legs and leaned

back against a bench covered with fading images of mermaids. "We all have those, honey. Emmett makes them. Supposedly, if he breaks yours, you'll disappear, but he's such a liar, who knows?"

"I was trying to get yours. I tried to trick him. But I think he tricked me."

"He's good at that. You've got to get out of here as soon as you can. If Hecate finds out about you, well, I don't want to think about it."

"I know. Val . . . a friend is taking care of me. But I don't know how I can leave. Do you?"

"No. But there has to be a way. Emmett comes and goes from here to the world all the time."

"Dad, it's good to see you." She moved over and leaned on the bench next to him. After a moment he put his arm around her shoulder.

"You, too. I'm so goddamn angry right now, but it's still good to see you."

"Why do you look like this, Dad? Are you sick?"

"Kind of. But it doesn't have anything to do with what you did back home."

"You sure?"

"Positive."

"I don't know if I believe you. Emmett took your record."

"Yeah, but not because of what you did," he said. "He took the record because of what I did."

"What did you do?"

"It's not important. All that matters is you getting out of here." Zoe's father took her face in his hand and looked hard into her eyes. "You can't ever come back here. I mean it. If you do, I won't see you. I won't talk to you. I won't acknowledge you. Do you understand me?"

Zoe nodded. "I understand." It hurt to have him mad at her, but felt good that he still wanted to help.

"Who's this friend of yours?" he asked.

"Someone I used to know back home."

"Do you trust him?"

"Yes."

"Then get to him and find a way out of Iphigene. Nothing else matters."

"You still haven't told me why you look like this. Why isn't the city how I remember?"

Her father started to answer, but was cut off by a strange howl in the distance. It reminded her of a foghorn, but this sound was rougher, darker, more like the deep wail of some wounded animal.

"Oh no," said Zoe's father.

"What was that?"

"Nothing. I have to go." He pulled himself to his feet. Standing, he looked even weaker than he'd been before. It took a few seconds for him to steady himself on his feet. Then he started off across the beach. Other people were walking in the same direction, a few other newcomers, but mostly people Zoe had seen on the streets by the newsstand and bar. Old-timers, she thought. She ran after her father.

"What's wrong, Dad? What was that sound?"

"Go to your friend and find a way out. I can't help you." Zoe grabbed him and his hand closed on her arm so hard it brought tears to her eyes. "Get away from me and stay away! I don't ever want to see you here again!" He pushed her hard enough that she fell back onto the sand.

Zoe lay there and watched as her father joined a long line of people walking into the dark heart of the city, following the wail that filled the sky.

Nine

Zoe couldn't stop her father. He was in a trance or under a spell or something, out of both her control and his. But she had to do something.

She sprinted down the beach away from the amusement park, zigzagging between the lost newcomers, moving in a wide circle to get a look at as many faces as she could. Then she saw Valentine, standing on the steps that led down to the beach, waving to her.

When she reached him, she tripped on the steps, but he grabbed her before she fell. "There's something wrong with Dad. He's hypnotized or something."

"Where is he?" asked Valentine.

Zoe pointed to the mob of souls trudging into the city. "He's with them. He changed when the sound started."

Valentine grabbed her and they ran after their father. "We can't let him get too far!" he shouted.

Zoe went as fast as she could, ignoring the pain in her ankle. Valentine, on his unsteady metal legs, couldn't keep up. Anger and frustration surged up in her. Didn't anything work here? Wasn't there anything she could rely on? She grabbed Valentine, putting his arm around her shoulders while she slid her arm around his waist. Together they ran as fast as they could, but when they turned into the street where the mob had wandered, no one was there. The wailing sound wound down, quickly dropping in pitch until it was gone. After all that noise, the silence that followed was deep and frightening.

"I think I know where they're headed," Valentine said. "This way." He loped away on his long legs and Zoe followed.

"Where are they going?" She was feeling tinges of panic now, more than she had since coming to Iphigene. "What's happening?"

Valentine pointed down a side street and they turned. "It's complicated." Zoe had the feeling that he didn't want to answer the question, but it wasn't like yesterday when she'd badgered him with a thousand queries all at once. She got the feeling that something had frightened him, something that he didn't want to talk about, ever.

"Tell me," Zoe said, her voice rising.

"Quiet. There are dogs at the corner." They slowed their pace as they passed the black beasts. Having to walk so slowly killed Zoe. She wanted to sprint away, but Valentine kept a firm grip on her until the dogs were well behind them.

"Tell me," she whispered.

"It's Hecate." Valentine looked away from her and his voice dropped so low she could barely hear him. "Her children are hungry."

Zoe took a quick step in front of Valentine. "What does that mean?" but Valentine wouldn't meet her eyes and stepped around her.

"You should go back to my house," he said. "If it's what I think, there's nothing you can do."

Zoe grabbed his coat and held him. "Valentine! Tell me!" she shouted. When he didn't answer, she grabbed her brother and shook him.

When he looked at her, his eyes were both sad and bright with anger. "Don't you know by now? You've seen how we are here. Ripped apart and thrown away like the garbage in the streets. Hecate's children need food and there's nothing to eat in Iphigene but us."

From far away, Zoe could just hear the sound of the buses pulling away after dropping off their last load of new souls. A light breeze blew drops of cold water down from the damp roofs onto her face. Finally, Valentine's eyes shifted to meet hers. "I lied to you earlier when I said I didn't know what Iphigene meant. It means 'sacrifice.'"

Zoe stared at him, her mind racing. "Is that what happened to you?"

Valentine looked around before answering. "It happens to everyone. You're here long enough, you end up with debts. Some mistake you made. A favor someone did you. But it's never just a payment the city wants from you. It's a sacrifice." He smiled, but it was cold. "And you're it."

Zoe shook her head as if movement might force what she was hearing into a shape that made sense. "I've seen Father's room. He doesn't have anything. He sleeps on the beach. What could he possibly owe anyone?"

Valentine's expression went dark. "We need to keep moving," he said, and started walking.

"What aren't you telling me, Valentine?" Zoe called. "Does it have something to do with me?"

He spun around, his hands balled into fists. "Shut up right now. This won't help anyone."

He started away again, but Zoe grabbed him. He kept walking, pulling her off balance. Zoe ran up behind him and punched his shoulder. He turned on her and grabbed both of her hands in a powerful grip. "You fucking need to be quiet."

"Valentine, please tell me what's happening. What debt . . . ?" she pleaded, her voice trailing off.

He took a breath and released her. Taking a step back, he pulled his coat tight around his body. "I think you know."

"For me," said Zoe flatly.

Valentine looked down and nodded.

"It was that day we spent together, when the city seemed so beautiful. Hecate made that for him."

Valentine shrugged. "What's important is that he did what he thought was right. Trust me, he doesn't regret it."

"I do," she said. "I was only trying to help, but I made things worse."

Valentine came to Zoe and put his stiff arms around her. "Father did what he did to save you from this." Zoe's head spun. "We should go back to my house. There's nothing we can do here."

"No," said Zoe firmly. "Take me to him. If he's sacrificing himself for me, I want to be there with him."

"We're almost there," said Valentine, pointing. "He'll be in one of the buildings around that corner."

"Let's go."

"I can't," he said. Zoe heard fear in his voice. When she looked, there were tears in his eyes. "I thought I could go there, but I can't. I'm afraid." He stepped back, holding out his corroded metal arms. "There's so little of me left."

She went to him and took his hand. "It's all right. I can go on my own from here."

"You should come back with me, where it's safe."

"I can't." She kissed his cheek. It was wet with tears and sweat.

"I'm sorry," he said.

"I love you," said Zoe. Turning, she sprinted down the street and around the corner.

Zoe didn't know what she'd expected to find, but it sure wasn't this. Where the rest of the city was alive with crawling, growing buildings, this neighborhood looked like nothing had changed in a long time. The buildings were as twisted as the others, but they didn't move. They were grimy and stationary. On a street where sacrifices had taken place for a thousand years or more, she expected bonfires, a church, maybe some kind of mysterious icons. All she found was a street of dusty, dead storefronts, like a small town on an old black-and-white TV show.

Zoe walked along the white line in the middle of the deserted street, peering into the empty stores without getting too close. She threw her hand up in front of her eyes, going blind for a second as all the lights along the street blinked on at once. When she could see again she ran from shop to shop, searching for her father in every window.

At the end of the street in a place with THE HALF MOON CAFÉ painted in cursive across the window, Zoe saw her father. He was sitting by himself at a table near the door. He'd taken his coat off and tossed it in a heap on the chair next to him. As she watched, he unbuttoned his shirt and took it off, too, tossing it onto the chair with his coat. Zoe saw other people in the café, men, women, and children, doing the same thing. All had the same glassy, resigned look in their eyes, and moved in slow motion, like sleepwalkers.

Zoe pushed on the café's door. It squeaked an inch forward and stuck. She pushed again, and when it didn't move, she slammed her shoulder into it. A few people inside looked sleepily in her direction. The light changed suddenly, grew dark for a second as if a hand had passed over the moon. When the lights came on again they were different, full of darting, jittery shadows that crawled on the walls like insects dancing before a flame. Zoe looked up and saw a dark, swirling mass descend from the ceiling. She stared in wonder as the mass broke apart. She realized then that it wasn't one giant thing she was looking at, but thousands of smaller things. They had the snarling pig faces and black membranous wings of vampire bats, but their bodies slithered through the air like snakes. Zoe slammed her shoulder into the café door and it burst open.

"Dad!" she screamed.

Her father's eyes met hers and went wide with fear. "Get out!" he shouted as a swarm of flying snakes settled on him like a boiling coat of writhing black tar.

The snake creatures chittered and squeaked in excitement, their voices high and painful in Zoe's ears. In a few seconds, everyone in the café was lost beneath seething piles of the hungry creatures. Snakes broke away from the pack and flew at her, tearing at her face and arms with needle-sharp teeth.

Zoe stumbled outside and ran back along the street. She stopped once at the corner to puke, but there was nothing in her stomach, so she just dry-heaved painfully. When she could get up, she started running again, heading back the way she'd come with Valentine. She ran back to the living, twisting buildings, over walkways that changed under her feet and through underpasses where the windows in sideways buildings showed her the inside of ghost kitchens and bedrooms. She ran until the pain in her leg forced her to stop. She looked around for landmarks. She was by a small park with broken benches and a jungle gym covered in cobwebs. Zoe didn't recognize any of it. She was lost.

She followed the empty streets back along a path that felt right, but that she knew in her heart wasn't taking her anywhere she knew. The streets grew narrower, the buildings older and more weather-beaten as she walked. The abandoned cars that dotted the other streets now became old single-speed bikes so choked with rust they were practically fossilized. Soon the asphalt gave way to wet cobblestones and the yellow light of gas lamps. This was an old part of town she'd seen earlier with Valentine, she was sure of it. If she could find her way through and back to her father's building, she knew she could get to the boardwalk and work her way to Valentine's home.

Along the way, she passed empty bakeries and a closed Laundromat full of rotting clothes. Occasionally, she'd catch a glimpse of someone ahead in the street, but they were always just stepping out of sight, turning down a side street or hurrying inside a building. The city was full of dead souls, but she hardly saw anyone. They're all hiding inside, she thought, afraid of their queen and her dogs. And worse. The image of her father covered in snakes flashed into her head and she had to push it out or she knew she'd scream. *Just get back to Valentine's. Get back where it's safe. Then I can think about it. But not now or I'll come apart right here and die.*

Jewels were scattered in the gutter. Diamonds. Rubies. Sapphires. She stopped to pick up some pearls, and when she stood again she saw three black dogs staring at her from the corner. As she started to cross the street away from them, one of the dogs raised its head and snarled. The others turned in her direction, showing their teeth and letting out deep, rumbling growls. Zoe was sure that the way to the beach was down the street where the dogs sat, so she walked a few yards past them, giving them a wide berth, hoping she could circle back and around them. One dog rolled to its feet and loped toward her. The others followed.

Zoe remembered a mean Doberman that one of the neighbors owned when she was a little girl. The first lesson her father had taught her was to never run from a dog. Zoe turned to her right and walked steadily away from the hounds, forcing herself to keep an even, unhurried pace, even as she heard the pack's snarls getting closer. Her heart felt like it was trying to punch its way out of her chest. She tried to stay calm and breathe through her nose, but she couldn't get air, so she gulped in lungfuls through her mouth. Could the dogs feel her fear?

Something tugged at the hem of her coat. As it pulled, it growled. Zoe tried to keep walking, but the growling grew louder and the pulling became more insistent. She couldn't pull back because she was afraid of her ankle giving way and of falling. She knew if she did, the pack would never let her get up again. Zoe did the only thing she could think of. She stopped. To her relief, when she did, the dogs stopped, too. She felt the tension on her coat ease as the one pulling her let go. Then the snarling started again, deep-throated and deadly. The pack was spreading out behind her and moving forward, starting to encircle her.

Zoe stood her ground. She could hardly breathe and her hands shook. As the dogs moved closer they looked bigger than ever, the size of bulls or lions, but she knew that this was just fear playing tricks on her mind. She forced herself to stay still and not run. The dogs growl and let out small choked barks. *Almost like they're talking to each other,* Zoe thought. *And they're not going to wait forever.*

"Now or never," she said. The dogs looked at her. She raised her right hand slowly. When it was chest-high, she threw the pearls she'd picked up as hard as she could. The dogs moved steadily toward her, but then the pearls began to fall, clattering and smashing apart as they hit the street, throwing gleaming shards into the air. The dogs leaped away from Zoe and tore after the rattling jewels. The moment they were gone, Zoe ran around the nearest corner.

The dogs turned as one and headed back for her, heads down, teeth bared. Zoe heard them behind her, barking and snarling. She ran as hard as she could, waiting for the attack, for the feel of the breath being knocked out of her as one leaped onto her back—the sound of the pack closing in on her when she went down. But nothing happened. Zoe stopped running and turned, looking back the way she'd come. Half a block back, the dogs paced impatiently at the entrance to the street. They whined and yelped, but refused to approach. Zoe turned in a slow circle, trying to catch her breath. She couldn't see much around her. All the gas lamps had been broken and the street was dead black. *Valentine said not to go down unlit streets.* But he wasn't here, and if he had been, would he be anxious to go back and face down a whole pack of the queen's dogs?

She could make out the shapes of three- and four-story small apartment buildings, similar to others in the old quarter. But these buildings were barely standing. Some leaned heavily to one side, threatening to collapse. Others were mere skeletons with open roofs, charred by fire. The desiccated corpse of a black dog was nailed to the door of what might have once been a small church. Zoe stopped and stared in amazement at the sight. Who was crazy enough to kill and display the corpse of one of the queen's spies for everyone to see? No one was going to come down here. Not unless they had to. She looked back and saw the dogs still pacing at the end of the street. Were they afraid, she wondered, or were they waiting for something? She turned back to the street, and understood instantly why the dogs hadn't followed her.

"They" shambled onto the street one at a time or in stumbling groups. Zoe knew who they were and Valentine's words came back to her. "There are souls a lot worse off than me," he'd said. "The dying dead."

They crawled from the doorless maws of crumbling buildings, clawed their way from under junked cars; they slipped from open windows and clambered from basements. They were thin beyond belief, less even than walking skeletons. They were sucked dry, empty, like papier-mâché ghosts on Halloween. But their teeth and nails looked hard.

It was too late to turn back. There were more behind her than in front. The souls were slow and she kept moving down the alley. Even on her bad ankle, when they reached for her, she was able to dodge their grasping hands.

As they lumbered out onto the street, the souls called to her. Their voices were barely a whisper. Not, Zoe knew, because they were trying to sneak up on her, but because they hadn't had a reason to speak for a very long time and their vocal cords had withered to dry reeds.

A woman in a nurse's uniform grabbed Zoe's arm.

She barely felt it and easily brushed the woman off. It was the same with the others. They were as insubstantial as leaves in a winter wind. But there were a lot of them and she could feel the weight of their numbers begin to press in around her. More souls poured from the buildings up and down the street. Fingers tangled in her hair and pulled at her legs.

A tall man in a rotting tracksuit reached out his snakeskin hand and raked his cracked fingernails down Zoe's throat. She felt blood where he'd touched her. She punched the man in the chest as hard as she could. Her hand went all the way through him and out his back. She let out a small scream, and when she pulled her arm back, the man flew apart like someone blowing on a dandelion. The souls backed away for a moment, then pressed in against her from every direction.

Zoe punched and kicked her way through the mob. Hands grabbed her coat. Teeth bit into her arms and legs, but she kept lashing out. The zombified souls flew apart around her, filling the air with a choking dust. Far behind her, she could hear the black dogs frantically howling and barking.

At the end of the block, she ran face-first into a chain-link fence. At the bottom was a section of torn links. She fell to her knees and squeezed herself though the small break. She felt dry, crumbling, insect-husk fingers grabbing at her legs. One of her pockets caught on the sharp edge of one link and she had to rip the coat to get free. The dead tried to pull her back through the fence. Chipped teeth, like ivory knives, bit her hands when she grabbed the fence to resist them. A man in a cop uniform tried to crawl under the fence after her. He caught his back on the link that snagged her coat, but it didn't even slow him. He ripped himself in half down the full length of his back and the two mirror-image pieces of him lay side by side, still grabbing for her. A woman in a bridal gown tried to push her way straight through the fence. Piece by piece, she fell apart, as the metal tore apart her papery skin.

Zoe ran a few yards in the dark, slipped, and rolled halfway down one of the cobbled staircases that led to the canals. Far away in the distance were lights. She limped along the narrow canal walkway until she came to a place where the black water slid under an old library coiled around one of the canal's docks. She clambered up the side of the embankment until she could see the boardwalk just a few blocks away. She ran toward it as fast as she could, glancing over her shoulder for signs of the dogs or the dying dead. But no one followed her.

There was some kind of street fair going on along the oceanfront boulevard. It seemed like all the inhabitants of Iphigene who had been in hiding were now gathered up and down the length of the boardwalk, pressed tightly together and cheering. They were a ragged mob, red-eyed and worn-looking, like an entire city coming off a three-day bender. Uncertain and overwhelmed, the new arrivals stayed together at the far end of the street, not far from where the buses had let them off. Maybe this was some kind of welcome party, Zoe thought. *What a fucked-up introduction to eternity.* As she looked down the crowd, with their improvised limbs waving over their heads, they looked to her like an army of broken marionettes, dancing out of step to a song no one could quite remember. Zoe had never seen anyone in Iphigene looking happy before, but here was a whole street of smiling faces. It made her nervous. She kept her collar up and hung at the back of the crowd, trying to see what everyone was looking at. They were staring in the same direction, toward the white palace at the far end of the street.

From nowhere, drums pounded in her ears. Complex rhythms. Three or four patterns piled on top of each other. Shrill double-reed horns played a quick discordant melody that made her ears hurt. The louder the crowd cheered, the louder the music became. There were no musicians or amplifiers in sight. The music seemed to just materialize out of the air. Zoe didn't want to cheer. She wanted to run, but she stood her ground.

"Look!" someone shouted. "Children. Her children!"

The crowd surged back onto the sidewalk as black cobras came roiling their way down the middle of the damp street. They were the biggest snakes Zoe had ever seen. Each one was easily the size of the crocodiles Mr. Danvers had shown her class, twelve feet long or more.

Their skin shone like obsidian in the moonlight, and their eyes were green-gold, like tarnished coins. Their enormous fangs were bone-white daggers set in up-curved mouths that made it look as if the cobras were always smiling.

Behind the snakes came dozens of the queen's hulking dogs, led by tall men with snouts and heads like wolves. Dressed in rough leather breeches and chain mail over dark jerkins, they held the snarling dogs with heavy silver chains, yanking them hard when one of the hounds would rear up on its hind legs as if it might lunge into the crowd. The spectators along the boardwalk cheered and screamed with delight as the dogs went by. The more the dogs snarled and charged them, the more they whooped and laughed.

The music stopped and the crowd grew quiet. The change was immediate and dramatic, as if it was something that had happened before. A kind of play or ritual in which everyone knew their part but Zoe. For a second, all she could hear was the endless pounding of the waves on the beach. She was still giddy enough with adrenaline that the abrupt change didn't scare her. It heightened her excitement. She knew what she was feeling wasn't exactly right, but she couldn't help herself. The rational part of her brain told her to sneak out the back of the crowd, but something else kept her rooted to the spot. It was like being a little high or what she imagined being under a spell would be like. She had to know what was going to happen next.

A murmur rose up through the crowd and all heads turned toward the palace. The cheering started again, harder, wilder, and louder than ever. Zoe stood on her tiptoes, trying to see over the crowd. When she couldn't, she crouched down and saw the legs of a horse moving down the boulevard. A protective circle of the wolf men surrounded the rider. When they were almost abreast of her, Zoe stood back up. She knew instantly that the woman who towered over the crowd on horseback was Queen Hecate. She reminded her of the shadow woman she'd seen in her dreams.

Her horse was black, but not like any black Zoe had ever seen before. It wasn't black like the snakes, who were shiny and whose scales shone like dark jewels. Queen Hecate's horse was black in the same way that darkness is black. The horse was the color of no light, as if the horse itself wasn't there and what the queen was riding was merely its shadow.

The queen herself was the most beautiful woman Zoe had ever seen. She was tall and wore a sleeveless tunic and leather breeches of silver and midnight blue dark enough that it was almost black. Her long braided hair and skin were as pale as moonlight, and her arms and shoulders were sculpted and strong. Her silver crown didn't encircle her head like an ordinary crown. It curved up and back from the center of her skull like a serrated shark fin. She wore knee-length leather boots with flat soles and sharp metal tips. Not the boots of a pampered princess, Zoe thought. Those were the boots of a warrior queen.

When Hecate reached Zoe, the girl looked up at her with awe. Every movement, every angle of Hecate's body presented a being of strength and power. The screams from the crowd grew louder and more demented by the minute. As Hecate drew abreast of Zoe, a wispy cloud passed in front of the moon. The light in the street shifted almost imperceptibly. As the cloud covered the moon's face, Queen Hecate's face disappeared. Gone was the gorgeous snow-queen profile, and in its place was the snarling head of a great, black she-wolf. The wolf's dark eyes scanned the crowd with a predatory gleam. Zoe stepped back, pushing to the rear of the crowd, not caring who she bumped into or which toes she stepped on.

A second later, the cloud moved beyond the moon, and Zoe chanced another look at the queen. She was a beautiful woman again, nodding and waving to her subjects.

"You aren't clapping," said a tall man to Zoe's right. She stared up at him, trying not to look too scared or shocked. Whatever spell or adrenaline high had kept her rooted to this spot was wearing off. She was tired and overwhelmed enough that her mind froze and she couldn't come up with a good lie for why she wasn't clapping. Then the man smiled down at her.

"It's all right. I'm not clapping either." He turned and looked back over the heads of the crowd, toward Hecate. He spoke quietly. "It's strange, isn't it? Seeing everyone here like this. The smiling, the cheering, their faces beaming up at our queen. Every soul here tonight hates her, and would like to see her ripped to pieces by her own hounds. Yet here they all are, screaming for her as if she were the answer to all the riddles that have ever plagued or terrified the human race." The tall man shook his head. "Why do you think they do it?"

Zoe's head was swimming with fear and confusion, but the man didn't do anything threatening, although it would have been easy to point her out to one of the queen's wolf bodyguards. The stranger had a sharp, bird-like face and heavy, unruly eyebrows. His skin was gray and sagged on his cheeks and under his chin, as if he'd been heavy once or, like her dad's aunt Irene, had spent most of the last twenty years drunk.

"Maybe they're afraid not to cheer," Zoe said.

The man shook his head again. "Silly girl, we're all afraid of her. But that's not why these people are screaming with such glee."

"Maybe they do it because they mean it."

The man looked at her, his expression open and curious. "Ah," he said.

"I guess, if someone was really kicking your ass, you'd want them to be special. I mean, I'd rather have Batman kick my ass than Mickey Mouse any day."

The man nodded. "A friend of mine once put that same thought a little more elegantly: does the smart sheep make friends with the wolf or with the other sheep?"

"The wolf, definitely," Zoe said.

The man smiled down at her warmly, patting her on the shoulder. "Good girl," he said. "Have a lovely evening." He turned and walked away, disappearing into the noisy crowd.

At the end of the street, Hecate stepped down from her horse and stepped onto a sort of stage. Zoe couldn't take her eyes off the woman as she strode to the front of the platform and raised her long arms for quiet. The crowd went silent in an instant.

"Welcome, my subjects, my friends, my children," Hecate began, her voice amplified magically so that it seemed as if she was speaking directly to Zoe, and to her alone. "Welcome especially to those newly arrived members of our family, new souls whose experiences and insights will, no doubt, reward and enrich us all."

The queen looked down on the crowd, nodding occasionally to someone near the front of the stage.

"To our new brothers and sisters still confused by your journey, you have come to Iphigene, the city at the end of the line. Your new home. I am Hecate, your queen and your protector, your sister and your mother. Iphigene, you will find, is both terrible and sublime." She bowed her head slightly, then looked up. "As am I." Zoe could tell that the head bob was a practiced motion.

"Tonight all you need take with you are these few thoughts: Iphigene, like all cities, is made more beautiful or more ugly by its citizens, and by my love for each of you. Never forget that we are in the most awful of places, a city forgotten, broken, and bleeding. And who has abandoned us here in this limbo? A repository for their trash, cast away, cast down, like so much filth." Hecate was at the very edge of the stage, pointing down into the crowd as if demanding an answer from every one of the tens of thousands spread out at her feet. The feeling of being high was coming on again. Despite herself, Zoe wanted to call out, so Hecate would be pleased and maybe smile at her. She was horrified at the thought, but couldn't help herself.

Hecate stepped back from the edge of the stage and opened her hands, palms out. Quietly, she said, "The living."

An anxious muttering started up from the crowd. Hecate's wolf men eyed the nearby crowd members restlessly from the sides of the stage.

"We are what they despise," Hecate continued. "We are the shadow they only see when they're alone. We are their nightmares and the secret fears they want to forget. So, they have condemned us to this dark and baleful place with nothing but our memories and the garbage that washes down to us." She shook her head slowly, in mock sorrow. "The living abandon everything when they're done with it. Even us."

The low sound of the muttering crowd kicked up a notch, rising into an animal rumble from thousands of throats.

"And now the living want to take from us the only thing we have left. Our home. Yes, my children, it's true. Iphigene has been invaded by the living."

The crowd roared and surged toward the stage, but the wolf men held them back. Souls bared their teeth, cursed, and spat. Hands were raised in the air, reaching for something . . . Hecate, the moon, or the living that they wanted to destroy. Zoe didn't raise her hands. The shock of Hecate's words had broken whatever spell the queen's voice had cast over her. She applauded and smiled, trying to look like everybody else, but she began to push her way back through the crowd, working her way away from the stage to where the crowd thinned at the back.

Hecate seemed to whisper right in her ear as she said, "At this moment there is a living girl child in Iphigene. For what reason, I do not know. You can be sure, though, that her presence is not for our benefit. Anyone who finds this child and brings her to me will receive a reward beyond their wildest dreams!" As Hecate's voice rose, so did the crowd's. The sound was deafening. Zoe wasn't being subtle anymore in her effort to escape. She pulled her collar up as high as it would go and shouldered her way through the mob. When she reached an open space, she turned to look back at the stage.

On a night when she knew there was nothing left that could shock her, Zoe found herself alone, her heart racing, a cold-fear sweat soaking her under her coat. Standing next to Queen Hecate on the big stage was Emmett. The queen cupped her hand under his chin and caressed his cheek, then mouthed a word. Zoe saw it clearly, though she wished she hadn't. "Son," she saw the queen say.

Emmett bowed as his mother exhorted the crowd to applaud. He raised his hands to his throat and dug his nails into his skin. As he pulled, the skin stretched like rubber. His face grew distorted and the skin slid upward, until it pulled all the way from his head and hung like a limp, flesh-colored rag in his hands.

What was beneath wasn't a human face that looked out over the crowd. It was the visage of a cobra, with its hood extended almost out to its shoulders. Hecate leaned in to kiss her son's true face. Zoe didn't need to see any more. She turned, hoping to disappear up a side street and work her way back to Valentine's house. Before she could move, though, something sharp pressed into her spine.

"There aren't many here tonight that I could threaten with a knife," came a man's melodious and oddly familiar voice. "My guess is that you're the only one."

Zoe turned her head as far as she could and peered up at the bird-faced man she'd been talking to earlier.

"You knew all along. And now you're going to turn me in for the reward," she said.

The man let out one barking laugh. "What's the fun in that? Besides, Hecate can't afford my wildest dreams. No, I have something more interesting in mind." Zoe felt a sharp pain as the knife dug into her back. "Come with me," he said, taking hold of her sleeve and leading her away.

Ten

His apartment wasn't far. The building was just a couple of blocks off the main street, and much closer than her father's room, lost in the tangle of anonymous buildings farther inland. He had to stop twice along the way to drink from a silver flask. He had a limp even worse than Zoe's and whatever was in the flask seemed to dull the pain.

When they reached his building, the sidewalk was clean and clear of any debris. The buildings stood relatively straight up and down. Oak trees lined both sides of the street and all the streetlights worked. Night-blooming jasmine climbed up trellises, filling the air with their faint ghost scent.

Inside the building, the carpets were clean and the elevator still worked. They rode up to the top floor and went to his room, which was at the front of the building. He had to stop once more in the hallway to nurse his bad leg. When he felt better, he took out his key, unlocked the door, and pushed Zoe inside.

His room was laid out like her father's, but that's where the resemblance ended. This room was clean and lived in. The floor was covered with a large Persian carpet in warm colors, and the walls were freshly painted. The dresser was made of a dark, ornately carved wood, decorated with dragons at each corner. The table and chairs in his little kitchen matched the dresser. A maroon silk duvet covered the ample bed. There was a large leather armchair with carved dragon paws for legs. Through the window, Zoe could see the ocean and the moon hovering overhead.

"Make yourself comfortable," he said, releasing his grip on her sleeve. He pointed with the knife. "On the chair, sit on your hands." Zoe walked to the chair and did as she was told, sliding her hands under her legs as she sat. The bird-faced man limped to the end of the bed and dropped down onto it. "What's your name?" He stretched out his leg and winced as pain stabbed through him.

"Zoe."

The man nodded. "I'm Prosper. Mr. Prosper to you." He took out the flask, unscrewed it with one hand, and drank deeply. He kept a tight grip on the knife with the tip pointed in her direction. Zoe could tell that he was exhausted. He was sweating just from the effort of bringing her to the room. His lips were as drained as his gray face, and his hands shook.

It didn't seem like a moment to be shy. "What's wrong with your leg?" she asked.

"Never you mind about my leg." Amber-colored apothecary bottles littered the top of a small bedside table. Zoe saw other bottles on the dresser and the floor next to the bed. She could only read one word on their labels, *Laudanum*.

Mr. Prosper was staring at her, studying her. A trace of a smile played at the edges of his pale lips. "Brilliant. I knew it the moment you arrived, you know. It felt like ice water running down my neck. Really, it was Hecate who felt you, but her excitement infected the rest of us. Made us all a bit mental. We've been waiting for you for a long time. How did you get here?"

"Through the sewers, then the tunnels. I followed Emmett."

"Emmett?" His eyes were wet and blank. He gazed out the window, then back at her. "Ah, Ammut. Well, you're the first who's ever made it all the way here, though not the first who tried. Remarkable girl."

"If you can tell me the way out, I'll leave and never come back."

He let out a deep, hard laugh, catching Zoe by surprise. He seemed so frail it looked like laughing might shake him apart completely. A moment later, the laughter dissolved into wet, phlegmy coughs.

"I'll bet you would." He stared past her, at the moon shining through the window. "It's a tempting idea, just to see Hecate's face. She's so counting on you."

That scared her, but she tried to keep it out of her voice. "Counting on me? For what?"

"Girlie, you're her chance to be reborn," he said. He pointed at her with the knife. "She needs a body. A living body. Oh, she has plans for you." He smiled, his sagging skin creasing around his mouth. The blade twitched in his hand. "She'll peel the skin right off you and wear you like a ball gown, all the way back to the world. And when she gets there, she'll use her considerable powers to take revenge on every living soul." He lifted the flask and drained it. "Of course, it's as likely that when she draws that first gulp of air into her lungs, she'll forget all about us down here and run off to be a girl again. It's so hard predicting the actions of the insane." His large, wet eyes were red at the edges. Beads of sweat, or maybe tears, slid down his sagging cheeks.

"You helped her trick me into coming down here?"

"Not me. Ammut." He set the empty flask aside. A few drops leaked from the open top, leaving a dark stain on the duvet. "You're not so special. Anyone would do. Anyone with the need to find him." He turned and looked at the bottles at the head of the bed. "A girl. A boy. An old man dancing the Charleston. It didn't matter. A body was all that mattered. Of course, a pretty young girl was the first choice, and here you are." He slid up the length of the bed, wincing as he dragged his bad leg. The first bottle he picked up from the bedside table was empty. He threw it to the floor in disgust. Still holding the knife, he took the next bottle in one hand and pulled the cork with his teeth. He drank deeply. Clear liquid trickled out of the corners of his lips.

"So, he did trick me into coming down here."

"Tricked. Trapped. Delivered you with a bow on to his mom. Yes, you were."

"That was him on our mountain. Watching Valentine and me," she said. It made her feel cold inside.

"What? Who?"

"Nothing. Emmett got me good."

"That he did. That he did."

Mr. Prosper let go of the knife and held the bottle with both hands. The blade glittered, resting against one thin leg. When he'd had his fill, he took a breath and said, "I was a powerful man back before your father or his father was born. I was mayor of Iphigene, back when it was still Calumet. She told me when she was gone, I could be mayor again. Just another lie."

He was far away from her, and looked worse than ever, Zoe thought. "But you fucked it up somehow, right?" she said.

Mr. Prosper leered at her angrily, dizzy, curling his lip and fumbling for the knife. He tried to stand, but his leg wouldn't take the weight, and he flopped back down on the bed. "Don't imagine that I'm done yet, girlie." He grabbed the knife and pointed it at her. "I won't let

Hecate have you, and if that means slitting your pretty throat, so be it."

Zoe wondered if she could get her razor out, and if so, could she use it on Mr. Prosper before he used his knife on her? She slid her hands out from under her legs and laid them gently on the arms of the leather chair. Mr. Prosper didn't seem to notice. Okay, she thought. "You were supposed to help Emmett, weren't you? But something went wrong. Were you always a junkie?" she asked.

"Watch your mouth, brat," said Mr. Prosper.

"That's when Emmett realized he didn't need you, isn't it?" Prosper frowned at her, but his eyelids dropped. He blinked, trying to keep them open. Zoe's heart beat madly in her chest. Instead of being afraid, she felt angry and reckless, fed up with all of Iphigene. She knew she was taking an awful chance, but she couldn't think of anything else to do. "Is that what happened to your leg? You were so high that you fell, and then everyone knew how useless you were."

When he didn't speak, she thought he might have fallen asleep, but his head snapped up and he gestured with the knife. *No. Wait. He's too awake and he already has his knife out. Forget the razor.* "She set the wolves, those man-beasts, on me. Her so-called children. Filth, all of them." He rubbed his bad leg. "Who knew that after death you could feel such pain?" He drank again and closed his eyes. His voice was light and high-pitched, as if he were talking to a child.

"When she first came here she was beautiful, the most beautiful creature any of us had ever seen. She came from the hinterlands with her black dogs. From over the farthest hills, somewhere very far, very ancient. At first, she was a powerful, reassuring presence among the new souls. She'd greet them when the buses dropped them off. She'd help them get settled and find places to live, places where they'd be comfortable—apartments, longhouses, stilt houses in the forest, and what have you. She was inexhaustible. Everyone knew her, her and her dogs."

Zoe started to say something, but saw that Mr. Prosper was somewhere else now, lost in drugs and memories.

"No one thought much about it when some of the newcomers went missing. It takes a while to settle in. We assumed they'd found family or somewhere more comfortable. At City Hall we dismissed the stories of the ravaged, sucked-dry souls she left behind while traveling here from the back of beyond.

"By the time any of us who were in a position to do anything about it were aware of the truth, it was too late. Her dogs were everywhere. Snakes, too, but they mostly stay hidden. The whole city was under her spell. They were her army . . . not that she needed one. When she marched into my office and told me that she was queen of the new city of Iphigene, I knew she was right. There was almost nothing left of Calumet by then. And when she stole the sun from the sky, we let her. Never fought her. We never even raised our voices. She didn't come here to lead a revolt. She came here to show us that our time was over. Once we understood that, once we saw that the she-wolf was truly our queen, there was nothing left to do but give her everything, even ourselves."

Zoe slid forward so that she was sitting on the very edge of the chair. The door was only ten feet away, but Mr. Prosper still held the knife.

"What happens now?" she asked.

His eyes snapped open, wide and red. "What happens is that I'm the one who gets reborn. I know her plans, and how she was going to sort you out." He slumped against the wall at the head of the bed. "God, the look on her face, if only she knew." He slurred his words and his eyelids drooped again. "Her face, when she figures it out." He slid to his side, down onto the pillows. The amber bottle spilled its contents onto the bed. "You're my treasure. The first one to make it all the way down. Such a clever girl."

She could hear him breathing, taking regular, shallow breaths. The knife slipped from his hand and fell onto the Persian carpet. Zoe stood and quietly left Mr. Prosper's room.

When she made it back to the boardwalk, Hecate and the crowd were gone. She didn't know how long Mr. Prosper had kept her in his room, but it was long enough for the streets to clear, so he might have done her a favor after all.

Zoe started heading to Valentine's rooftop home feeling less afraid than before. She wasn't stupid. She kept her head down and steered clear of any dogs, but something had broken inside her in Mr. Prosper's apartment. The steady, gnawing dread she'd felt since coming to Iphigene was gone. Maybe it was learning what had lured her to the city and why. Knowing she'd been manipulated made her feel a little less guilty. And walking out of Mr. Prosper's room without a scratch proved something else. That the entities that ran Iphigene, for all their power and sinister magic, were far from infallible. They were fuckups and losers, just like people she knew back in the world. That was something she could understand and find comfort in.

She found the twisted garage where Valentine lived and limped up the fire escape to the roof. He was coming around the far side of the shack when they saw each other. He ran to her, his homemade legs pumping at crazy angles, and threw his arms around her.

"I'm sorry. I'm sorry," he said over and over again. "I should never have left you alone."

"It's all right. I'm all right," she said.

He let go and took a step back to look at her. "I thought Hecate had you for sure. All those people in street, they're all looking for you."

Zoe nodded. "I know, but no one saw me. No one even looked at me."

"I'm kind of not surprised," said Valentine. "The way

Hecate talked about you, they're probably all out looking for someone ten feet tall and riding a tank."

"That's me all right," she said. She couldn't believe how good it felt to see a friendly, familiar face. She tried picturing Julie and Laura, even Abysnthe, here with her in Iphigene, but their faces all came out blurred and indistinct. Valentine took her hand and pulled her toward the shack.

"We should keep away from the edges of the roof. Someone might see you."

Zoe followed him inside his crowded little home. Valentine got out a teakettle and started rummaging around the shelves for cups. "I went back looking for you just a few minutes after I left, but you were already gone," he said.

"I kind of freaked out," Zoe said, picturing the scene in the restaurant. The black creatures swirling in the air. Her father disappearing under them. "I ran off and got lost. It was stupid."

"I came back for you," Valentine said, his voice a little high and strained. "I really did come back."

Zoe looked up at him. "I believe you."

He lit the camp stove and put water on to boil. "So, you saw Father."

Zoe nodded. "You were right. There was nothing I could do for him. Hell, I couldn't even watch."

"I'm just glad you got back here in one piece."

Zoe took off her sneaker and rubbed her sore ankle.

Her whole leg was burning. It wasn't until she was sitting here, where she felt relatively safe and at home, that she noticed.

"I can't leave Dad like this, paying for my mistakes," she said. "I have to do something."

Valentine picked up the teakettle from the stove and slammed it down hard. "Yeah? And what are you going to do for him? You going to bring him back with you to the land of the living? Maybe he can live under your bed or be the monster in your closet."

Zoe looked down at her sore ankle as she adjusted the rag. "I can't leave him here, being eaten piece by piece. I saw the dying dead. I won't let him end up like that."

"Yes, you will. You'll leave him just like you're going to leave me, because it's what Father and I want and it's the right thing to do," shouted Valentine. "You keep trying to change things you can't change. Some things are just too big. They are what they are and there's nothing you can do about it." He came over to her and bent down, pushed Zoe's hands out of the way, and retied the cloth around her ankle until it was snug and comfortable. "If you love Father, do what he told you when you first came here. Go home. Be safe. Have a life."

"How can I just run off and leave you?"

Valentine got up, went to a pile of dishes, and put two cups on the table. "Just put one foot in front of the other and keep doing that until you're far away from this shithole."

"I don't even know how to leave."

"Yeah, that's a problem," he said. "I've learned to sneak around the edges of things. Get far enough out of town to sneak into your dreams, but that's because I'm dead. You need some other way back."

"Emmett . . . um, Ammut, he's alive, isn't he? I could go out from the place where he goes."

Valentine turned away from her, rummaging for the sugar. "If we knew where that was."

"I might know someone who does," said Zoe.

Valentine turned and looked at her intently. He reached over and turned off the stove. "Let's go."

Traveling with Valentine made Zoe feel safe and they didn't see any dogs along the way, so it wasn't more than half an hour before they were standing in front of Mr. Prosper's building.

Valentine looked up and down the bright, clean street and gave an exaggerated whistle. "Damn. I've seen these buildings, but I've never had the nerve to go inside. I always figured they had some kind of alarm that could smell street scum."

"You're not street scum."

"I'm sure not one of *them*," he said, looking up at the top of the building.

They went through the lobby and took the elevator up to the top floor. Zoe led the way to Mr. Prosper's apartment. She turned the knob slowly, and when she could feel that the door wasn't locked, she pushed it all the way open. Mr. Prosper was still asleep on the bed where she'd left him. She went over and sat down on the edge of the bed, facing the sleeping man. Valentine remained in the doorway, his gaze taking in the room and its opulence.

Zoe gestured for him to come in and close the door. Valentine nodded and did as he was told. Inside, he spotted Mr. Prosper's knife on the floor and picked it up. Zoe watched him weigh the blade in his hand. He shrugged off his greatcoat and let it fall to the floor. Zoe hadn't seen his arms in the light before. They really were pipes. His hands were a crazy combination of metal scraps all fitted together like a rusted jigsaw puzzle. It didn't make sense that they could work, but they did, by whatever magic ruled Iphigene. Plus, they looked formidable.

Valentine smiled at her. Zoe reached over and shook Mr. Prosper's shoulder. "Wake up! Hey, wake up!"

Mr. Prosper jerked violently away from her and raised his head. "What?" he said hoarsely. He opened his eyes and looked at Zoe, but didn't seem to recognize her. His gaze moved past her to land at the foot of the bed, where Valentine was standing, the knife held tightly in his metal hand. "Gah!" shouted Mr. Prosper, scrambling back farther on the bed. "Go away!"

Zoe gently put a hand on Mr. Prosper's leg, and that seemed to get his attention. He jerked away from her, his eyes wild with fear. "You!" he said in wonder.

"Me," said Zoe. She glanced up at Valentine. "I told

my brother how you kidnapped me and how you said you were going to slit my throat. Know what he wants to do to you?" She leaned in closer and spoke in hushed tones. "With that bad leg of yours, he wants to drag you down to one of those dark streets and leave you for the dying dead. How does that sound?"

Mr. Prosper put his hands over his face. For a second she felt bad for the man, blubbering and terrified, stripped of his dignity and everything he valued by Hecate and now by her. *But he did threaten to kill me and steal my body and we really won't give him to the dying. Maybe scaring him a little is payback.*

"No! Go away, please! I'm sorry," Mr. Prosper said.

"If you're really sorry, tell me how Emmett gets back to the world. What's the way out for someone who's alive?"

He looked at her in horror. "No. I can't."

"Tell me how to get out of Iphigene," Zoe insisted.

"She'll know it was me. She'll feed me to her dogs."

"She will if I go and tell her what you did."

"What?"

As Zoe and Mr. Prosper talked, Valentine went around the man's room taking small things and stuffing them in his pockets. He slipped the empty flask off the bed, took a silver bottle opener off a table and a faceted glass paperweight off the top of Mr. Prosper's dresser.

"I've been thinking about it," Zoe said to Mr. Prosper. "I bet I can make a deal with Queen Hecate. My brother and father would like living in this building. Would you like this room, Valentine?"

Valentine looked over at her and Mr. Prosper as he was slipping a cigarette lighter into his pocket. "Very much."

"I can do more," said Zoe to Mr. Prosper. "If you worked for Hecate, I bet Emmett has one of those records with your soul on it. I'll get her to tell Emmett to break it. What will happen to you if your record breaks?"

The man's wide, wet eyes swiveled in their sockets, looking first at Valentine and then at Zoe. "Please. You can't."

"What will happen to you?"

"I'll fall apart," he said in a tone that was more of a plea than a statement. "It's horrible. I'll burn up from the inside out and disappear. Forever."

"It doesn't have to happen. Just tell me how to go home. But first tell me this. If Emmett can get to the real world, why doesn't Hecate take *his* body?"

Mr. Prosper seemed horrified by the question. "He's her child. She'd never hurt him."

"Why can he go back and forth to the real world when no one else can?"

"For the same reason that he holds the records. He's Ammut, the eater of the dead. The keeper and destroyer of lost souls. Some spirits are ushered into this world and others—"

Zoe nodded. She didn't want to hear the rest of the sentence.

"I understand. Now, how do I get out?"

Mr. Prosper held up a hand in Valentine's direction, palm out, defensively.

"I'll tell you what I know," he said miserably. He pulled one of the pillows from the bed and clutched it to his chest. His face contorted. "Please, my leg," he whispered.

Zoe took one of the laudanum bottles from his bed-side table and handed it to him. Mr. Prosper tore out the cork with trembling hands and downed half the bottle before coming up for air. "Thank you," he said, gasping. He pointed out the window. "On the beach, near the far end of the boardwalk, is a rocky outcropping. At low tide there's a drainage pipe. You can't miss it. It's big enough for a man to stand up in. Follow the pipe for perhaps a quarter of a mile and take the left fork." He took another drink from the bottle. A smaller one this time. "Soon you'll come to an underground entrance to the palace. Only Emmett ever uses it, so no one will bother you. When you see the door, you'll know you're on the right path. Keep going until you see light. When you reach the end, you'll be back in the world of the living."

Valentine came over and leaned on the wall at the top of the bed. "Are there any tricks or traps along the way?" He weighed Mr. Prosper's knife in his hand.

"Why would there be?" Mr. Prosper clutched the pillow tighter as Valentine loomed over him. "No one knows about the tunnel but Hecate's most trusted advisers."

"I hope you're not lying," Valentine said. "If anything happens to my sister . . . well, those unlit streets are already calling your name."

"Thank you, Mr. Prosper," said Zoe. She started to turn away, but stopped. "I'm sorry about what Hecate did to you."

"Go away now, please," Mr. Prosper said. He lay down and curled up on the bed, clutching his bottle and pillow.

Outside, it was starting to rain again. Clouds of silver and midnight blue roiled over the rooftops as a few fat raindrops fell onto their faces. It's going to be a downpour, Zoe thought. She was struck again by how beautiful Iphigene could be in the right light. There was something wrong with that. It didn't seem fair for there to be any beauty in a place like this. She was about to say something to Valentine when he shoved her back against the building. She tried to move, but his hand swept back and held her in place. She was getting annoyed when she saw something across the street coming toward them.

She could make out three of Hecate's wolf men in the rain, which was coming down hard and steady. As the wolf men advanced, Valentine shifted, keeping Zoe behind him. He reached under his coat and pulled out Mr. Prosper's knife. The wolf men hesitated. Moving away from the apartment building, Valentine pulled her along, shifting his stance with each step, keeping himself between Zoe and the wolves. She looked around for a way out, a place to run. She couldn't see anything. This wasn't fair, not after they'd learned how she could get home. She held on to Valentine's coat sleeves.

"Zoe?" whispered Valentine.

"Yeah."

"When I tell you, I want you to run. Find Father. He'll take care of you."

Zoe held on to him harder. "What are you going to do?" She felt his body tense.

"Now!" he said, pushing her away and leaping at the wolf men, slashing the closest one. The knife flashing streaks of silver streetlight as the air filled with Valentine's shouts, the wolf men's howls, and the hissing of the rain.

As the wolves closed on Valentine, Zoe looked around for something to hit them with. A branch or pipe, anything.

"Go!" yelled Valentine.

Still, her mind screamed for her to stay, to help him, but she knew what this was. It was Valentine's sacrifice for her. To stay now when she couldn't help and would only get in the way would turn him from a hero into a fool. So she turned away from the fight and ran as hard as she could. The pain in her ankle grew steadily worse, but this time she was grateful. It was something to focus on, something to enable her to shut out the voices telling her to turn around and go back. In her mind, she drew a circle, then she eased the white-hot pain in her leg into its center, letting the hurt propel her through the storm all the way to the sea.

She walked out onto the beach and her feet sank into the wet sand. Each step hurt her ankle and the usefulness of pain had passed a couple of blocks back. Now pain was just pain and each time she had to drag her injured leg out of the heavy sand, the pain made her breath catch in her throat. But she didn't stop walking until she made it to the abandoned carousel.

She stepped up to the crooked platform and dropped immediately to the floor, breathing hard. Rain seeped through the cracks in the carousel's wooden roof, dripping onto the faces of some of the nearby animals. The horses looked like they were crying. Zoe lay down and pressed her ear flat to the floor. Overhead, the rain was a high-pitched patter, while the sound coming into her ear on the floor was deep bass mixed with the pounding of the waves. There were no monsters here. No mad queen. Just the rushing of the water. There was no reason for her to ever get up, she thought. *I might stay just like this forever.*

Out of the corner of her eye, she saw something move. She rolled over and saw a man's legs. He was sitting on the floor smoking, his back against the carousel's hollow central core, the spindle room where the ride's motor was housed. Zoe couldn't see the man's face, but she knew him immediately.

Slowly, she rose and limped over to her father. "I wondered if you'd be here."

"Zoe," he said. He lowered the cigarette and rubbed his red eyes. "Damn. I hoped you be gone by now."

She leaned on the pole connected to a pink-and-silver shark. "Nope. Not yet," she replied. She shrugged and looked out at the boardwalk, a bit more paranoid now after the wolf men's sudden appearance. She looked at her father. There were fresh scars on his face and hands. He looked even more gaunt than before.

"I'm sorry I ran," Zoe said.

Her father patted her leg. "You did the right thing."

"At least we found a way out."

"You and your friend?" Her father took a puff of his cigarette. In the dark, the red glow lit up his whole face. Worn and weak, he suddenly reminded her a little of Mr. Prosper.

"Yeah. Val—" she started to say, but broke off, reminding herself of her promise not to tell her father about him. She could at least keep her word about that. "He really saved my life. Hecate's cops or whatever they are—those wolf assholes—they arrested him."

"I'm sorry, honey. You all right?"

Zoe nodded. She knew it was silly since he was already dead, but it bothered her to see her father smoking. Still, there was something comforting and normal about

it all. Having a cigarette at the end of a long, hard day.
It's what regular people did back in the world. The real
world. It seemed so far away now. Like Iphigene was the
new normal and the other was a dream. Would she ever
see the other world again? She felt a sudden, unexpected
twinge of homesickness. "I'm okay," she said. "You
know, I thought you were dead back there at the café.
Like dead dead. You know what I mean."

He smiled up at her, a weak, exhausted smile. "It's not
as bad as it looks. I just need to rest for a couple of days
and I'll be fine."

"Then she can do it to you all over again." Zoe hugged
her coat tightly around herself.

Her father didn't say anything for a few minutes. "If
you know a way out of here, you need to go. The whole
city is looking for you. How the hell did you get here?"

"I ran. I really wasn't thinking about it. It was raining hard. I don't think anyone noticed me," she said,
looking back toward the boardwalk again. "I guess
someone must have seen me before and told the cops,
right? But I was so happy to have found a way out. I
should have been more careful."

"You know, if Hecate arrested your friend, he isn't
coming back," her father said.

Her injured leg made it too hard to stand anymore.
She slid down the pole and sat facing her father. "So, I
just run off back to Sweet Valley High? I leave him in a
dungeon and you to get sucked dry."

Her father leaned forward and touched the dirty toe of her sneaker. "If Hecate finds you, she'll kill you."

Zoe felt herself laugh, but nothing felt funny. "She'll do worse than that, from what I hear."

"What?"

"Nothing."

Her father finished the cigarette and tossed it away. The glowing tip arced high, making burning red loop-the-loops through the rain out into the sand. "You can't just sit here, honey. You have to go."

"Don't worry. I am," she said. "But the beach is the way out. I have to wait for low tide."

"Oh." Something in his voice surprised her. After he'd told her to go home God only knew how many times, there was a hint of regret in his voice. It made Zoe happy, in a quiet, sad way. She said, "Is it okay if I sit here with you while I wait?"

"That would be nice."

As she went over to him, he put one arm out and she laid her back against it, leaning against him as he wrapped the arm around her. She held on to his jacket as she had to Valentine's.

As she sat there quietly in the dark with her father for what would be the last time, the ice inside Zoe began to crack. She'd felt nothing for so long. The numbness was comforting, even though it brought the guilt of not really feeling how she knew she should, how she would feel normally. About her mother, about her brother's arrest, and this last meeting with her father, doomed to be food for Hecate's children. And then what? He would just wander away with the dying dead forever?

If leaving was what everyone wanted, why did it feel so bad? The truth was that a part of Zoe wanted to leave Iphigene right then. To run away and forget about it, about everything she'd seen and heard. Even father and Valentine. How could she live with herself knowing she couldn't save them and that she was partly responsible for the horror that was their lives?

The cracking ice inside her was being replaced with a spongy fear, as if a monster were trying to swim up out of her guts and swallow her whole. She bit her lower lip and breathed hard, trying to drive the monster back into the void. If she allowed the monster to touch her, she knew that she would begin to cry and that she'd never stop. What good was crying now? It was a child's trick that kept her from having to deal with the hard things. She wouldn't hide from the hard things anymore. Never again. *I owe it to Dad to be here with him now. And to Valentine. My shit, I can deal with later.* She hugged her father harder while feeling furious with herself for being so weak and confused.

No crying. Nothing. Just be here.

They sat on the broken carousel without talking, just looking out at the moonlit sand.

• • •

Zoe drifted, halfway between sleep and daydreaming. She was on the mountain overlooking the almond grove and the tree fort behind the house in Danville. Black dogs prowled among the trees, sniffing the air. She wasn't surprised or even particularly scared to see them. They were a part of her world, both in life and now in her dreams. Every now and then one of them would look up to where she was sitting on the mountain. *They know I'm here. They're waiting for me to come down. They're not in any rush. They can wait forever.* Could she? Half buried in snow, a rusty telescope lay at her feet. Emmett's telescope. The one he used to watch Valentine and me. She picked it up and looked for their tree fort. It took her a while because she didn't recognize it at first. The fort was falling apart. Half of it lay on the ground in a heap. What was left looked like scrap lumber that a hurricane had blown into the tree a hundred years ago. The wood was black, pulpy, and rotten, the nails rusted and barely holding what was left of the fort together. Unlike the dogs, that sight scared her. It was all being taken away, the good things in her life and now her dreams, too. And when even her dreams were gone, would there be anything left of her? Finally, the dogs started up the mountainside. They aren't going to wait, after all, she thought. Zoe set down the telescope and clutched her knees to her chest. She watched the dogs come all the way up the hill.

• • •

There was a sound. Then something moved, brushing against her leg. Beside her on the carousel, her father sat up. He turned his head, looking as confused as she felt. "No, it can't be," he said.

Zoe looked at him, waiting for her head to clear. She'd drifted farther away than she'd meant to and the world was fuzzy around the edges. Her father stood slowly, pulling himself up on a bright yellow sea horse. "Not now," he said quietly.

She finally heard it. The rain had stopped and the sound was replaced by the soothing white noise of the ocean. Then slowly, as the world came into focus, there was something else, the animal-like wail of a siren that Zoe knew was calling her father to another feeding.

"But you just did it," she said. "You said you're supposed to rest now. They can't call you right back. Can they?"

Her father looked down at her. "It's never happened before." He leaned his head on his arms, propped on the sea horse's back. "I know what this is. It's Hecate. She wants to trap you and she thinks if she calls me back you'll follow. You have to leave now. Right now. To hell with the tide. I have to go to the café." He let go of the sea horse and collapsed onto the carousel platform.

Zoe scrambled over to him and pulled him upright. "Look at you. You can't even stand up," she said. "I'm supposed to watch you walk off and get bled to death?"

"Neither of us has a choice."

She stood and pushed her father back against the carousel pole. She smiled at him. "Listen to me. Don't go."

"I have to. I can't help myself."

"Try. I know what to do. It's so simple," she said. She stopped at the edge of the platform. "Stay here. Don't follow the siren. Fight it. Everything is going to be all right."

She jumped down onto the sand. Her father said something as she went, but she couldn't hear him over the wailing of the siren. Zoe felt good, energized, better than she'd felt since the funeral. For the first time she saw things with total clarity and knew exactly what she had to do. It was so simple. She was a little scared as she fell into step with the souls marching to the café, but she was excited, too. It felt good to be doing something real after having lived so long in a stagnant gray gloom. She wondered if it hurt when you were covered with the snakes. A few had bitten her the last time. The bites stung a little, but it wasn't that bad. She remembered that Mr. Danvers had said there were bats and snakes with anesthetic in their saliva, so their prey wouldn't feel their bite. Maybe these snakes were like that. She took a deep breath and let it out, knowing that she'd have the answer soon enough.

This is was what I should have done the moment I got to Iphigene. It's what the city wanted—blood and sacrifice—and it would have it. Not a pale ghost version, but the blood of a living person. *That should make Hecate happy enough to leave Dad alone.*

She fell into step with the other dazed spirits, jostling and being jostled as she pushed her way to the middle of the throng. She was nervous, but she knew that was all right; normal, even. Zoe let go of everything she'd been clinging to and let herself be swept along by the tide of dead souls.

In front of her was an older man who was nearly bald. A few bristly sugar-white hairs on the back of his head were pressed flat by a plastic bag pulled tight onto his scalp. Reading upside down, Zoe made out the words WHITE RABBIT and saw a picture of an overly cute bunny. She remembered White Rabbit candies. They sometimes came with the check when her family would go out for dinner in Chinatown. The old man in front of her was using the bag as a makeshift rain hat. Next to him was a girl just a few years older than Zoe. Her head was shaved and she had large Chinese-style dragons tattooed on her scalp above each ear. The dragon on the left was red and the one on the right was blue. Zoe wondered what that meant. She wished she'd met the girl somewhere else so she could ask. She looked like someone who would have been in the club the night her mother and father met.

The steady sound of the siren soon melted into the background and everything seemed to go very quiet. Zoe's gaze flickered back and forth between the twin dragons and the cartoon rabbit as she splashed through the silent streets.

Time was moving in funny ways. A block could shoot

by in a second, but passing a single building could take hours. It was the fear, she knew, playing with her head. Zoe closed her eyes and let the crowd guide her with the motion of their bodies. She felt like an overwound guitar string, vibrating at some unnaturally bright and delirious frequency, knowing she could snap at any moment. She hoped they reached the café soon.

A moment later, the siren stopped, for real this time, leaving the street in unsettling quiet. Zoe opened her eyes. There in front of her was the café. Scared though she was, she smiled to herself, suddenly remembering something her mother had once told her: "Be careful what you wish for." Without a word, the crowd began filing through the open door. Zoe followed them in.

Inside, she went to an empty table near the front window. It felt important that she be able to see outside and not be suffocated by the Half Moon Café's drab walls. The gray street through the window might be dead, but at least it looked a little bit like the world and home.

Zoe took off her coat slowly. She had to. Her hands felt thick and clumsy, like she was wearing mittens. She took a deep breath, her face filling with heat. She ignored the sensation, refusing to think about it. She didn't allow any thoughts to form in her mind at all. What she needed to do was to keep her body moving and not think about anything.

She stood and folded her overcoat, but as she dropped

it over the back of her chair, the straight razor clattered to the floor. She grabbed it up and stuffed it into the pocket of her hoodie, hoping that no one had seen it, but it gave her an idea. She checked her pants pockets, and when what she was looking for wasn't there, she checked the pockets of her coat. Nothing. Valentine's compass was gone. Somewhere, through all the running and hiding, she'd lost it. It was too bad. It was something of his and something from home. And so she wrapped her fingers around the razor. She needed something to hold on to when it, and *it* was the only word her mind would permit her at that point, was happening. She unzipped her hoodie and pushed it back, exposing her shoulders and neck. She pushed up her sleeves and rested her hands on the table, waiting.

Nothing moved outside the window. Everyone was inside. The café was about half full. Zoe turned around in her seat. No one was talking to anyone. Most people were staring off into space, either still under the hypnotic effects of the siren or just wanting not to make eye contact with anyone. Zoe looked around for the man with the White Rabbit bag on his head, but she couldn't find him. She spotted the girl with the tattoos near the back of the place, under a dusty cuckoo clock. Zoe smiled at her, but the girl turned away.

Without her wanting it, an image of her mother popped into her head. She wondered where her mother was right now. In a funny way, as far as Zoe was from home, she felt close to her. She'd made her own sacrifice, given up so much, and now here was Zoe about to do the same and she wanted to talk to her mother about it, maybe thank her and maybe get some reassurance that she was doing the right thing. *I don't even know what's going to happen next. Wish I'd had the chance to say something to her in case I'm not going home.*

"Look at the brave little princess all alone. Where's Daddy? Did he abandon you again? First in the world above and now here. He's not a very good daddy, is he?" Zoe knew who was speaking without turning around, though his voice was different now. It was more of a whisper, and he had a slight lisp that turned each *s* into a hiss.

Zoe looked up into Emmett's cold snake eyes. He was a horrible sight—a glistening cobra's head perched atop a man's body. His tongue shot out every few seconds to taste the air. Ugly as he was, seeing him now, she wasn't frightened as she had been the first time she saw him. The awful thing she'd been dreading was happening and was no longer a crippling imaginary terror. As scared as she was, she could hide it. Don't give him the satisfaction, she thought.

"I like you better like this," she said brightly. "It really suits you. All slimy and crawling through sewers, eating shit and rats. Who taught you that? Your mother?" She cocked her head coyly at those final words.

"My mother is a goddess," said Emmett.

"Your mother is a dumb dead bitch!" Zoe said, her voice getting louder with each word.

Emmett lunged at her. Zoe jumped back, almost knocking over her chair. Emmett grabbed her before she could fall and held her, his warm, wet snake breath in her face.

"I was going to take you out of here," he whispered. "But now, princess, you get to bleed. Not die, but you get to bleed like Daddy."

Zoe shook herself free and leaned her elbows on the table. She didn't care about anything at that moment except shouting loud enough for the whole café to hear. "That's your threat? I get to bleed? That's why I came here! You can't threaten people with what they're already doing, you fucking retarded lizard!"

Emmett took a step back. Zoe got the feeling that no one had ever yelled at him in such a way before. It felt pretty damned good. The feeling didn't last long, though. Emmett's eyes turned upward to the ceiling then back down to meet Zoe's. "It's starting."

Zoe looked up. It was happening just the way she remembered. A dense black cloud swirled around the ceiling, and as the cloud descended, it broke apart into individual, chittering, batlike snake things. *This is it.* She closed her eyes. Maybe she could fool Emmett by not letting him see her fear, but she couldn't fool herself. She took deep breaths and squeezed the razor. Her stomach was full of ice. The chittering grew louder and the light grew dimmer. She braced herself for the first bite.

Something slammed into the window and someone was shouting, but it didn't sound like anyone in the café. Zoe opened her eyes and froze. Her father, pale and sweating, his hair plastered to his forehead, was pounding his fists against the window near where Zoe was sitting. He was yelling to her.

"Zoe! Get out of there!" he screamed.

Emmett turned and let out an airy little chuckle. "A day late and a dollar short, Dad," he said.

"Zoe! Don't do this!"

Emmett laughed merrily.

Then the first snake landed on Zoe's shoulder and dug its fangs into her neck. The pain was electric. Hot and dizzying, it shot through her, making her whole body shake. A bat landed, and then another. Through the pain, she could hear her father calling her name. Emmett was right beside her. She could hear him laughing.

Something snapped. The taut string she'd felt like earlier finally frayed and came apart. Before she knew what she was doing, Zoe was on her feet and screaming. She had the razor in her hand and she was slashing at Emmett's arms. He whirled and backhanded her across the face. She fell back into the table, then ran at him again, screaming and hacking away at his arms and hands, driving the razor into his chest and slashing his face.

Emmett bellowed, a horrifying, deep-throated roar of pain and fury. But the snakes, which had ignored him until then, were on him. Driven into a feeding frenzy by the scent of his blood, they flew away from Zoe and the others to attack Emmett. An immense, writhing horde of flying snakes forced him to the ground. His hands burst from the ravenous black mass, scattering snakes and reaching for Zoe. She leaped back as Emmett rolled over, crushed under the weight of his starving brothers and sisters.

Zoe turned and burst out of the café door, running to her father. They held each other while, behind them, the other spirits dashed from the café, scattering down the wet, gray street. When the street was clear, Zoe's father took off his overcoat, wrapped it around her, and they ran back into the city.

Eleven

They went back to his room. Zoe's father kept his arm around her the whole way, as if a strong wind might carry her off. It felt good. It felt conspiratorial.

Her father's coat was big enough that it was easy for her to keep her face hidden behind the collar. She wasn't sure where they were headed, at first. She was worried that it might be back to the carousel, and was relieved when her father steered them the other way, onto the twisting route to Ouroboros Street. Once they were inside, Zoe limped up two flights of stairs before she realized that her father wasn't with her. She went back down and found him at the top of the first-floor landing, on his knees and leaning heavily on the wall.

"Dad?" she asked uncertainly.

"I'm all right," he said, blinking up at her. "I just needed to rest a minute."

She came down to him. "Let me help you." They started up the stairs slowly. This time he leaned on her.

"Look at us. A couple of wrecks."

"If Mom could see us now."

That made him laugh. They made it up to the fifth floor and Zoe opened the door to his room. Her father collapsed on the bed.

"You need to rest," Zoe said.

"I think you're right," he replied. Then he smiled at her weakly. "You saved me back there. Another feeding right then would have finished me."

Zoe was looking through the drawers in her father's unused dresser. She found a couple of worn-looking towels in the bottom drawer and looked up at him as he spoke.

"You'd have done it for me." She took the towels and went to the bed. She handed him the larger of the two, tossed his overcoat onto a chair, and used the smaller towel to dry her hair.

"Of course I'd have done it for you. I'm your father. It's part of my job description," he said, unfolding the towel and wiping his face. "But I don't know that every kid would have done what you did."

" 'Course they would. You would have."

"Yeah, right," he said quietly. He looked away from her, balling the towel in his hands. "I'm not so sure I would have done it for my old man."

Zoe looked down at him. She couldn't believe what

she was hearing. Part of her was shocked, but another part felt sad for him. Why would he say something like that? She remembered seeing her father differently just a few days earlier, when she'd put on the Animagraph and seen the world through his eyes. It was the night he'd met her mother. She recalled flutters of drunken excitement when he first laid eyes on her, but the feeling was mixed with others Zoe hadn't paid attention to at the time. Confusion. Silent, sullen rage. And fear, buried way in the back of his mind under all the beer. Something that had happened between him and his father that night. His back and arms ached where the belt had hit him, where it always hit.

Zoe sat down next to him on the bed. He suddenly looked younger to her.

"Yeah, you would have," she said. "In the end."

"I'd like to think so." He turned back to her, took her hand, and smiled. "In case I haven't told you, you're a pretty good kid. A pain in the ass, but a pretty good kid."

"Thanks."

"It always cracks me up how much you're like your mom."

Zoe let go of his hand and went back to drying her hair. "Really? How?"

"No one could ever tell her anything either." He followed Zoe's lead and started drying his hair. "Not her parents. Not me. No one. She just did what she thought she had to do. A lot of the time she was right, too."

"What about when she wasn't?"

He shook his head and set the towel aside. "Craziness. Complete fucking madness. She got us into as much trouble as she got us out of." He looked at Zoe. "Just like you."

Zoe took their wet towels and draped them over the tiny sink in the kitchen area to dry. "I never thought we were much alike."

"Believe me, kiddo. You are."

"Sounds like a lot of trouble."

"It sure as hell is," he replied. "But you don't mind. We admire people for the smart things they do, but we love them for their craziness, all the ridiculous little things they do." He laughed a little to himself. "She used to let the air out of the cops' tires outside the clubs. She'd pile up all the baby corns and hide them under her napkin whenever we had Chinese food. She'd scream like a banshee whenever she heard Barry Manilow."

Zoe laughed, too. "Yeah, I've heard her do that." She walked back over to where her father lay. "It's just really hard to picture her like that."

"Try it sometime. You'll both be happier." He looked at the window. "The rain's letting up a little. You should be getting down to the beach for low tide."

"Yeah, I know." Zoe looked around her father's dusty, dank little room. "I just need to know that you're going to be all right."

"I am. Really." He sat up in bed and leaned against

the wall. "I said before that I was mad that you'd come here. Well, I was wrong. You didn't just save me tonight. I'd kind of given up hope down here, but blowing up Hecate's feeding tonight, leaving Emmett in a world of hurt . . . that was beautiful stuff." He gave an exaggerated shrug. "And I'm not afraid of them anymore. And that's because of you. Thanks."

Zoe looked down at the floor. "You're welcome."

Her father swung his legs onto the floor and got up. "Come on. I'll walk you downstairs."

Her head snapped up and she looked at him. "You're not coming with me?"

He shook his head slowly. "Look at me. I'm a mess, darlin'. I wouldn't be able to help you and I sure as hell can't run right now. I'm sorry."

Zoe nodded and went to the window, looked down into the street. "I'm a little afraid of those dogs, Dad."

He sat back down, his legs already shaking. "Yeah, I wondered about that. You don't smell like us. That's why the dogs notice you. It's probably how Hecate plans to catch you."

She turned and looked at him across the dim room. He looked more like a ghost than ever before. "What am I going to do?"

He didn't say anything for a minute, and seemed to be thinking. Then, "Wait here."

He went out into the hall and Zoe heard him walk down a few doors and knock. A door opened and there were voices. A minute later, her father came back and sat on the bed, leaving the door to his room open.

A few minutes after that, a young woman walked into the room holding a small cut-glass bottle full of an amber liquid. She handed the bottle to Zoe's father and turned to Zoe. The pale evening light through the window illuminated her fine features and high cheekbones. Zoe couldn't believe what she was looking at.

The woman crossed the room to Zoe with her hand extended. "Hello," she said. "I'm—"

"Caroline Lee Somerville," said Zoe, remembering her first experience with the Animagraph and the pregnant woman who Emmett had explained would die soon after that particular memory.

Caroline Lee Somerville's eyebrows drew together, puzzled. "Have we met?"

"No," said Zoe. She didn't know if she should talk about having seen the woman's life so intimately. *Would I want to know that someone had been inside me like that?* No, Zoe decided. "Someone mentioned you to me."

"Really? Was it a relation?"

Zoe shrugged. "Probably," she said.

Caroline Lee Somerville nodded. "Of course," she said, and turned to Zoe's father. "You were right when you said that she was a lovely girl," she said. Then added in a stage whisper, "But she's not quite as good a liar as she supposes she is."

Zoe's father smiled. "Usually she's much better at it,

but she's had a long day." He turned to Zoe, still grinning. "Come here," he told her.

Zoe went over to them a little reluctantly, not sure if she was in trouble or if this was "Adult Humor," as Julie used to call it. The kind of jokes that no one under thirty ever found funny.

"Remember when you got here and I told you that some of the spirits liked and used things from their lives? They read newspapers and eat food at the restaurants?"

"I know about them," she said.

"Caroline here is like me: she doesn't eat or drink, but she does have a vice."

"I still love perfume," said Caroline. "I used to wait each season for the new scents to arrive by ship from Paris."

"Caroline has agreed to let you use this perfume. It should help you get past the dogs. Or anyone else, really." He handed Zoe the bottle.

She pulled out the glass stopper and sniffed. "I can't smell anything."

Caroline gave a silent chuckle. "And why should you? This is a folly for the dead. Something to make a ghost feel a bit less like a ghost."

Zoe held the bottle to her chest. "Thank you."

"It's my pleasure," said Mrs. Somerville graciously. "Go back to the world. Be happy. Be sad. Be whatever you want to be. Just be."

Zoe's father took the bottle from her hands and said,

"Put on my coat." Zoe did as he said. Her father came over and splashed perfume on the coat and her head. A little trickled down into her eye. She expected it to burn, but it felt like water. She wiped her eye with her finger.

"Is that it?" she asked.

"That's it," her father said. He handed Zoe the rest of the bottle. "Keep it with you. If anyone notices you, just put on more."

"Thanks."

Caroline took a roll of gauze from the pocket of her floor-length skirt.

"Now, your father told me that you have a bad ankle, so take off that filthy shoe and let me see it. My brothers were athletes one and all. I know all about injured joints."

Her father brought the chair from the window and held it out for her. She sat and pushed her sneaker off with the toe of the other one. Caroline took her foot in her hands and moved it up and down and around. Zoe winced. Caroline nodded.

"Lucky you, I don't think anything's broken. It's just a sprain, is all. This should help."

Caroline took off Valentine's rag and dropped it on the floor. When her father picked it up and threw it in the trash, Zoe almost stopped him, but how would she explain wanting a filthy rag without explaining that it was from her brother? She couldn't, so she sat and said nothing as Caroline wrapped a bandage tightly around her foot and her father threw away her last physical connection to Valentine.

"There. That should do it. Try standing on it," said Caroline.

Zoe got it. The foot felt good. She put her weight on it. The bandage was tight and there was almost no pain.

"It's great. I've been hobbling around here for days."

"Well, if we couldn't make your time here comfortable, the least we can do is make your exit a bit more bearable."

Bearable, Zoe thought. What a funny word when she was never going to see her father or brother again. There was nothing very bearable about it. "Thanks," she said.

Zoe's father gently put the sneaker back on her foot, stood, and turned to Caroline. He took her hand in both of his. "Thank you again," he said.

"I'm glad to help." Caroline nodded and briefly laid a hand on his shoulder. She looked at Zoe. "And you, young lady, have a fast and unexciting trip home," she said, and walked out of the room, leaving Zoe and her father alone.

"You'll be safe now," said Zoe's father. He let out a low sigh. "So, now it's really time for you to go."

"Dad—" Zoe started.

Her father cut her off. "Listen, we've had way too damned many good-byes at this point. Agreed?"

Zoe smiled a little and nodded. "Agreed."

"Then all I'll say is this: have a safe trip home, and I

don't want to see you again until you're white-haired and wrinkled."

"Okay," she said, wanting to say more, but nothing would come.

"Now get out of here before I get disgusting and start tearfully good-byeing all over." They held each other for a moment, and then he pushed her gently away. "Go on," he said.

Zoe gave him a quick peck on the cheek and ran from his room, not looking back. It was the hardest thing she had ever done.

Zoe made it to the beach without anyone paying the slightest attention to her. A pack of Hecate's black dogs passed her on the boardwalk. One stopped to sniff the air as it passed, but didn't turn around before moving off to catch up with the others.

She went down to the beach, all the way to the waterline, turned right, and kept walking. The sea left white foam trails on the sand ahead of her, like the snowy peaks of distant mountains.

A chilly wind that blew in off the sea had replaced the rain from earlier in the night. There was no one else on the beach. Even the broken-down amusement park looked deserted. *They're probably all out looking for me.* So, this is what it's like to be one of the popular kids, she thought.

The drainpipe that Mr. Prosper had told her about

was there by the waterline, but still half submerged. The idea of wading an unknown distance up to her waist in seawater and whatever else might be floating or skittering in the pipe wasn't very appealing, so she decided to wait awhile and let the tide continue to pull back from the shore.

She really envied Absynthe right then. Absynthe smoked, and when you smoked, you always had something to do. When you were outside with a cigarette, people knew why you were there. You weren't waiting for a ride home or standing nervously on the corner, hoping your date hadn't stood you up. No, you were taking a moment to indulge your nicotine addiction. Besides, smoking always gave you something to do with your hands, she thought. Zoe thrust hers deep into the pockets of her father's coat. Maybe I'll start smoking again when I get home. Mom would love that.

There was nothing to do now but wait. She didn't want to attract attention by pacing, so she sat in the damp sand behind the ruins of a collapsed pier a few yards from the pipe.

She was so tired from running around being afraid. Zoe thought about what her father had said about her and her mother. That they were alike. That no one could tell them anything. She thought again about her mother. What was she thinking? What did she do when she realized that Zoe was gone? Did she call the cops or was she playing it cool, expecting Zoe to come home snarling and high on something some strange boy had given her at a party she was too young to be at? Wouldn't she be surprised if she knew the truth. *What the hell am I going to tell her when I get home?*

Or did she know anything at all? Did time work the same way in Iphigene as it did back in the world? Maybe only an hour had passed back home. She felt a quick jolt of relief at the notion that she might not have to explain any of this when she got home, but it would be frustrating after having seen what she'd seen and done what she'd done that, at home, it amounted to little more than the running time of a couple of sitcoms. She felt a twinge of guilt, too, but dismissed it. Guilt was just a natural by-product of thinking about her mother at all . . . in any world. Zoe took a breath of cool salty air to clear her head. Don't lose it now, she thought. Not when the way out is so close.

A few minutes later, she checked the pipe again. A few inches of water still pooled at the bottom. Fuck it. She couldn't stand waiting any longer. She splashed into the pipe and plunged into darkness.

The dark gave way to a thin gray light as her eyes adjusted to the interior of the pipe. The pooled water reflected the moon and stars far enough inside that she could keep moving in something like a straight line without too much trouble. After two or three minutes the light changed. The anemic glow was now in front of her, not behind. She kept walking, slower now, straining her eyes to see where it was coming from.

She found an old wooden door. A couple of steps leading up to it had been chiseled into the drainpipe. Dim light leaked from where the bottom of the door didn't quite meet the floor. Zoe walked up the steps and stood before the door. It was warped and pulpy from the dampness in the pipe. She didn't need to see the crest in the door's center to know where it led, but the image of twin snakes supporting the moon on the back of a great black she-wolf confirmed it. This was Emmett's door, the one he used to get from Iphigene to the world.

Zoe thought about Valentine fighting the wolf men. How he'd kept her behind him, protecting her. He was probably in there right now, she thought, somewhere behind this door. She put her hand around the doorknob and just held it for a moment, feeling the weight of the cold brass against her palm. Then she slowly turned the knob. She heard the latch give. The door swung open.

Inside was a small, tidy room, like an oversize closet. There were shelves and bins holding stack of neatly folded men's clothes. This is where he gets ready to travel back to the record shop, she thought. She went to one of the bins, touched the shirts and jeans, and picked up some of the black Nikes. Next to it, like a sick Halloween joke, lay a pile of human faces. Men's. All the same. Emmett's disguises, Zoe thought. She reached out a hand and touched one. It was warm and soft, like real flesh. There was even beard stubble along the chin. If this is real skin, she thought, where did Emmett get it? She thought again of what Mr. Prosper said about the other people who'd tried to find their way to Iphigene and failed. Is this what's left of them? She pushed the thought out of her head.

Zoe picked up a shirt, took off her coat, and dropped it on the floor. She put the shirt on over her hoodie. It was made of worn red flannel and was much too big for her. She took a clean pair of pants from an adjoining bin and slipped them over her jeans. There were belts hanging from a peg on the wall. She used the straight razor to cut a new hole in the leather, allowing her to pull the belt tight and keep Emmett's pants reasonably on her hips. She put the coat back on and looked around.

A broom stood near the exit to the drainpipe. The door had hidden it when she'd come in. Zoe picked it up and opened the door that led into Hecate's palace.

She remembered that the palace had once been Iphigene's city hall. She expected something like the basement of Show World High, a collection of dull cinder-block corridors dotted with anonymous storage rooms and covered at the top by white acoustic tiles. An elephants' burial ground for wobbly desks and steam-powered PCs. What she saw, however, took her breath away.

The interior of Hecate's palace resembled a vast subterranean cavern with tunnels branching off in all directions. The walls weren't smooth like cinder blocks, but were sliced from soft soil and sloped gracefully to the loamy floor. Arthritic-looking fingers of roots trailed down the walls in twisted bundles, tangling themselves in outcrops of limestone and glistening quartz.

Though the palace seemed to be underground, the ceiling overhead was the night sky and it luminesced with the same stars she'd seen over Iphigene. The moon hovered over it all, shimmering high in the star field. The light was a quivering milky blue that drained the color from all objects, leaving them and everything that moved in the cavern looking as if they were made of mist and ice.

Zoe took the broom and pulled her collar up. She felt like an idiot sweeping the packed dirt and stone floor, but reasoned that if there was a broom around, someone must use it. She made her way around the wall, sweeping quietly and trying to look as boring and blank as possible. She glanced down each staircase and corridor as she came to it. There were no markings or signs anywhere, and all the other rooms looked the same to her.

As the excitement that had pushed her into the palace began to fade, she kept up a slow mantra in her head, repeating it over and over again. *Valentine is brave. He would do this for me.*

It hadn't occurred to her until she was inside and sweeping that there might not be any humans in the palace. All the residents could be wolves and black dogs. Her face flushed with fear. Some of the little snake-things, like the ones at the café, flew in lazy circles around the ceiling.

When she finally saw a man and woman walk by, Zoe let out a long breath. The perfume still seemed to be working. No one paid any attention to her, including the black dogs that roamed the place, pissing and shitting where they wanted, marking their territories as they went. Still, she had no idea where to go from here, and she knew she couldn't keep sweeping this one room forever.

A few minutes later, three of Hecate's wolf-headed enforcers came in and fell into deep conversation with two human men. The men were both large, like wrestlers on TV, and wore identical blue uniforms that looked vaguely like something you might think a cop or prison guard would wear if you hadn't seen one in a hundred years. Their thick leather belts caught Zoe's eye. Dangling from each belt was a set of heavy old-fashioned keys, the kind she'd seen in a dozens of old movies, whenever a princess was being held prisoner in a magic tower.

Soon the wolves and the two human men walked off in opposite directions. Still sweeping, Zoe followed the human guards into one of the room's side tunnels. There was a spiral staircase carved from pink quartz that gave everything a faint reddish glow as she followed them down.

When she reached the bottom of the steps, the guards were gone. Human souls, wolf men, and black dogs roamed the corridor. Zoe wasn't sure she could just turn around and go back up the stairs without someone noticing, so she started sweeping, hoping she'd catch sight of the guards.

She went into the nearest open room off the main corridor, and immediately wished she hadn't. The room was too hot and it stank of something wet and rotten. The walls were made from large interlocking gray stones, like a massive jigsaw puzzle, and were covered in strange hieroglyphics. Giant black cobras, like the ones she'd seen in Hecate's procession, slid quietly around a set of low stone enclosures filled with straw and large white eggs. Nests, thought Zoe.

A moment later, one of the eggs cracked open and a small hatchling, not much bigger than a pencil, wriggled out. It spread its wings and hissed and the big snakes hissed back. Another egg opened a moment later and another snake slithered out, wet and glistening. It was much larger than the first hatchling. As other eggs began to crack, it slid across the straw to the first young snake, reared back, exposing its fangs, and struck. Once, twice, three times, until the smaller snake lay dead. The large cobras twisted around the nests faster, hissing excitedly. More eggs opened and the scene repeated itself over and over. The larger hatchlings attacked the smaller ones and killed them. When all the smaller ones were dead, the young snakes began to feed. The black cobras reared up over the nests, hissing and tasting the air with their tongues. Proud parents, thought Zoe. She backed out of the room as quietly as she could.

She clutched the broom to her chest and went to the end of the corridor, hoping to find the guards. A group of wolf-men enforcers and human souls stood before a wall-size map of what she was sure was Iphigene. The humans pointed to spots on the map with wooden or rusted metal stumps of hands. Each time they did so, one of the wolves would mark it with an *X*. *I wonder if those are for me?* These are souls who thought they'd seen me and are trying to collect Hecate's reward, Zoe thought. One of them might be the one who saw Valentine and me going to Mr. Prosper's apartment and told the wolves.

"Hey, you."

Zoe squinted at the map, trying to see if there were any marks on the beach near the drainpipe. Please don't be following me already, she thought.

Someone grabbed her arm. Zoe looked up into a man's face.

"You. Didn't you hear me calling you?"

He wore an old uniform like the guards, but he didn't have a belt and the insignia on the front was different.

"No. I'm sorry."

"Never mind that. Clean up this mess over here."

He led her to another room and pointed to a pile of clothes and shoes that filled the corner of the room.

"Gather these up and take them to the incinerator," he said, and left.

Zoe leaned the broom against the wall and went to the clothes. Coats, dresses, and pants were scattered across the floor. Children's clothes, glasses, and jewelry. Zoe didn't know what to do, so she began sorting things into piles.

At the far end of the room was a big screen showing the image of a woman laughing. It looked almost like a music video at a club. The woman had dark coffee-colored skin and bright eyes. In front of the screen another woman was strapped to a chair. Wires ran from her head to a big brass device with spiderlike legs moving over a spinning platter. The machine reminded her of the Animagraph but was much larger. The woman screamed.

"Please. No. It's mine. You have no right."

This is it, she thought. This is where they make the records for the secret room of Emmett's shop. Images of the woman's life flashed on the screen as the machine transcribed them all.

A couple of men and a woman in white lab coats clustered around the brass machine, making tiny adjustments here and there.

"Queen Hecate will enjoy this one," said the woman.

"A lovely specimen," said one of the men.

The woman strapped to the chair cried quietly as every small moment of her life was transcribed onto the record.

Hecate will enjoy this one? What does that mean? wondered Zoe. Is that what the records are really for?

Not just traps for idiots like me, but things for Hecate to play so she can feel like she's back in the living world?

The screen was dark now. Another body, covered in sweat, moved over the woman. Hands and lips caressed her. Memories of sex. The three technicians laughed.

"Please," said the woman. "Let me have something for myself. I'm not chattel. I'm not here for your amusement."

"Yes, you are, my dear," said the taller of the two men.

Four more souls stood in a line against the wall. Three women and a man. At the front of the line was a girl not much older than Zoe. Over the collar of her shapeless overcoat, Zoe could see her wide brown eyes and bleached-blond hair. The girl was holding her hands over her mouth, as if stifling a scream. Zoe continued sorting the clothes.

Without warning, the blonde bolted from the line and ran for the exit. Before she'd gone six steps, a black hound leaped from the door and sank its jaws into her throat. Another dog followed and grabbed her legs. The girl screamed as the dogs tore into her. The other woman's life, the life of the woman who was strapped to the chair, flashed by on the screen. She was eating cake and people were singing "Happy Birthday." The song mixed with the blond girl's screams. Zoe's stomach churned. She wanted to throw up. She grabbed the broom and a handful of clothes and headed for the door.

Out in the corridor, she fell back against the wall.

She wanted to curl up on the floor, close her eyes, and scream like the woman strapped to the chair. She wanted to throw up or to cry. Instead, she kept her head down and looked for a sign or mark, anything that might point to an exit.

Zoe heard a faint metallic jingling of keys. Turning, she saw the two guards she'd seen upstairs. They were going into a stairwell at the end of the corridor. Zoe held the clothes in front of her and followed them. The moment she was out of sight of the door, she dropped the clothes. She almost left the broom behind, but at the last second decided to keep it.

At the bottom of the stairs, rows of prison cells spread out as far as she could see in all directions. Most were empty, but the blood on the floor and red trails of slithering snake bodies made her wonder if the prisoners down here had suffered the same fate as the hypnotized souls at the café. This isn't a palace, thought Zoe. It's a feeding trough.

Voices echoed faintly from the far reaches of the dungeon. Sweeping again, she moved through what seemed like miles of empty, bloody pens.

She weaved her way between rows of filthy timeworn cells with bars so corroded that the rust was pitted and black. It almost looked as if with a little help, you might be able to snap one of the bars in two. But the guards would hear you, she thought, and you'd have to get past them. And the wolf-men enforcers. And snakes.

And Hecate.

At a crossroads where a cellful of dying dead hissed and grabbed for her as she passed, Zoe stopped. The low voices were much closer. When she started sweeping down a new row of cells, the sound stopped. But it didn't matter. She'd already seen them.

A hundred people were locked in a hundred separate cells. Men and women, old and young. None said anything as she went past. They seemed too afraid, not sure if she was one of them or one of Hecate's spies. "Valentine?" she asked quietly. An old woman in a cell to Zoe's right pointed her bony finger farther down the line. Zoe nodded thanks and ran from cell to cell whispering, "Valentine?"

"Here!"

She rushed to the corner cell, and there he was. Valentine looked even dirtier and more ragged than before. The wolf men's claws had shredded his clothes and he had a bloody gash across his forehead. When he stood, one of his metal legs was bent badly to the side. He dipped and rose with each step. Still, he smiled when he saw her and they hugged each other as well as they could through the bars.

"What the hell are you doing here?" he asked.

"I'm not really sure. I was on my way out of the city," said Zoe. She added hopefully, "Rescuing you, maybe?"

"That so?" asked Valentine. "Did you bring an army? Do you have keys? Do you have a plan?"

Zoe knew his voice well enough to hear the undertone of sarcasm, and it hurt, mostly because she knew he was right.

"No. Nothing," she said finally. "I just couldn't leave with you thinking that I'd run off and forgotten you."

Valentine wrapped his metal hand around Zoe's where she clung to one of the bars. "I'd never think that," he told her. "Not in a million years. Which is about how long Hecate will lock you up if she catches you here."

Zoe looked around. "Is Mr. Prosper here? Maybe he knows a way out—"

"Prosper's gone," said Valentine. "They gave him to those things. The ones that live on the unlit streets."

"Oh." Much as Zoe hated Mr. Prosper, she didn't figure that even he deserved that kind of end. "Can't you get out on your own? Your arms are metal. Can't you break these old bars?" She grabbed the one she'd been holding with both hands and pulled. It didn't budge.

Valentine shook his head. "We've all thought that and we've all tried. The bars might be rotten, on the outside, but they're still solid. Forget it."

Zoe stepped back from the cell, looking it over, hoping she could find a weak spot. One of the little snakes swooped down and chittered around her head. She swatted at it with her hand and it flew away.

"They've seen you. You have to leave here," said Valentine urgently. "Please, you've made it this far. Go back to the tunnel and keep going."

A couple more of the snakes flew down at Zoe. They dive-bombed her head and yanked strands of hair painfully from her head before flying off.

"I'm sorry. I don't know how to save you," Zoe said.

"Yeah, but you tried. No one's ever done that for me before. Thanks," said Valentine. "Now go, before someone else spots you."

From far away came the sound of a rough, angry voice. "What?" it yelled. "Where?" This was followed by the squeaking of the snakes and the sound of thundering footsteps.

Valentine squeezed Zoe's arm.

"Show us where she is!" Angry wolf growls joined in with the human voices.

"Run!" shouted Valentine. He released her arm and pointed to the rear of the prison. "That way. Go to the end of the row and bear right. There's a door. I saw stairs on the other side."

Zoe wanted to say said something, but the stricken look on Valentine's face stopped her. She dropped the broom and began to run as fast as she could.

"Where is she?" Zoe heard the guards screaming at the prisoners. "Which of you was talking to her?" She heard something snap and break. She slowed and almost turned back, but ran again when she realized that the sound was the broom.

Ahead was a rusted metal door of decayed diamond plate. She pushed through and ran into the gloom. The stairwell looked normal, like you'd see in any office-building basement. Zoe noticed a slide lock on the door and threw it, sealing the dungeon level closed. She craned her neck trying to get a a sense of whether there was anything dangerous up the stairs, but she couldn't see anything. The sound of crashing in the other room got louder. She started up the stairs. Her footfalls on the metal steps echoed off the walls. She tried running in a lighter way, putting her weight on the balls of her feet and not her heels. Even with the new bandage, this hurt her ankle, but she kept going.

From below came the high, eerie low of wolf calls. A second later, answering calls came from over her head. They were trying to trap her, catch her between two wolf packs. She stopped for a second and tried a door. It was locked. She tried another at the next landing. It was locked, too. Below her, someone pounded on the dungeon door, trying to get through.

Zoe ran up to the next floor. The stairwell was cluttered with boxes and old desks and chairs. She fell against the door and opened it a few inches. A wolf man's arm shot through the opening and grabbed for her. She tried to slam the door shut, but caught the wolf enforcer's arm. There was nothing she could do but brace one leg against the stairs and lean her shoulder against the door to hold it closed. Sharp claws ripped at her coat as the wolf man's arm flailed in the small opening, trying to pull free. She was trapped. She couldn't let go of the door and she couldn't get it closed. Snarls and howls resounded through the opening and filled the stairwell with animal fury. As hard as she pushed, the wolf man was too strong. Inch by inch the door crept open.

She took a chance and reached into her pocket. Her hand landed on the straight razor. She pulled it out and snapped it open, slashing at the wolf man's arm with all her strength. The enforcer howled in pain. Warm red blood ran down the wall and splashed into her eyes, but she kept slashing. The wolf grabbed the blade, but Zoe pulled it free, slashing its hand. With one more howl of pain, the wolf arm pulled back through the opening and Zoe slammed the door shut.

She fell back against the old furniture. Footsteps grew louder below, but before she could run, a snake darted down from overhead and bit her cheek. Then another. There were six of them overhead. They dive-bombed her, hitting her face and forehead. *They're trying to get my eyes.* Zoe threw her hands up and kept her head down. That's when saw what was happening. She might have closed the door and locked the wolves out, but the little snakes wriggled underneath, slithering into the stairwell.

Zoe slipped off her coat and threw it at the bottom of the door, kicking it into place with her heels. Still, the snakes that had made it in were coming at her. Running upstairs wouldn't help because they could just follow her. Their high-pitched chittering was like ice picks in her ears. She slashed at the snakes with the razor, cutting a wing off one, so it crashed into the floor. She stamped on it until it stopped moving. Keeping her hand in front of her face, she slashed overhead, hitting two more snakes. They slammed into the wall and tumbled onto the stairs. The snakes' chittering went up an octave and the whole flock rose into the air, too high for Zoe to reach. They circled the ceiling a couple of times and flew up the stairs.

Howls came down to her from above. The enforcers below were closing on her and the door she'd locked shook more and more as the wolf men in the hall rammed it over and over again. Zoe looked around frantically. There was another door by the stairs. She ran to it and opened it a crack. Beyond was an empty office. There were marks on the floor where souls had once worked. A few windows showed the moon high in the Iphigene sky. Zoe went back into the hall and got Caroline's perfume bottle from her coat. Back in the office, she unscrewed the top and threw the bottle as hard as she could at the far wall. It shattered. The glass shards looked like jewels in the moonlight. Behind her, the door on the stairs started to splinter. Zoe ran back to the stairwell and crouched down behind an old desk just as the door burst open.

A crowd of wolf men charged into the stairwell, their snouts in the air, sniffing. A second later, they tore open the door to the office and ran inside. Zoe stood up in the stairwell and slowly came out from behind the desk. At that very moment the wolves from the dungeon level broke through and ran up the stairs. She threw herself back down onto the floor as the wolf men pounded past her, following the others into the office. Zoe got up and ran through the splintered door.

She was in a hall that looked like something she'd expect to see in an old office building. Tiled floors, wood-paneled walls and glass-fronted office doors, piles of unwanted chairs, boxes, and tables pushed against the walls.

"Excuse me," came a voice from over her shoulder. "Are you supposed to be here?"

Zoe spun around, sweating and bleeding, gulping in big lungfuls of air. A young man stood there with a pile of large ledgers in his arms. He wore a tight gray suit, a bow tie, a starched collar, and small round metal glasses. Zoe thought he looked like a character in a Dickens novel.

"Who are you?" asked the young man more insistently.

Zoe's mouth moved, but nothing came out. Then, "There's trouble downstairs!" she said. "Prisoners have escaped. Get help!" The young man's eyes widened. He turned to go, but came back and grabbed Zoe's arm. "Come with me so you can explain what's happening to the head clerk."

Zoe grabbed the ledgers and threw them up into the air. They popped open and papers flew everywhere. The young man stood in shock, watching the pages float down like a slow-motion snowstorm. Zoe shoved him from behind so that he fell over a small table leaning against the wall. She never saw him hit the floor. She was already running the other way. At the end of the hall was an imposing set of double doors. She pulled them open and ran through.

The room she entered looked like a large auditorium. At the far end was a dais on a low stage. The middle of the room was empty, but folding chairs were stacked neatly by the door. Overhead, an enormous wrought-iron-and-glass dome let in spectral moonlight.

Zoe thought that the auditorium must have been converted into a storeroom when Hecate took over. The walls rose thirty or more feet above her head, but they were piled all the way to the ceiling with books, old desks, chairs, statues, plaques, crumbling, yellowed records, lamps, bookshelves, rolled carpets, and hundreds of unmarked boxes. The contents of the old city hall spilled up the walls like a tidal wave of junk. Towering over it all was a mammoth ornamental mirror, as tall as the room. Its old silver face was peeling and speckled with grime, but its ornate gold-leaf frame glowed like candlelight.

Zoe looked around, but didn't see any exits. She realized that the piles of discarded office equipment probably blocked any doors. For a moment she panicked, but she couldn't go back into the hall. The young man would have gone for help by now. Looking around, she saw windows dotted around the room above the piles of detritus. One window stood just above the enormous mirror. If she could get up to it, she could use the ornamental frame like a ladder and climb to the window. She climbed onto a desk, then up onto a bookcase, and onto a pile of filing cabinets. Nothing fell. Nothing wobbled. The pile felt firm under her feet and her ankle felt strong enough to keep going. She started up.

Below her, Zoe heard the auditorium doors slam open and the sound of running feet. Human voices and wolf howls filled the air. Zoe didn't look back until she heard someone climbing up behind her.

Balancing on a couple of boxes of books, Zoe looked down. Wolf men and human souls in uniforms were clambering up the mountain of junk, eyes flashing, thrilled by the hunt. Zoe tried climbing faster, but the higher she got, the more careful she had to be. Every movement felt like it could start an avalanche. But she was going too slowly and looked around for a way out. On each side of her were boxes of books. Bracing her back against a big desk, Zoe dug in her heels and pushed a stack of boxes over. They rained down on her pursuers, catching a couple square in the face and knocking them to the ground. She pushed over more boxes, kicked over lamps and rolled office chairs over the edge at them. A few of the humans fell back off the pile. The remaining wolves retreated, but more came up behind them. Zoe kept climbing, stopping only to push over a drafting table or an unstable desk on the mob below.

"Leave her!" came a woman's voice, cool and commanding. It echoed around the room, repeating the order until it finally faded, leaving a charged silence behind.

"What are you doing, child?" came the commanding voice. Zoe didn't want to stop and look, but she couldn't help herself. She had to see the woman. Carefully, moving only a few inches at a time so she wouldn't fall, she turned and looked down at Hecate. The queen was dressed in a long flowing gown of black and red. She wore a beautiful metal crown that looked to be made of silver wolf teeth.

"What a brave girl you are," said the queen. "And resourceful, too." Her smile was like the night sky—cold, beautiful, infinitely deep. "No one has ever made it this far into my palace before. Do you know why?"

Zoe didn't want to answer, but couldn't look away from the queen. "No," she said.

Hecate gave her a dazzling smile. "Because no one has ever dared to. But you did." The queen approached the pile of junk. The wolves and human souls fell back, creating a lane for her to pass. "That's why I like you. That's why you and I can be friends. Because we dare. We do what these blackguards and minions wouldn't dare dream of."

Zoe didn't want to listen, didn't want to talk to the queen. There was something in her voice, something seductive and compelling. Something hypnotic. "I could use someone brave and resourceful for a friend. But to be my friend, you will have to come down here and stand beside me."

"I . . ." Zoe said weakly, "I can't."

"Of course you can, dear," said the queen lightly. "Don't worry about falling. My men will catch you."

"Catch me," said Zoe. The words bounced around in her mind until she saw their true meaning. "Yes, you want to catch me. You want to use me to get back to the world." She backed away, knelt on a filing cabinet, and started climbing again.

"Nonsense. Did that fool Prosper tell you that? He was mad as a hatter," said Queen Hecate. "That's why I dismissed him."

Zoe's was dizzy. It was hard to move forward. Each step she took, each handhold, was an effort. Even though the queen didn't tell her to stop, the sound of her voice weighed Zoe down and made moving almost impossible. She said weakly, "I don't believe you."

"One day, it will be my time to leave Iphigene, you know," the queen said. Her tone was conversational. "When I do, a new queen will have to take my place. Until now, I haven't seen anyone worthy of the title. But you could be that queen."

"No" was all Zoe could muster.

"I have your brother and soon I'll have your father," said Hecate in a deadly tone. "My men are already on their way to arrest them."

Zoe ignored her. This angry Hecate was less hypnotic than the cajoling one, and easier to fight. Zoe's head began to clear, so she climbed faster. She could see the edge of the giant mirror just a few yards above her.

"I will not let you leave!" Hecate cried.

Zoe paused, picked up a box of glass paperweights, and hurled it down to the floor. The box split open and sharp shards flew in all directions, forcing Hecate's troops back.

The queen turned and spoke to one of the wolf men. "Very well," she said. "But only wound her."

An arrow sliced the air by Zoe's head and embedded itself deep in the side of a heavy oak desk. She threw herself down behind the desk and looked for a way out.

The edge of a nearby bookcase that was tall enough to hide behind. She put her shoulder into the side of the desk and pushed, feeling it slide slowly forward. Finally, it toppled down the mound, scattering Hecate's men. Zoe ran the few steps to the bookcase and jumped on top as more arrows shot past her.

From there she was up high enough, she thought, that if she kept low and crawled, the archers on the ground wouldn't be able to get a good shot at her. She started forward on her belly. Arrows still flew at her, but they all landed too low or whizzed by overhead.

"Enough," said Hecate impatiently. The arrows stopped flying. "Come, my children. Feed. Fill your bellies."

Zoe heard an awful sound in the air above her. She looked up just in time to see a swarm of Hecate's winged baby snakes swarming into the room and filling the space under the glass dome. Their high-pitched squeaks and chirps sounded even madder than before. The bats circled the dome once, twice, and then dove for her.

Zoe stood and scrabbled up the pile of junk as quickly as she could. The giant mirror was just ahead. If she could reach it, she'd be close enough to the window that the bats and archers wouldn't matter.

When the first wave of snakes swarmed around her, they hit hard enough to knock her down. She had to grab the base of a withered old potted palm to keep from rolling over the side. The next swarm hit her just as she got to her feet. Zoe was ready this time and ducked, so she was able to take the blow and stay standing. She made it up the pile a few more feet before they hit her again. From where she stood, it was a straight line to the mirror. If she leaned forward far enough, she could almost touch it.

This time when the swarm slammed into her, the snakes didn't fly away. They dug in with their fangs and beat her with their wings. Zoe covered her face, trying to protect her eyes. She swung her free arm before her, trying to keep the snakes off as much as she could. She couldn't breathe. It felt like she was drowning, drowning while being eaten alive. It took her a second to realize that the screams she heard were her own.

Zoe fell to her knees as more snakes landed on her. She closed her eyes and crawled a few feet, using one hand to move and the other to cover her face. Every inch was agony. Covered with snakes, her arms felt like they weighed a hundred pounds each. Then her hand landed on something glassy. Zoe tilted her head up and opened one eye. Through the trembling mass of serpents, she saw the gold frame. With her free hand, she reached out, grabbed the edge of the mirror, and pulled herself up. When she stood, the snakes lifted off her as one.

Her legs shook but the snakes were gone. Relief flooded through her. She looked down on the wolf men and humans below. *I'm too close to the window to stop and they know it.* She raised her bloody hands and gave them all the finger. It wasn't until she lowered her hands that she saw Hecate, and by then, it was too late.

In the split second before it happened, she remembered the first time she'd seen the queen. Zoe had known instantly that she was more than a simple ruler. She was a warrior. That's why it was so frightening, though not at all surprising, to see Hecate aiming a longbow up at her.

There was the slightest of sounds, as if someone had delicately plucked a string on a classical guitar. A second later, something slammed into Zoe's chest. It didn't feel like an arrow, what she imagined an arrow would feel like. It was more like being punched with a fist made of fire. When she raised her hands, however, she felt the arrow's shaft buried deep in her chest. She looked down at Hecate and watched as a satisfied, feral smile split her face. The sight made Zoe's head swim.

She stumbled back, grabbing on to the mirror. One of her legs slid from beneath her and slammed into something.

Zoe felt the junk mound move ominously. Boxes shifted and settled. Something cracked. She didn't care. She slid down onto her belly as her vision collapsed into a long dark tunnel. From somewhere a million miles away, she heard Hecate scream "Don't let her fall! I need her body!"

Zoe tried to push herself back to her feet, but her bones had turned to rubber. She leaned back onto the boxes and felt them slide away from her. A roaring, crashing sound filled the room. It took her a second to realize that she'd started an avalanche. A whole section of the junk mountain was beginning to move. A fault line opened in a lower section, wobbled from side to side, and slammed into the mirror. She heard a scrape and a screech as it shifted and began to slide.

Boxes cascaded around her and over her. The hand she'd been resting on the mirror was suddenly empty as the enormous slab of silvered glass toppled forward.

"No!" shrieked Hecate in a new voice, one more fearful than angry. "What have you done, child?"

Zoe didn't answer. She lay on her side, one hand on the arrow buried in her chest. Her arms and legs didn't work anymore. She couldn't see much more than gray outlines below. Each breath she took was harder than the last. Something wet sloshed around inside her, filling her lungs. Each breath hurt more than the one before. She couldn't keep her eyes open. Zoe knew that she was dying and she was so tired, she was happy to just let it happen.

At least I'll be with Valentine and Dad, she thought.

When the mirror hit the floor, it shattered with a sound like the earth bursting open, of the sky cracking. Everything shook, like all of creation was trying to rip itself apart from the inside.

Light burst from beneath the shattered glass and wood. Even at the edge of death, the light was so bright that Zoe had to raise a hand to shield her eyes from it.

Her body began to fill with a strange warmth and she found that she could breathe again. The dull pain in the center of her chest began to fade. When she touched the arrow, it crumbled in her hand. Through her closed lids, the light that filled the room faded, drawing in on itself until it was a floating ball of burning gold. Zoe opened her eyes.

Rising slowly from the floor of the auditorium, from the middle of the broken mirror, was the stolen sun. It moved slowly, elegantly, rumbling and sizzling, filling the room with a brilliant healing light. Zoe pushed herself into a sitting position and touched the skin between her breasts. Though the front of her shirt was damp with her blood, the arrow wound was gone.

"No! I beat you! You're mine!"

Zoe looked down and saw Hecate shrieking at the burning star floating just a few feet over her head. Around the queen, her wolf men ran from the light, bursting into flames as they went. The floor was already covered with them. Hecate's snakes sizzled like sparklers, floating in the air like thousands of fireflies, before falling to the ground at the queen's feet.

"You're mine!" Hecate screamed. She had been looking at the sun, but now turned her gaze on Zoe. "You're all mine." Hecate's face went soft and the bones seemed to shift under her flesh. Her hair and dress were already beginning to smolder. She paid no attention to any of this as the human part of her melted away like candle wax, leaving only the snarling she-wolf behind. Hecate's dress was burning now and the flames spread quickly over the fabric and onto her coarse black fur. Burning, she leaped from the floor onto the boxes and desks and began to climb.

Zoe fell back against a card catalog. Looking around, she saw that there were enough boxes to reach the window. Still weak, she began to climb. She'd only gone a few feet when she felt a blistering heat rising behind her.

Hecate stepped onto the platform just below Zoe. The queen was a pillar of pure flame now, and the furniture that was nearest to her immediately began to smoke and smolder. Hecate reached up, but Zoe pressed herself into the wall. It was so hot that she was afraid of her own clothes bursting into flame. The queen braced herself to climb onto Zoe's level, but as she moved to rise up, her leg collapsed. She lunged at Zoe with both arms and froze in place. Her ashen body wouldn't move. Not much more now than a statue of orange-blue flame, she raised her burning snout in the air and let out one last long and ferocious howl. Then her body caved in on itself, crumbling and drifting away to the floor in a cloud of burning ash. Zoe lay still, unable to think or move.

Silently the sun rose, swelling as it went. When it reached the ceiling, it was as big as the glass dome. It burst through without slowing, gliding away, growing larger and more dazzling by the second. Zoe looked up at the window. Outside, the moonlit sky gave way to a deep blue.

She climbed up to the window and pushed it open. Swinging her feet over the sill, she dropped onto a fire escape. Leaning against the railing, she looked down on Iphigene, seeing it lit up like it had been on that one perfect day she had spent with her father. The air felt lighter, the atmosphere clearer. She could feel it. Some powerful spell had definitely been broken. Souls poured from the restaurants and bars, out of the alleys and backstreets. They ran past the boardwalk and onto the beach to watch the sun rise over the city.

Zoe rested on the metal steps and watched the city come to life. She stayed there a long time, just breathing. When she was ready, she got up and went down the fire escape to the street below.

Whatever the sun had done to her back in the auditorium, she sensed that it was still doing it. She felt stronger with each step she took, not at all tired. The dozens of little bat bites were healing, though the marks were still visible. She was glad of that and secretly hoped that some would scar over. She didn't want to have gone through all this without something to keep so that when she was back in the world, no one, not even she, could tell her that it had all been a dream.

People streamed out of City Hall. Papers, uniforms, and broken glass were scattered among piles of ashes where more of Hecate's guards had met the sunlight. Just inside the front doors, she spotted a belt that held some old prison keys. She retraced her steps to the staircase by the auditorium. Downstairs, she released Valentine and the other prisoners. The ones who could run took off for the stairs. Zoe and Valentine were the last to leave. She held on to her brother's shoulder as he hobbled up the stairs on his bent leg.

It was slow going, but they made their way down the boardwalk, neither of them talking because there was nothing to say right then. Things were changing quickly in the city, as if its residents had been poised to move for a thousand years.

Buses were already lining up to take souls to . . . well, Zoe thought, wherever it was souls went to from here. She looked at Valentine and a smile spread across both of their faces. She knew what he was thinking, that wherever the buses were going, it was somewhere else, somewhere new. An adventure. And it was no one's choice but his own whether to get on or not. Valentine asked her what had happened back at City Hall and

Zoe told him. He nodded as she talked. When she was done, he just laughed, leaned over, and kissed the top of her head.

It took them an hour of wandering through the crush of excited souls to find their father. He grinned happily when he saw Zoe and took her in his arms. "I take it back," he said. "The last time I said I didn't want to see you for fifty years, it was just practice. But I'll mean it the next time." He let go of her and looked at the sun, shielding his eyes with one hand. "I don't know what just happened or how, but I have a feeling you had something to do with it," he said fondly.

"Hecate's dead," she said.

Her father's eyes widened.

"You did that?"

"No. The sun did. All I did was find the sun."

"That's my girl," he said, and pulled her to him.

She took Valentine's hand and pulled him forward. "This is the friend I told you about. The one who helped me."

Zoe's father smiled at the boy and took him into a big bear hug, saying, "Thank you for taking care of my little girl." Zoe saw Valentine stiffen the same way he had when she'd first touched him. Then she saw him relax just a little and tentatively put a hand on his father's back.

"There's something you should know, Dad. A secret," she said. Valentine's body grew rigid again and he took an awkward step back from them, but she grabbed his hand and held him there.

"You said you wouldn't tell," Valentine said through clenched teeth.

"The secret is stupid. Look," she said, pointing at the buses, "everyone is moving on. You have to, too."

"I can't," said Valentine. "Look at me." He pulled her hand, but Zoe held him tight.

"What is this, Zoe? What's going on?" asked their father.

"Dad, you two don't know each other, but this is Valentine, your son."

Zoe's father stared at her with a blank, uncomprehending look. He turned to the boy as if hoping for some kind of explanation, but Valentine kept his head low in his torn coat collar. "Trust me, Dad. I've known him all my life, but I didn't know who he was until I came here." She looked at Valentine. "You can be mad at me for telling." She turned to her father. "You can be mad at me for not telling, but there's no way I was leaving here without you two meeting." She let go of her brother's hand. To her relief, he didn't try to run away. "Valentine, say hello to Dad. Dad, say hello to Valentine."

Their father stared at the boy. "Valentine?" He turned to Zoe. "How is this possible?"

She nodded at Valentine. "He can tell you. He's smart."

Their father put his hands on both their shoulders. "I'm lost here," he said. "I don't know what to say."

"I can explain it, if you like," said Valentine quietly. He stared down at the ground. "Will you be getting on one of the buses?"

"Yeah," said their father. "I suppose I will."

Valentine nodded. "Maybe we could ride together," he said. "If you want, I can tell you as we go."

"I'd like that."

From out of the crowd, Caroline appeared. Like the others, she looked a little dazed by the sunlight, but she was smiling. "There you all are," she said merrily. "Isn't it a lovely day?" She looked up at the sun, squinted, and looked away. "I need to practice what one does and doesn't do on sunny days, I think." She touched Zoe's shoulder. "I've been sent to fetch you, dear."

"Fetch me for what?" asked Zoe.

Caroline cocked her head slightly. "There's a bus waiting for you," she said. "It's time for all little living girls to go home."

Zoe looked at Valentine and her father. "She's right, Zoe," her father said. While keeping one arm out so that Valentine could lean on him, he took Zoe's hand and they followed Caroline to the last bus in the row. The door hissed open as they approached. Gently, but firmly, Caroline urged Zoe up to the bottom step of the bus.

"I guess I'm really going this time," said Zoe, feeling a little overwhelmed and lost; so much was happening so fast.

"Yeah, kiddo," said her father. "And this time I really mean the fifty-year thing."

"It's a deal," she said.

Valentine limped to the platform and hugged her. "I'm glad we really, finally met," he said.

"Me, too," said Zoe. "Will I see you again, in the tree fort?"

Valentine shrugged. "I don't know. Where we're going, I don't know if I'll be able to get there." He brightened a little. "Anyway, you don't need me there anymore. You can take care of yourself."

She leaned down and kissed him on the cheek. "Don't worry, I'll always need you."

Zoe's father took a coin from his pocket and dropped it into Zoe's hand. "You know how I told you that some spirits cling to things from life? I liked to pretend that I was above all that, but the truth is, I wasn't," he said. "The club where your mother and I met had these drink tokens they sometimes gave to regulars. I had this one with me when I died. Give it to her for me, will you?"

Zoe turned the coin over in her hand. It was penny brown, but as large as a quarter. On one side was a ragged anarchy *A* in a circle. On the other side were a skull with crossed beer bottles and the words *Fuck You Very Much*. Zoe grinned, remembering the same words on her mother's jacket years ago.

"I'll give it to her first thing when I get back," she said, slipping the coin into her pocket.

"Time to go, dear," said Mrs. Somerville.

"But wait," said Zoe. "What happens to all those people who helped Hecate?"

Valentine, Caroline, and her father all looked at one another. "I have no idea," her father said. "Some of them probably didn't want to help her. We all did things we didn't want to do here. The ones who did side with her, maybe they'll have to answer for it somewhere, sometime. I don't know. My guess is they'll stay right here hiding in the city forever, afraid to move on." He looked around at the growing crowd. "But it's not my job to worry about it and it's not yours . . . so fuck them all."

Caroline gave Zoe a small wave. "You have a good trip home, and a long and lovely life when you get there."

"Thank you," Zoe said. She called to her father, "When I come back old and wrinkled, you'll recognize me because I'll be the old lady in the Germs T-shirt."

The bus doors hissed closed and the engine ground to life. Zoe sat up front and slid across the seat to the window. She waved to Valentine and her father as the bus pulled away. It moved slowly through the dense crowd of smiling faces. She turned for a last look at the beach just as they were passing the abandoned amusement park. It looked kind of cool in the sun, she thought. Absynthe would love the place, she thought. Maybe Julie and Laura, too. What was she going to tell them about all this? If she told the truth, they'd think she really was crazy or, worse, showing off by pretending to be crazy.

It was a strange kind of problem, she thought. Then the light faded from the windows and the interior lights on the bus dimmed. Suddenly everything was very soft and dark and quiet. For a second it felt like falling, but she wasn't scared at all.

Twelve

She awoke just as the bus was pulling up outside the liquor store down the street from her apartment house. It was dark out and she saw the night clerk step outside to stare at the bus that had pulled up where there was no bus stop.

"Last stop. Everybody out," called the driver. The back door opened and Zoe stepped down onto the street. The door closed and bus rumbled away in a cloud of smoke, turned the corner, and disappeared.

Zoe headed for her building halfway up the block. Everything felt weird here. The air . . . the acrid street smells and lights assaulted her. Buildings stood straight up and cars hissed by, honking and belching music. Everything was more real, but less so at the same time. She thought of Caroline having to get used to the sun again. She felt like coming home was going to be something like that.

The elevator wasn't working, so she had to walk up the four flights to the apartment. Standing by her door, she realized she'd lost her keys. And her father's razor. Except for the clothes she had on, she'd lost pretty much everything she had. There was nothing else to do. She knocked on the door.

It opened halfway on its chain and part of her mother's face appeared in the crack. Her mother's eye, the one she could see, was red and rimmed with dark circles, like she hadn't slept in days. "Zoe?" her mother said. The door closed for a second, then burst open again. Her mother stood there for a moment. Zoe didn't move, not sure what to expect. Then her mother flung her arms around her, hugging her so hard she couldn't breathe.

"I knew you were all right. I knew you were going to be all right," she said.

"It's good to see you, too, Mom. Can I come in? I'm pretty tired," Zoe said.

Her mother stepped aside so Zoe could enter the apartment. The living room looked as odd to her as the street outside had looked. Nothing had changed, except for the overflowing ashtrays on every flat surface and the smell of stale smoke. Zoe felt so different, so utterly and irrevocably changed, that it seemed to her that everything else should have changed, too. She shook off the feeling and turned to her mother.

"Hi," she said feebly. "I'm glad I'm home."

Her mother still stood by the front door, almost as if

she was afraid to approach. Her hands were balled up in front of her mouth, and she regarded Zoe with wide, wet eyes.

"You're hurt," she said.

"It's all right," said Zoe. "Really, it's not as bad as it looks." Then she added, "But it was a rough couple of days."

"Couple of days? It's been a week," said her mother. "Tomorrow would have been eight days." She dropped her hands to her sides, but she was still tense and didn't seem able to move from the door.

Zoe sat down on the edge of the couch. "It didn't seem that long. Just a day or two, at most."

"Well, it *was* that long!" yelled her mother, breaking down into red-faced sobs. She tried to speak, but she had trouble breathing. "I thought you were dead."

Zoe got up from the couch and went to her. Her mother took a step back.

She held out a hand and after a minute her mother took it, as if she wasn't sure that what was happening was real. "I'm sorry," Zoe whispered. "I'm so sorry." Her mother's sobbing let up a bit and she stroked Zoe's head.

"You're filthy," said her mother. "You look like you've been dragged behind a truck."

Zoe laughed a little. "Just about."

"Where have you been for a week?"

"Far away," said Zoe. "Farther away than I ever meant to go."

"What does that mean?"

"Can we do this sitting down?" Zoe asked. "I've been running for days. I've hardly eaten anything."

"Running? Are you in trouble? Did someone do this to you?"

"Do I look that bad?" Zoe asked. She turned and caught her reflection in the hall mirror. It took her a moment to recognize the young woman looking back at her. This young woman had wild, dirt-caked hair. Her face and arms were covered with cuts and bruises. She still wore Emmett's baggy clothes over her own. They were torn and the front of her shirt and pants were splattered with blood and Hecate's ashes.

"Let's sit down," Zoe said. She took her mother's hand and they sat on the couch.

"I know you want to know where I've been, what happened to me, but I'm afraid to tell you."

Her mother let out a short, harsh laugh and took her hand back. "Just say it. What kind of trouble are you in?"

"It's not that kind of trouble. And all the blood is mine, so you don't have to worry that I murdered anyone," Zoe said. "I'm just afraid that if I tell you the truth, you won't believe me. I haven't been real good with the truth lately."

"That's for goddamn sure," said her mother. She reached for a pack of cigarettes on the living room table, took one out, and lit it with a disposable plastic lighter.

"Please don't do that. It's not good for you," said Zoe.

"You don't get to tell me what's good and not good for me," her mother said. "Sitting around for a week thinking you were dead, that's what's not good for me!"

"I'm really sorry. Nothing quite went the way I thought it would," Zoe said. She held on to the back of the couch. The fabric was cool and scratchy against her hand, but it felt a bit more real than it had when she first came in. The world felt like it was slowly shifting back into focus.

"Look," said her mother, exhaustion and anger framing each word, "just fucking tell me what's happened to you, where you've been."

Zoe looked away, gathering her thoughts, not sure where to begin. She took something from her pocket. "Someone told me to give you this," she said, handing the coin to her mother.

It took her mother a few seconds to register what she was holding. She turned the coin over and over in her hands. "This club's been gone for something like fifteen years. Where did you get this?"

Zoe took a breath, held it, and said, "Dad." They sat in silence for a minute.

Finally her mother sighed and shook her head. "Zoe, what are you—"

"Do you want to hear where I've been or not?"

"I don't want to hear a load of shit that's supposed to make me feel guilty about your father being dead."

"I'm not trying to make you feel guilty, I swear."

"Don't play games with me. Not after what I've been through. You could have found this coin on eBay."

"But I didn't. Dad gave it to me to give to you because it's from the club where you first met. You even had the words on the back, 'Fuck You Very Much,' on the jacket you were wearing that night."

Her mother stared at her. "How do you know all that?"

"I know about it because I was there. I told you, I went somewhere very far away, and when I was there I saw a lot of strange and horrible, and even some kind of wonderful things." She put her hand on the low table where her mother's cigarette butts spilled over the sides of a saucer. The sight of the ashes swept her mind back to Iphigene for a moment and she pictured Hecate burning, reaching for her. "One of the things I saw was my brother, Valentine."

"What?"

"Why didn't you or Dad ever tell me about him?"

Her mother stared at the cigarette smoke curling in the air between them. When she turned back to Zoe, her eyes were red and unfocused. "It hurt too much," she said. "We didn't tell anyone I was pregnant, at first. We were going to have a big party and tell people there, but then I had the miscarriage."

"I'm sorry," Zoe said, suddenly seeing the young girl from the club lying in a hospital gown, scared and heartbroken, knowing that her baby had died.

"When the doctor told us how far along I was, your dad and I counted the weeks and realized he'd be born about Valentine's Day. So that's what we called him." She reached for the ashtray and stubbed out the cigarette. "No one knew but us and the doctor. How did you find out?"

"Remember the boy in my dreams I used to talk about? My imaginary friend? That was Valentine. He came to me in dreams in this world, and then I met him for real in the other world."

"What other world?"

Zoe took a deep breath. "Iphigene," she said. "You see, there was this record shop and a man named Emmett. Well, really Ammut, but I'll get to that part later." She talked for hours, and told her mother everything.

When she was done, she could barely keep her eyes open. She was too tired to even take a shower, so her mother helped her to bed. After she had slipped under the covers, her mother sat beside her. "Do you believe me?" Zoe asked.

Her mother stroked Zoe's hair and nodded. "I used to believe in things, once," she said. "God. Ghosts. Guardian angels. I used to believe the world was a crazy, bad, beautiful game we were supposed to play forever." She shrugged. "So, yeah, I guess I believe you, because it's the best thing I've heard to believe in a long time." She got up from Zoe's bed, went to the door, and flicked off the light. "Besides," she said, "you've had a week to come up with a better lie than that. So, how can I not believe you?"

"Love you, Mom," said Zoe.

"You, too," said her mother, and pulled the door closed.

Even though she was still covered in grime and dried blood, it felt wonderful to lie in her bed between the cool, clean sheets. Zoe was in her body again, in this world, and she had to admit that she was happy to be back.

As sleep swept over her, she heard a strange sound, like something scratching at her bedroom window.

When she awoke the next morning, the covers were pulled tight and wrapped around her like a cocoon. In the night, her dreams had shifted randomly from Iphigene to this world, until she wasn't sure which was which or where she was, and Valentine wasn't there to help her figure it out. It was a relief to wake up in one place and have it stay that way.

Zoe was wearing her underwear and an old "X" T-shirt she must have found on the floor the night before. She didn't even remember changing. The clothes she'd worn in Iphigene lay in a pile at the foot of her bed. She laughed when she saw them. Her mother had been right. It really did look like she'd been dragged behind a truck. She kicked them over by her closet. The hoodie and T-shirt she'd wash later. The jeans might even be salvageable, but the sneakers were so caked with sewer filth that they were probably a total loss. She hated the idea of giving up a good pair of Chuck Taylors while she and her mother were broke, but she told herself they could probably find a used pair down at Goodwill.

The sound of the television, the smell of coffee, and the noises her mother made in the kitchen seemed as out of place and exotic as a circus in the living room. Give it time, she thought. Iphigene sort of made sense by the end. This will, again, too. She went into the kitchen, where her mother was in a terry-cloth robe, putting milk into her coffee. Zoe hugged her briefly from behind.

"Morning," she said sleepily.

"Morning. Sleep okay?" her mother asked.

Zoe nodded, still trying to shake away the last few cobwebs.

"Want some coffee?"

"In a little while. I think I need a shower."

"Thank God," said her mother. "I'm going to have to burn your sheets. I didn't want to have to boil the rest of the house, too." They both cracked up a little at that.

In the bathroom, Zoe thought about how weird it was to laugh with her mother. Their relationship had become based so much on tension, that the absence of tension, even for a while, felt odd. Maybe not a bad odd either. It was kind of nice not to have her stomach tied in knots as she waited for the next explosion.

The hot water in the shower stung her cuts and scrapes, but still felt great. As she washed, she felt between her breasts and found a small, round patch of raised skin—a scar from where the arrow had gone in. Zoe smiled. When she turned eighteen, maybe she would have something tattooed around it. What? A snake, maybe. An ouroboros. She stayed under the hot water until it ran out and turned cold.

Her mother suggested that since it was already Thursday, Zoe take the next couple of days to rest before going back to school on Monday. It would also give them time to work out some kind of family emergency to use as an excuse for Zoe's absence. At around noon, her mother dressed and headed out for another interview at the design company where she'd applied for a job before Zoe had left.

"Good luck," Zoe called as her mother left.

"Thanks. There's food in the fridge, if you get hungry."

"Thanks."

Her mother started to close the door, then came back in the living room. "Look," she said, "I'm not going to lock you up or anything, but for the next few days, do me a favor and don't go too far, okay?" She smiled at Zoe a little sadly. "I'll be back in a couple of hours and I'd really like it if you were here when I got back."

Zoe smiled and picked up a cup of coffee she'd brought in from the kitchen. "Don't worry, Mom," she said. "I'm not going anywhere."

"Thanks. Is my hair okay?"

"Perfect."

After her mother left, Zoe watched cartoons and then

part of an old black-and-white Fred Astaire movie. After that, *The Wizard of Oz* came on. She fell asleep just as the flying monkeys were taking off to attack Dorothy and the others.

When she woke up a couple of hours later, her mother still wasn't back. She hoped that was a good sign. Maybe the guy at the design company had put her to work right away, she thought.

While she'd been asleep, the flying monkeys had invaded her dreams. They'd circled overhead, just above the clouds, waiting for their chance to take her away. It didn't feel exactly like a regular dream, more like something she was trying to remember. That night, she lay in bed, willing herself to stay awake. And then she heard it—a scratching at the window. When she went to look, there was nothing there, but the window frame was torn and splintered, as if by claws.

Her mother was already dressed when she got up. She moved around the kitchen in an anxious rush, gulping coffee and wolfing down mouthfuls of buttered toast.

"Choking to death is not a good way to start a new job," said Zoe, pouring herself some coffee.

"I'm so nervous," said her mother through a full mouth. "I know I can do the work, but I haven't worked in an office in so long, and everyone else there looks like they're twelve years old and have been doing design since they were a fetus."

"You'll do great," said Zoe, stealing a half slice of toast from her mother's plate.

"Hey!" her mother said. "Now I'm going to starve to death!"

"Don't worry. It's your first day. They'll take you to lunch," said Zoe cheerfully.

"You think so? That would be nice," her mother said, her voice dropping into a low, thoughtful tone. "If they don't and I faint at my desk, I'll tell them it's my daughter's fault."

"Say, do we still have that old Polaroid around?"

"The camera? Yeah, it's in one of those boxes behind the couch. The one marked 'Random Household,' I think. You going to take some pictures?"

"Yeah. I thought maybe I'd shoot some stuff around here for Julie and Laura."

"Great idea," said her mother distractedly. She set her coffee cup and plate in the sink. "Is my hair okay?"

"Great."

"See you tonight."

After her mother left, Zoe thought about what she could to do to get ready. She should have known Ammut wasn't going to let her get away. She'd killed his mother, even if she hadn't meant to. And Valentine had warned her that the snakes wouldn't finish him off. He'd marked her window for two nights running. She was certain that he'd come for her tonight. He liked threes.

Gathering the clothes she wore in Iphigene, she left

them in a pile by the window. In the bathroom, she checked the cabinets for rubbing alcohol, but didn't find any. She dug through the boxes in her closet and found an old diary with a few dollars hidden in the spine. She got dressed and walked to the corner.

The liquor store sold cigarettes individually, for a dollar each, and on the counter were little glass tubes that were labeled as cigarette holders but which everyone with two brain cells knew were actually crack pipes. On the shelves were brightly colored candles set in tall glass holders with pictures of Jesus and saints she'd never heard of. There were dusty boxes of ancient laundry soap and pet food, but she couldn't find any rubbing alcohol. But she noticed that the store seemed to have every kind of liquor known to man. She went to the counter, where the bored clerk was watching a talk show on a small television propped up on a milk crate, and pointed to a pint bottle of vodka on a lower shelf, a cheap off-brand with a white plastic screw-on cap.

"How much?" she asked.

"You got ID?" asked the clerk.

Zoe leaned around the man and saw a hand-lettered sticker reading "$3.99" by the vodka. She put five dollars on the counter, took another five from her pocket and set it on top. It was all the money she had. The clerk looked her over for a moment. Zoe looked right back at him, hoping her scratches and bruises made her look older. The clerk took a small bag from under the counter, slipped the bottle inside, and twisted the top closed. As he handed it to her, he swept the ten dollars off the counter and into the pocket of his baggy chinos.

"There's no drinking in front of the store," he said.

Zoe took the bottle back to her room and hid it under the mattress. In the living room, she found her mother's cigarettes and the disposable plastic lighter. She threw the cigarettes in the trash and took the lighter to her room, slipping it under the mattress with the vodka. She went into the kitchen and found a small box of laundry detergent and put it in the pocket of her heaviest winter coat.

She napped as much as she could during the afternoon so that she could stay awake later. She tried to will herself not to dream, but it didn't work. When the dreams came, they were confusing, a murky combination of Iphigene's worst sights—the dying dead, the flying snakes descending on her father—and the tree fort where she and Valentine had played. The fort and tree were burning and the snakes she'd seen there once before had overrun the field.

When she got into bed that night, Zoe wore her old, scuffed combat boots, along with her winter coat, her jeans, and Ammut's oversize pants that she'd stolen in Iphigene. She was hot and uncomfortable fully dressed under the covers, but if what Mr. Danvers had told the class about snakes was right, it could work. She lay down and closed her eyes, but she didn't fall sleep.

After all her preparations, she still didn't know if she

was ready. Not "ready as in having no plan." She had a plan for once, as ridiculous as it was. No, she wasn't sure she was ready mentally to act, to do what needed to be done. It had been easier in Iphigene, threatening a kidnapper, taunting Emmett in the café, fighting the dying dead with her bare hands. None of it was completely real, and the parts that were real worked within a whole different set of rules from this world. She wasn't the same person here. She felt smaller and more vulnerable. The thought of going back to school the following week made her queasy. Would anyone have even noticed her absence? Absynthe, probably. Maybe Mr. Danvers, still the most interesting adult she knew. If everything worked out tonight, she'd see if she could find him a tooth to pay him back for the one she'd stolen.

She lay in bed for hours, listening to every footfall and creak in the building. Someone was playing some techno very quietly. All that came through the wall was the rhythmic thumping of the bass. A baby wailed miserably, stopped, and then in ten minutes started crying again. Car alarms and sirens went off distantly in the street below.

Sometime after two A.M., a shadow crossed her window. She opened her eyes a little more, but kept very still. There was definitely something outside the glass. She heard scratching noises and the sound of ripping nails as something pulled at the window frame. Then it stopped, and everything seemed to go quiet.

Her window exploded into the room, in a shower of glass and splintering wood. Something heavy landed near the foot of her bed. Zoe rolled to her right, onto the floor and away from the shadow that was rushing toward her. All the extra clothes she was wearing seemed to be working the way she'd hoped. They hid enough of her body heat that the shadow ignored her and attacked the warm spot on the bed where she'd been. The shadow brought down its knife, stabbing the crumpled sheets over and over again, until the box spring underneath cracked.

Zoe slid toward the window with her back pressed against the wall. As she reached the end of the bed, one of her boots came down on some broken glass, crunching loudly. The shadow looked up and lunged across the bed for her.

The flash on the old Polaroid blinded him, but in the millisecond before she dropped the camera and ran for the window, Zoe got a good look at him. The white glare of the flash lit up Ammut's cobra head in stark relief. His face was more monstrous than ever. When the young snakes had smelled his living blood back in the café, they must have gone wild. Most of Ammut's face had been torn off, exposing the bones and taut muscles around his mouth. His black tongue darted out, tasting the air, but Zoe was already climbing out the window. Ammut lunged for her, but she got her foot out just in time and he tore his arm on the shards of glass rimming the window frame.

Zoe banged up the fire escape, trying to keep her head clear and not to panic. As she put her foot down on the top step, the old metal gave way, and the step collapsed under her. She fell on her face, and when she rolled over, Ammut was almost on top of her. She kicked at his injured face with her boot and he howled in pain. As he fell back he slashed the air with his knife, catching the side of her injured ankle. The cut hurt, but not enough to stop her. She hopped the last couple of steps to the roof and looked back. Ammut wasn't there. Zoe turned in frantic circles trying to find him. She didn't see anything. There was a scrabbling sound behind her and she turned just in time to see Ammut leap at her from the drainpipe he'd climbed.

He landed on her hard and they rolled over and over across the roof, coming to a stop with Ammut on top. Zoe could smell the thick snake blood trickling from the wound she'd opened up when she kicked him. His tongue darted out, tasting the air. Trying to taste my fear, she thought. Ammut grabbed Zoe's throat, digging his dirty human nails into her skin, and raised the knife over his head.

"For Mother," he hissed.

Zoe took her hand from her coat pocket and threw a handful of the dry laundry soap into Ammut's eyes. He screamed, this time more in fury than pain, and swung the knife down in a shimmering arc at Zoe's head. She bit his wrist and twisted her head. The knife slammed into the roof, burying itself up to the hilt, close enough to tear away strands of Zoe's hair. She dug her teeth into Ammut's wrist and threw the rest of the soap. Ammut let go of her throat and she squirmed out from between his legs while he rubbed the soap from his eyes with one hand and twisted the knife from the roof with the other.

Zoe got up and limped to the far side of the roof as quietly as she could. A few seconds later, Ammut managed to pry the knife loose from the roof and he stood up. Zoe held her breath. He still rubbed his eyes, squinting and cursing, trying to get the last of the soap out. He knelt down on his haunches and blinked. What looked like an extra, transparent eyelid came down, clearing the soap to the bottom of his eye, where he wiped it away with the back of his hand. Zoe knew she didn't have much time. Ammut was already turning his head this way and that, scanning the roof for her body heat.

The cool San Francisco night was touched with fog, and there was a slight breeze that carried the smell of car exhaust and pizza from the joint around the corner.

Zoe took the vodka from her back pocket and poured it on the T-shirt she'd left to air out days before. The smell caught Ammut's attention. His tongue darted out, trying to find the source of the smell. Zoe's pounding heart felt as if it was going to crack her ribs. This was it.

She unbuttoned her heavy winter coat and let it fall to the ground. Ammut's head immediately snapped in her direction. He charged forward, his jaws wide and distended, as if he wanted to swallow her in one gulp. Zoe took a step back so that her heels were hanging off the edge of the roof. She waited until he was halfway to her.

As Ammut reached out to grab her, Zoe flicked the plastic lighter once, twice, and held it to the vodka-soaked shirt. She threw herself down hard as she tossed the burning shirt high into the air behind her. With her eyes closed and blood pounding in her ears, she heard Ammut run past her and off the roof.

Zoe's heart wouldn't slow down. She was paralyzed where she lay, afraid to open her eyes, afraid to move, imagining Ammut standing over her, his jaws gaping wide. But nothing happened.

Finally, she forced her eyes open and looked around. She'd heard right. Ammut wasn't there. She was alone under the stars. Too out of breath to stand, she crawled the few feet to the roof's edge and looked down. The shirt was still burning faintly in the alley five floors below, but there was no body. A pillar of gray ash eddied and danced in the crosscurrents as the night breeze swirled in the narrow alley. A few minutes later the ashes were gone, drifting into the street, waiting for the first rain to wash them down the sewer all the way back to Iphigene.

She limped back down the stairs to her room. Her bleeding ankle was hurting, and she'd jammed her shoulder when she'd hit the roof. Inside, Zoe's mother was standing in the middle of the wrecked bedroom looking lost, one hand clamped over her mouth. As Zoe climbed through the window, her mother asked uncertainly, "Zoe?"

"It's okay, Mom. It's me." Zoe limped over and dropped onto the edge of her broken bed. Her mother came and knelt beside her, moving her hands over Zoe's face, her arms and legs, checking to see that she was still intact. Zoe winced when her mother touched her shoulder. Her mother drew her hand back.

"We should get you to a doctor," she said.

"And pay for it with what?" Zoe asked.

"Don't worry about that," said her mother. "I've got a job now."

"Listen, Mom," Zoe said, feeling down beside the bed. Every part of her hurt, but there was something left to do. "Everyone in the building probably just heard that window break and someone's already called the cops."

"Good," her mother said. "Let the cops do something useful for a change."

"When they get here, I'm going to tell them it was a crackhead who followed me home from school the other day. But that's a lie, okay?" She looked into her mother's eyes and saw growing fear and suspicion. "The other night when I told you about seeing Dad and Valentine in Iphigene, and Queen Hecate and Emmett, you said you believed me, but you didn't really, did you?"

Her mother rubbed Zoe's back in small circles. It was a comforting feeling, something she'd done when Zoe was a little girl and sick. "I do believe you. Mostly. I want to believe it."

Zoe nodded. "It's okay. I know how crazy it all sounds," she said. "But it wasn't a crackhead who broke in here tonight." She handed her mother the Polaroid photo she'd picked up off the floor. "It was Emmett," she said.

When the police arrived, Zoe told them the story about the crackhead. By the time he'd escaped to the roof, the crackhead must have panicked and disappeared. She told the police that he'd made all kinds of disgusting sexual remarks and threats the day before. She told them everything she knew they wanted to hear. The cops nodded and took notes without seeming particularly interested in any of it. Before they left, they gave Zoe's mother a little card with a case number on it. The one thing the cops did that made Zoe grateful was shoo away the other tenants who'd clustered outside the apartment door, gawking and trying to get a look at the crack girl.

When everyone was gone and she'd locked the apartment door, Zoe's mother took the photo of Ammut from the pocket of her robe and stared at it as if trying to force a rational answer out of the flat, overly lighted image. Finally, she dropped it onto the living room table and shook her head. "I believe," she said. Then she turned to Zoe and asked, "Did you throw all my cigarettes away?"

"Yep."

Later, when Zoe fell asleep on the couch, there was nothing but peaceful blackness. She didn't dream at all, or if she did, none of it was important enough to remember.

That Monday, while Zoe was getting ready to go back to school, the insurance company called. They'd located her father's paperwork and were finally processing the claim. Considering how important that had been to her at one point, it felt sort of weird and anticlimactic.

They didn't bother with the story about a sick relative. Zoe was still bruised and scraped enough when she went back to school that her mother gave her a note about a car accident during a family road trip.

"I hope everyone is all right," said the woman in the school office who took her note. She was a nice older woman who wore a gray sweater over a white blouse covered in small yellow flowers. Pinned to the blouse was a silver rhinestone pin in the shape of a fluffy cat. Two greenish-yellow rhinestones set into the cat's face served as its eyes.

"That's a nice pin," said Zoe.

"Thank you, dear. It reminds me of my poor deceased kitty, Fuller."

"I once saw a snake with green eyes like that."

The woman gave a shudder. "Oh," she said, "I don't like snakes."

"Neither do I," said Zoe.

The school day passed in the same vague way that

they'd all passed before she'd left. The classes weren't bad. They just hadn't become any more interesting while she was gone. Besides, she knew she could pass most of them by reading the textbook the night before any big tests, so she didn't worry about it. The teachers were all coolly polite when she handed each the permission slip allowing her back into each class. Some clearly didn't remember that she'd even been in their class, which, she had to admit, made sense considering how much school she'd cut in the weeks before she'd followed Emmett into the sewer. The good news was that since she'd allegedly been in a car accident, she was exempt from making up all the homework she'd missed. Each teacher gave her an outline of what the class had covered during her absence. None of it looked very hard. Zoe had no doubt that she could get caught up with most of her classes by the weekend.

Mr. Danvers's class was in the afternoon and she was nervous about going back. Did he know that she'd stolen from him? She hoped he wouldn't make a scene in front of the whole class.

He'd just finished taking the roll when she entered the class and handed him the permission slip. Zoe kept her gaze on his desk until he spoke.

"Our wanderer's returned. How are you doing?" he asked. When Zoe looked up, he was smiling down at her.

She relaxed a little. There wasn't going to be a scene after all. "Pretty good, thanks," she said.

"You look like you were doing stunts for the next *Mad Max* movie."

"I feel like it, too."

He signed her form and handed it back to her. "I'm glad you're okay, Zoe. It's good to have you back."

"Thanks."

"I'll get you the information on what you missed after class. Stick around for a couple of minutes, okay?"

"Sure," she said, and headed for her seat in the back of the room. She didn't want to make eye contact with anyone else in class, so she looked at the anatomy charts on the back wall. Out of the corner of her eye she spotted Absynthe and turned to give her a rueful little smile. Absynthe had added purple extensions to her hair while Zoe had been gone. They looked really nice over her blue hair. Absynthe pointed to her face and lifted her hands to mime *What happened?* Zoe mouthed, "Later," and sat at her usual seat in the back.

After class, Zoe hung around while Mr. Danvers copied some notes from his lesson plans for her. When he handed them to her, he said, "Don't go getting in any more accidents for a while, okay? You don't talk much in class, but it's nice to know that at least someone smart is out there listening."

She tried to suppress the smile that wanted to break out on her face. Instead she blushed and said, "Thanks. I'm not going anywhere for a long time."

After stashing her books in her locker, she went outside and around the corner of the building to Absynthe's secret hangout. The other girl was there already, smoking a pink Sherman Fantasia.

When she saw Zoe, she jumped down from the steps and hugged her, then took her hand and looked her over appraisingly at arm's length. "Let me get an eyeful of you," she said. After checking Zoe out for a minute, she said, "Scars on children are wolves in their skin; the scars of young lovers are the moon shining in; old scars are the damage and the medals we win."

"Who said that?" asked Zoe.

"Nick Valéry, an old poet who wanted to fuck Patti Smith. It didn't work."

"What does it mean?"

Absynthe drew her over to the steps and they both sat down. "It means you've got a story to tell me," she said. "What the hell happened to you? I was starting to think you were dead or kidnapped by a satanic cult or something."

It made Zoe happy when she heard the genuine concern in Absynthe's voice. It was funny. Absynthe didn't seem quite so formidable anymore, or her look and public persona something to aspire to. Yet Zoe found that she also felt more affection for her now that she didn't see her as the zenith of cool, but just another high school kid trying to figure out how to cut through the boredom, frustration, and bullshit of it all.

"You sound like my mom," said Zoe.

"Oh no," Absynthe said, wagging a black nail-polished finger at her. "Don't change the subject on me, young lady. Tell me a story."

"I want to tell you the truth," Zoe said, leaning forward, resting her elbows on her knees, and wincing a little. Her shoulder still hurt, but she refused to wear the sling the doctor had given her to school. "But I'm still trying to wrap my brain around some of it and I don't know if I'm ready to talk about everything yet. I hope that doesn't sound too weird."

"From the way you look, I know it will be a hell of a story. I'm cool with waiting," said Absynthe quietly. Then, in a more serious tone than Zoe had ever heard her use before, she asked, "What'll it take for you to know when you're ready?"

Zoe thought about it for a minute and nodded to Absynthe's necklaces. "All that stuff you wear, the crosses and pentagrams and magic symbols. Do you really believe in any of it?"

Absynthe took a puff of her cigarette, held it, and let the smoke out slowly. "Sometimes." She shook her head. "Sometimes not. I'm not really sure."

Zoe sat back on the stairs, using her finger to loosen the tops of the new, used leopard-print Chuck Taylors that her mother had bought her at Goodwill over the weekend. "When you know and can tell me absolutely truthfully, I'll tell you everything. Okay?"

Absynthe nodded thoughtfully. "Deal," she said.

"Some friends from my old neighborhood, Julie and Laura, are coming to town this weekend. They're having a punk night at an all-ages club downtown. You're invited, too, if you want."

Absynthe looked at her appraisingly. "Sounds like fun," she said. With two fingers, she flicked the remains of her cigarette away. "So, do you ever listen to music recorded in, I don't know, your lifetime?"

"Not so much," Zoe said. She'd been so nervous about going back to school that she'd only had some toast for breakfast. Her stomach rumbled with hunger. "Do you want to get some lunch?"

"Sounds good," said Absynthe.

Zoe stood up and said, "I guess I don't know that much about any new bands."

Absynthe smiled one of her big feral smiles and looped her arm in Zoe's. "Will you let me play you some? As much as I love old-school punk, living in the past is kind of a dead end, don't you think?"

"Yeah, I do," said Zoe. "I'd really like to hear something new."

About the Author

New York Times bestselling author Richard Kadrey has published eight novels, including *Sandman Slim, Kill the Dead, Aloha from Hell, Devil Said Bang, Butcher Bird,* and *Metrophage,* and more than fifty stories. He has been immortalized as an action figure, his short story "Goodbye Houston Street, Goodbye" was nominated for a British Science Fiction Association Award, and his novel *Butcher Bird* was nominated for the Prix Elbakin in France. A freelance writer and photographer, he lives in San Francisco.

BOOKS BY RICHARD KADREY

The *New York Times* Bestselling
Sandman Slim Series

Available in Paperback and eBook

New in Hardcover and eBook

Available in Paperback and eBook

HARPER
Voyager

www.richardkadrey.com

FIND RICHARD KADREY ON
FACEBOOK AND TWITTER

Discover great authors,
exclusive offers, and more at hc.com.

**AND THE
BRILLIANT
STAND-
ALONE
NOVEL**

Available in Paperback and eBook